KATHRYN ERSKINE

SEEING
RED

Scholastic Press / New York

Library of Congress Cataloging-in-Publication Data Available

978-0-545-46440-6

10 9 8 7 6 5 4 3 2 1   13 14 15 16 17
Printed in the U.S.A. 23
First edition, October 2013

The text was set in Adobe Garamond.
Book design by Nina Goffi

Discover the past,
understand the present,
change the future.

Chapter One
The Sign

Folks don't understand this unless it happens to them: When your daddy dies, everything changes. He's not around anymore to teach you how to drive a truck when Mama isn't looking, or tell you man stuff that J isn't old enough to hear, or listen to you holler when you're mad, and say, "I hear ya, son," while he lets you figure out what you're going to do about it.

Even if your brother is seven years old, he goes back to being a baby and acting more annoying than usual. Your mama turns into some kind of zombie, walking around aimlessly, in between fits of crying. And you want to cry, too, except you're the man of the house now and you know your daddy said he could always count on you, so you can't let him down.

PORTER'S: WE FIX IT RIGHT! That's what the sign above our car repair shop says. It was the truth, too. Daddy said us Porters had been taking care of vehicles around Stony Gap ever since cars were born. That's how come our street is called Porter's Shop Road. Daddy could tune an engine, fix a flat, smooth your dents, jump your battery — he even managed to keep Miss Georgia's Rambler running, and that sickly old thing was held together with spit and prayers. I didn't know how anything could get fixed right again, now that Daddy was gone. Why couldn't the doctors fix him? How hard could it be to jump-start a heart?

I closed the shop door behind me and pushed the hair off my sweaty forehead. "It sure is a hot one, isn't it, Daddy?" Inside the shop I could talk to him out loud and nobody heard me. Not that there was anything wrong with talking to him. Heck, Miss Georgia still spoke to her husband and he died about thirty years ago.

I walked up the stairs in the back where Daddy had his office, taking in a deep breath of everything I loved. The shop was oil and gas and paint and dirt. It was brake pads, hoses, filters, and about any kind of tool you'd ever need to fix a car or truck. It was Lava soap, old rags, and a sink with a faucet you could turn on with just your elbow. It was the last place I saw Daddy.

I sat down in the swivel chair at my great-great-granddaddy Porter's rolltop desk. Old Man Porter built our house, shop, and convenience store way back over a hundred years ago. Daddy called it the "holy trinity" because with the house and store on the road, and the shop in the middle behind them, the buildings made a triangle. "Don't worry, Daddy," I said, "I'm going to take care of this place. You know you can count on me."

At the back of the desk was a brass plate screwed into the

center drawer: FREDERICK STEWART PORTER. I was named after my great-great-granddaddy, even though everyone just called me Red. I'd inherited his red hair, too. Daddy always said I'd inherit his desk because "it has your name written all over it."

A shotgun went off across the creek, and I jumped. "It's Mr. Dunlop," I said, "after those raccoons again." As if Daddy wouldn't know. I wanted to close the window and block out Mr. Dunlop's hollering even if the August heat killed me. But I sat back down when I heard Beau's voice rising from our convenience store, singing that hymn *Rock of Ages*. It was good to hear some singing coming from the What-U-Want, even if it left a lump in my throat. Daddy used to sing there all the time. And he used to sing to drown out Mr. Dunlop, just like Beau was trying to do.

Sometimes when we heard Mr. Dunlop swearing at his family, Daddy would pull a lock of hair over his forehead so he'd look like a rock singer and strut over to the food shelves. He'd wink at me, pick up a can of beans like it was a microphone, and belt out that Aretha Franklin song. Moving his hips like they belonged to Elvis Presley, he'd dance to the back door, throw it open, yelling, "What you want . . . huh . . . huh . . ." and sing about wanting a little respect, spelling out the word loud enough to zing all the way past Mr. Dunlop's shed, the Confederate flag on his front porch, and right into his ignorant head. The Dunlops were a whole line of bad blood, and we'd hated them since forever. Except for Rosie, of course. It was hard to believe she was a Dunlop. Everyone loved Rosie as much as they hated her daddy. Like

Miss Georgia said, "That girl is so full of love, even her face is shaped like a heart."

I heard a car crunch onto the gravel between the house and the shop, and I sat up straight. Me and Daddy always tried to guess the type of car by the sound it made. He called me the Boy Wonder of Cars because I have a knack for understanding them. I guess it's in our blood. I listened to the car door as it opened and slammed shut. It wasn't as heavy as a pickup. It wasn't a high-performance car like a Corvette, either. "What's your guess?" I asked Daddy.

The kitchen screen door whined open, and Mama's voice gave a shaky hello. After that she called, "Red? I need to talk to you, honey!"

She probably needed help fixing some mess J made. That kid was like a tornado, running wild, causing havoc, and leaving everyone feeling bad. I took in a giant whiff of Goodyear tires as I walked down the steps from the office and headed for the door. Before I opened it, though, I told Daddy what kind of car I thought was outside. "Late model four-door sedan, V-8 engine." I scrunched my face up to think real hard. "Chrysler or Chevy."

When I opened the door, dust was still settling from Mr. Harrison's '71 Chrysler 300. "Yes!" I couldn't help smiling because Daddy would be proud.

Mama waved at me and opened her mouth to speak, but Mr. Harrison said, "I know you want to get to Ohio as soon as possible, Betty, so I'll get to work right away."

Ohio? What was he talking about? We hadn't been to visit Mama's family in years. Besides, they'd come to the funeral not two months ago. And with only me and Beau to run the shop and the store, it seemed like a funny time to go on vacation.

The screen door banged open and J screamed, "Ma-*maaaa*!" even though she was standing right there at the bottom of the steps. "The TV's all fuzzy and I cain't see a thing! I wanna watch *The Flintstones*!" He was half naked, wearing only his green briefs, and he leaned his head so far back, bawling, that his curly black hair touched his bare shoulders.

"It's all right, baby, I'm coming!" Mama looked at Mr. Harrison, then me, and said, "Just give me a minute." I wasn't sure which one of us she was talking to, and she ran up the steps and into the house, her wrinkled black dress disappearing behind the screen door.

Mr. Harrison puffed his fat stomach out and looked everywhere but at me. It was like I had some disease and grown-ups didn't know what to say or do around me. So I looked at his car. He could afford a new one every other year seeing as how he was both a real estate agent and an insurance agent. He had what Daddy called a "healthy business," which is a polite way of saying he was rolling in dough. Daddy said there were only two things slimier than Mr. Harrison: a leaky oil pan and a big-city lawyer.

I heard J screaming another tantrum inside and Mama saying, "I'm trying, baby, I'm trying."

I decided to take charge, since I was the man of the place. "You want your oil changed, Mr. Harrison?"

He acted all surprised, like he'd just noticed me. "Oh,

well, son, that's nice of you, but I think Beau's got enough to handle over in the store right now."

I tried not to let my voice sound like I thought Mr. Harrison was ignorant. "I know that, sir. I can change your oil for you."

Mr. Harrison stared at me for a moment. His eyes moved over to the What-U-Want and back to me, like he was deciding which was worse, having a dumb kid change your oil or a retarded grown-up. Not that I thought Beau was a retard, but most everyone else did. Daddy said Beau might be on a different track from the rest of us but sometimes he was way ahead, and that Beau's mind raced around so much, you could get whiplash just trying to keep up.

Finally, Mr. Harrison made his choice. "Beau!" He yelled so loud Miss Georgia could probably hear him even though she lived half a mile away.

I heard the jangling bells on the front door of the What-U-Want and Beau's lumbering footsteps coming down the stairs and across the gravel.

"Yes, sir, Mr. Harrison, sir?"

"You got time to let young Red here help you with an oil change?"

I looked at Beau hard, not because I was mad at him, but because I was mad at Mr. Harrison. Still, Beau gave out a little moan and sank his three hundred pounds lower into his baggy jeans and giant blue shirt. He reached a hand up and tugged at the tufts of gray hair that stuck straight out from under his Quaker State cap. "I-I guess so."

A couple of minutes later, the three of us and the Chrysler were in the shop.

Mr. Harrison was stuffing his red tie underneath his vest but there was barely enough room in there for him, never mind his tie.

"Yes, sir," Beau said, "Red is real good at oil changes. I-I think he might could be better than me." He fingered the fancy red letters Mama had sewn on his shirt: BEAU. "Plus, I should go back to the What-U-Want." He said it almost like a question.

Mr. Harrison squinted his eyes at me. "How old are you, boy?"

"Almost thirteen."

Beau coughed and tugged his hair again.

The truth was, I'd just turned twelve. "Well, I'm a good solid twelve, and I've been changing oil since I was nine. By myself." I wanted to say, *Who do you think has been changing your oil for the past three years?*

Mr. Harrison shook his head, chuckling. "Huh, I think an oil change is too much to handle even if you're a good solid twelve."

How come when it's something you want to do, grown-ups say, "You're only twelve," but if it's something you don't want to do, like homework, it's, "You're almost thirteen years old, for heaven's sake!" and they act as if you ought to have been doing it since the day you were born.

"I can hack it," I said loudly, and picked up a new filter from the shelf for a '71 Chrysler 300 and the right-size wrench, along with the oil pan and some rags.

Mr. Harrison was wiping the sweat off of his face and eyeballing me. "What about oil? Don't forget to put the new oil in."

I took a deep breath the way Daddy always did when customers said ignorant stuff like that, and answered slow and patient, "Yes, sir, Mr. Harrison, but I can't reach the top of the engine to pour in the new oil while your car's up on the jack. We'll need to bring her down to ground level. Then I'll be putting four quarts of top-of-the-line Quaker State 10W-40 in your engine to keep this baby running real smooth."

Mr. Harrison grunted like he was a pig and I was a low-class piece of dirt not worth rubbing his nose in. After he watched me drain the oil, he followed Beau out of the shop, still grunting. I swear, he made me want to do something bad, like leave the oil out of his engine on purpose, but messing up would only let Mr. Harrison say he was right all along that no twelve-year-old can change oil. I let out a sigh. "I know, Daddy. We fix it right, and I will."

I'd already lowered the Chrysler on the jack and was pouring the new oil in when I heard a pounding outside and figured Mama must've given Beau another job to do or J was up to no good. Either way, I decided to ignore it. Until the shop door opened and I heard Beau's voice, nervous-like. "Red?"

"Almost done, Beau," I said, screwing on the oil cap.

"Red?" He said it so pitiful, my scalp prickled.

I turned around fast. He was tugging at his hair with both hands and his face looked fit to start bawling.

"What's wrong, Beau?"

"Out there." He looked over to where the pounding was still coming from. "Your . . . your mama . . ." We heard a few more taps. Like the final nails going into a coffin.

I felt as if my insides were turning to ice and I froze for a moment. Then I pushed past Beau and ran out the door.

I stopped dead when I saw Mama. She was standing there with Mr. Harrison. There was nothing wrong with her. It was the sign that was wrong. The new sign in front of our house. FOR SALE.

Chapter Two

Rosie

Mama called after me, but I took off and didn't look back. I jumped the creek and ran into the woods behind Rosie's house. I stomped up and down, kicking every little acorn, leaf, or stump I could find. I picked up stones and ran back toward the creek, throwing them across, aiming at our house. "No!" The sweat on my skin was making me feel hot and cold at the same time, like when you stick your foot in real hot bath water and you can't tell for a second whether it's freezing you or burning you.

I shook my head hard, walking in circles, trying to get my brain to work. What was Mama thinking? Bad enough we'd lost Daddy, now she wanted to sell our place? "No way!" Daddy's heart and soul were still here. My mind went back to late June and tried to put the pieces together.

The first week after Daddy died, Mama sat on his La-Z-Boy recliner, clutching its padded arms, staring at nothing. By the second week, she was curled up in the La-Z-Boy underneath an afghan so we wouldn't see her crying. But we could still hear her, day and night. I felt real sorry for her until, come the third week, she boxed up Daddy's clothes, threw his *Motor Trend* magazines in the trash, and dragged his La-Z-Boy out for the Salvation Army pickup. As if that weren't enough, she painted their bedroom, her and Daddy's, pink. Pink! It was like she was trying to paint Daddy clear out of our lives. "No! I won't let her!"

"Red!"

I whipped around to see Rosie standing there, all out of breath. "I heard you yelling. Are you OK?"

"No, I'm not!"

"What's wrong?"

I started pacing. "Mama's trying to sell our place."

Rosie's dark eyes opened wide as she tied and untied the strings on her peasant blouse. "Are — are you sure she's really aiming to sell or is she just talking about it?"

"Well, she's talking about it to Mr. Harrison and there's a For Sale sign in front of our house right now!"

Rosie sank down to the ground like her legs were as faded and frayed as her cutoffs. Her face went whiter than pale against her black hair, and even her lips lost their color. "Where would you go?"

I stopped pacing. I hadn't thought of that. And then I remembered what Mr. Harrison said about Mama wanting to go to Ohio as fast as possible. Did that mean permanently? "Ohio," I breathed. Then I shook my head. "No, it couldn't be."

She raised her eyebrows and pressed her lips together like she was a math teacher waiting for me to give the answer to a simple division problem.

"What, Rosie?"

"That's where your mama grew up."

"So? She's lived in Virginia since before I was born!"

"But Ohio's her home. When Mama's feeling poorly and your mama brings food over for us, she sits by Mama's bed and talks about her sisters, Nancy and Patty. Your mama misses them, Red."

"Well, I miss my daddy, and that's a whole lot worse!" My lip started quivering, so I turned away from Rosie, picked up another stone, and threw it toward our house. Hard. Ohio? "We're not moving to no Ohio."

"How are you going to stop her?"

"I don't know, but I'll think of something."

She picked at the pink nail polish on her thumb. "Maybe we need to talk to your daddy."

I stared at her. Was she making fun of me for talking to him? I expected that from her brother because that's what Darrell was like, but not Rosie.

"We'll have a séance," she explained. "That way we can bring your daddy back. So you and me can talk with him." She looked past me. "And Darrell, too."

I looked over my shoulder and there was Darrell. Tall, skinny, with hair as dark and dirty as his boots. You'd never think he was Rosie's brother, although you'd figure out pretty quick that he was Mr. Dunlop's son. The way he lounged against a tree, he looked like a snake waiting to strike. Darrell loved sneaking up on people and scaring them. He'd done it to me I don't know how many million times.

Darrell chuckled. "The kid already talks to his daddy."

Rosie sniffed. "Well, I never had a chance to say good-bye to Mr. Porter."

"Yeah, dingbat," Darrell said, "because when someone has a heart attack they can't exactly stop to say good-bye."

Rosie shot Darrell her killer vampire look she learned from that *Dark Shadows* TV show she'd been watching for years. She stared at him so long I figured she was putting some kind of hex on him. It almost made me smile.

"How does a séance work, exactly?" I asked her.

She sat up on her knees. "I'll bring my Ouija board, and you be sure to wear some of your daddy's clothes."

"Why?" I thought about how Mama had given all Daddy's clothes away, but as Rosie was explaining how spirits worked, I remembered that not long ago he'd given me one of his old work shirts since I'd outgrown my ripped-up T-shirt I used to wear in the shop. "I can wear his old shirt. It's even got his name sewn on it."

"Perfect! We'll meet at your daddy's grave tonight at midnight."

"Why does it have to be by his grave? And why midnight?"

She rolled her eyes. "Red, it's a good thing for you I know how to call up spirits. First, they only come out at night because they sleep during the day."

Darrell snorted. "I thought that was vampires."

Rosie shot him another of her looks. "Second, we have to be right by his grave because that's where his spirit lives. And third, he can't talk like we talk anymore, what with being . . . you know, not alive and all, but he can move the plastic eye over the Ouija board and spell out words so he can talk to us."

"Will he be able to hear us? Or do we have to spell stuff out, too?" I was thinking it would take a while to spell out, "What should I do about Mama's dumb plan?"

"He'll hear us. That's how a Ouija board works. You say something and then the spirit responds by pushing the plastic eye around the board."

Darrell snorted again.

"You don't have to come, Darrell," Rosie said, "if you don't believe."

He sighed. "Yeah, I'll come. Who knows? You might get lucky. Besides, you kids are too young to be in the graveyard at night. Never know who you might find there."

Rosie crossed her arms. "Darrell Dunlop, you better not have your gang show up."

"I didn't say that, I'm just —"

"ROSIE!" It was Mr. Dunlop's voice, followed by a whole bucket load of swear words.

Rosie stood up fast, her face going pale.

"Where are those sandwiches? Can't you do anything around here?" Mr. Dunlop came storming down the front steps of their house — his boots like to bust each one, he was stomping so hard — and strutted past the shed toward us.

Rosie took a step back. So did I.

"I forgot to make his lunch," Rosie whispered.

Darrell's expression turned serious as he hissed, "Don't say a word."

He spun around and faced Mr. Dunlop like he was a

bullfighter and his daddy was the charging bull. "Hey, Daddy! I'm real sorry. Would you believe it? I ate those sandwiches."

Mr. Dunlop stopped, like bulls do while they're getting up steam before they charge. He growled. "You ate my sandwiches?"

"I thought they were for me," Darrell said with a nervous laugh. "I'll go make you some right now."

Mr. Dunlop swore some more. "You got exactly two minutes or else I'll meet you in the shed, boy." And he pointed to the shed like we didn't know what that meant.

"Coming right up!" Darrell grinned like it was all a big joke, but he moved fast and by the time he reached their porch he took the steps in one big leap.

I heard a whimper out of Rosie.

"Next time," Mr. Dunlop said, his forefinger punching the air in front of her face, "you deliver the sandwiches directly, you hear me?"

"Yes, Daddy," Rosie squeaked.

His head jerked over to me so fast I flinched.

"What are you looking at, Porter?"

"Nothing."

"Well, take your nothing and get on out of here." Mr. Dunlop turned and stormed back to the house.

I heard Rosie squeak again, and I was sure hoping Darrell had those sandwiches ready.

"I better go," she whispered.

"I'll see you tonight, Rosie," I whispered back.

She nodded but was already heading for the rickety steps.

Chapter Three
The Séance

That night I lay on my bed, waiting for midnight and wondering what Thomas would think of Mama's idea to move.

I was real little when me and Thomas became friends, but I still remember when we met. He'd just finished kindergarten and had come to spend the summer with his grandparents. They came to our store, and I followed Thomas up and down the aisles as he read some of the words off the packages, something I was a long way from doing, so I was amazed that he knew more about my own store than I did.

"That's 'big,'" he said. "That's 'red.'"

"That's me!" I told him. "Big Red." It wasn't really my name, but I guess I wanted to feel big and smart like he was, since he was a couple of years older.

He stared at me for a moment. "Wanna play?" And we ran outside.

We tried playing leapfrog, but I kept getting stuck trying to jump over Thomas, since he was bigger. That set us off giggling so much that, as I struggled to get over him, he fell down with the weight of me. Mama came running over, but we were full-blown laughing by then. Little kids don't get hurt that much when they fall. Plus, Thomas has this laugh that's like birds chirping and the creek gurgling at the same time. Maybe because it's so crazy hearing those sounds coming out of a person's mouth that it just makes you laugh. As she brushed the dirt off of us, even Mama started laughing.

"It's OK, ma'am," Thomas said, "I'll take care of him."

Mama smiled at him, but I frowned. "I'm Big Red! I can take care of myself!"

Thomas, his dimples showing, looked at me, then at Mama, and back to me. "OK. Let's be friends!"

After that, we spent every summer together, and he called me Big Red like it was my real name. Daddy called us the Dynamic Duo because we were always up to some adventure or science experiment, like when Thomas wanted to see if a whole newspaper would burn if you shine sunlight on it through a magnifying glass. It does. Both of us stared at the flames, and Thomas even let slip a curse word because we knew we'd get in trouble, especially if we caught the whole woods on fire. Right as I was wondering how we could stop it, Thomas yelled, "Fire hoses!" and just like that I knew what he meant. We stood there and peed the fire out. After we stomped on the embers, we looked at each other and started laughing, more and more, because that's what Thomas's laugh does to you.

His laugh infected you however old you were, from J to Miss Georgia and everyone in between. Except Mr. Dunlop.

He didn't like Thomas hanging around our place because, as he told Daddy, he didn't want a black boy so close to his property. Daddy told Mr. Dunlop to get over it. When Mr. Dunlop said, "I have a *daughter*, you know!" Daddy narrowed his eyes at him and said, "That doesn't even deserve a response."

Mama was red-faced when Daddy told her what Mr. Dunlop said. Her foot tapped the kitchen floor real loud and she turned to me and J, saying, "You boys should try to be as much of a model citizen as Thomas." I figured she meant because he was nice to J, even teaching him how to climb a tree. And he always remembered to say "ma'am" and "sir." And because of his clothes.

Thomas's grandmother made him wear school shorts and a white button-down shirt, even for playing. Once I asked him if he was ever embarrassed being dressed up like that. He shrugged. "It doesn't matter what I look like, as long as I get to do what I want." And that day we built the coolest fort out of old car parts, played *Mission: Impossible* in the woods, crawled under logs, and then ran into the creek to cool off, and I realized Thomas was right. He could do anything.

A few years ago, Thomas decided we should earn enough money to buy what we both really wanted: Rock'Em Sock'Em Robots. We made lemonade, which we sold out front of the What-U-Want, mostly to Beau, and even paid Mama back for the lemons, sugar, and paper cups — "Otherwise, it's not right," Thomas told me. We took turns "owning" the Robots, and as soon as Thomas got in town this summer I gave it to him because this was his year. We used to play it all summer. Sure, we were getting old for it now, but it was a tradition. Until this year. We hadn't played it at all.

Thomas hadn't been friends with me since the first week of summer, right before Daddy died. Mama said it was his age, being a teenager and all, and Daddy said Thomas would come around. But I knew better. There was a reason. And it wasn't even my fault, which made me real mad.

I looked over at my dresser where the Rock'Em Sock'Em Robots had been until June, and I saw my alarm clock. *Shoot!* It was almost midnight. I had to get to the séance!

I jumped out of bed and put on Daddy's old blue shirt. On the left side of the chest Mama had sewn FRANK in fancy red letters. It smelled like the shop and Daddy, and I put my arm up to my nose to take an extra big whiff of the sleeve.

Carefully I snuck out through my window. Dang if I didn't rip Daddy's shirt because of the raggedy old pitch pine that was stuck to the side of our house right by my window. "Sorry, Daddy," I whispered, and I cursed the tree.

J wanted Thomas to teach him how to climb that stupid pine, but Thomas said it was a tough one and J would get pretty scratched up trying. But he also said that one day J could handle it. Mama always said it should be cut down on account of it was a fire hazard. Daddy didn't like it, either, but he figured it had practically grown into the house so as to be a part of it, and he didn't know what would happen if we tried to tackle it. So he had trimmed away the branches that were trying to get in the windows or fill up the gutters, but he never did get around to hacking the whole thing down.

I rolled up my ripped sleeve and forgot about that mess of a pine tree pretty quick, though, as I headed for the graveyard. It's no fun being out alone in the middle of the night when the owls are hooting, every twig you step on cracks like a gunshot, and the moon is spotlighting down on you, showing all the black bears where you are.

I hadn't been in the woods at night since Thomas quit hanging out with me. That night in June we were playing *Mission: Impossible*, as usual. Thomas was Barney because he was going to be an electronics whiz like that someday, and I was Willy, the strong guy. Our impossible mission that night, should we choose to accept it, which of course we did, was to infiltrate Mr. Dunlop's shed and disable the weapon — a horsewhip — that he used for beating Darrell. Thomas didn't much care for Darrell, but he said it wasn't right for a daddy to beat his son. He also didn't like how Mr. Dunlop spoke to Rosie, but we didn't have any ideas for disabling that.

We had a great cover because raccoons had been getting into the shed and messing things up since the spring. Still, my heart was pounding as we creaked the shed door open, and I swear every shadow looked like Mr. Dunlop ready to jump out at me. I could even smell his sweat. I hung back by the door as lookout while Thomas got the can from the shelf, right where Rosie said it was, and took off the lid. I wrinkled my nose up at the stink. The moonlight came in through the window, so I didn't need to use my flashlight, which was good because I didn't want to risk Mr. Dunlop's noticing anything. Thomas felt for the whip, on the same shelf by the cans, and tipped the can of contact cement so that stuff poured over the whip like honey on a wound.

And it was as slow to pour as honey, too. I glanced at the Dunlops' house. "Hurry up, will ya?" I hissed.

Thomas was slow and steady. "I want to make sure it's glued to the shelf real well."

"It's glued, OK? Now let's get out of here!" My voice was quiet but shaking.

"Don't worry," he whispered. "I won't let him hurt you."

"I'm not scared," I whispered back, which we both knew was a lie.

"Remember, raccoons have been here," Thomas said, as he finally put the can of contact cement on its side by the whip and set a few cans of spray paint on their side, too.

"Oh, yeah." I took the strawberry stems out of my pocket and threw them on the floor. The raccoons were always in Mr. Dunlop's garden patch, stealing his food.

"Done!" Thomas said, and we hightailed it out of there and didn't look back.

The next morning, Rosie said Mr. Dunlop was fit to be tied, and that he believed the raccoons did it. He switched to a piece of wood for walloping Darrell, though. I guess me and Thomas knew that disabling the whip wouldn't end the problem, but we hoped it might make Mr. Dunlop stop and think for a minute.

I sure wished Thomas were with me now. He would've said something like, "Why are you walking so slow? You didn't spill contact cement on your shoes, did you?" And that would've made me laugh, and then he would laugh, and I'd still be laughing now.

In the distance, I heard Rosie and Darrell bickering, so at least I was close to the cemetery. When I opened the wrought iron gate, its squeal made me shiver.

Rosie stopped talking and smiled at me. She looked like a fortune-teller with a scarf around her head and bead necklaces hanging down, making a racket whenever she moved. Darrell had on black pants, a black T-shirt, even a black knit hat.

"Got to hide from the spirits so I can jump out and scare 'em." He chuckled.

"Sit down right there," Rosie said to me, "by your daddy's headstone."

I sat down like I was in church. The breeze picked the hairs up on my arms and made me shiver. I wondered if it was Daddy's spirit touching me.

Mama stopped making me go to church after Daddy died. I guess she didn't have enough fight in her to make me go. She and J visited Daddy's grave after church every Sunday, and I felt kind of guilty about not going. I looked at it now and swallowed hard when I saw the mayonnaise jar with white roses in it. Daddy always gave Mama white roses for their anniversary. Now she was giving them to him. It didn't seem right. Still, I hoped she never switched to plastic flowers like some people did. There wasn't anything sorrier than seeing faded plastic flowers on a grave. It was like looking in a dime-store window at all the old junk that had faded so much no one would want it.

"Red, are you listening?" Rosie was staring at me. "I said, hold hands and close your eyes." She linked one arm around Darrell's elbow and the other around mine, which left Darrell and me to hold hands with each other.

We both looked away.

"Come on," said Rosie.

"No way," Darrell snorted.

Rosie got all huffy. "We have to close the circle!"

"Listen, dingbat," said Darrell, "boys don't hold hands."

"But you have to for a séance!"

"Not for a séance, not for nothing. You got any brains in that fat head of yours?"

I put my foot on Darrell's ankle. Hard. "There. That'll work, won't it?"

"Oh, all right." Rosie shook her head at us before looking down at the Ouija board in front of her. She closed her eyes and started humming as she reached her hand out toward the plastic triangle with the "eye" in it, pulling my arm along with hers since our elbows were linked.

Quick as a flash, Darrell took his free hand and pushed the plastic triangle with the clear circle in it across the Ouija board. He whipped his hand behind his back and said, "Hey, look! It's moving!"

Rosie's eyes popped open. "What?"

Darrell couldn't hide a laugh.

Rosie's mouth got tight, and she gave him a squinty-eyed look. "Quit it, Darrell!"

She closed her eyes again, and the humming started. Only this time it was Darrell.

Rosie gave Darrell's elbow a tug. "Darrell, I swear I'm going to smack you!"

"Ooh, I'm so scared."

I gave Darrell a little kick. "Give her a chance."

After a moment, Rosie started breathing heavy and her face looked all funny. Her voice was real shaky and spooky. "Mr. Porter, Mr. Frank Porter. Please come back to us. We need to talk to you. Your son Red is here." She squeezed my arm hard.

I jumped. "What?"

"Talk to him," she hissed.

"But — what do I say?"

"Ask him about moving."

I froze. I talked to Daddy all day in the shop, but I felt weird being put on the spot like this, especially in front of Darrell. "Can — can't you ask, Rosie?"

I swear she rolled her eyes even though they were closed. "Mr. Porter? Mr. Porter, please tell us how can we stop Mrs. Porter from moving." Her hand rested on the plastic triangle and it started jerking around the board. Rosie's voice was breathy. "Call out the letter every time it stops."

"What letter?" I whispered back, as her arm dragged mine by the elbow.

"The letter in the see-through circle, stupid!" Darrell said.

"Shhhh!" Rosie cautioned.

I looked through the little circle when it stopped. "*P*."
Next, it hovered over the *E*, so I called that out, too. When it went back to the *P* again, I thought it might be a mistake. "*P*?"

Darrell snorted. "Do you need to go, Red?"

"Not that kind of pee!" I snapped.

Rosie made a warning rumble in her throat, and her hand started moving again.

"OK," Darrell said, "so far we got P-E-P. Pep? What kind of answer is that?"

Rosie's hand stopped, and I read out the letter. "*T*, I think. Maybe it's an *S*. It's kind of between *T* and *S* —" But it moved again and I followed it with my eye. "Not *P* again! It must be *O*."

Darrell shook his head. "This ain't even a word. P-E-P-S-O. Pepso?"

"I think it was *T*, not *S*," I said.

"Doesn't make any difference," Darrell answered. "P-E-P-T-O. Pepto. That's — wait a minute!" He hooted. "Pepto-Bismol! That's what'll keep your mama from moving! Get it? Like bowel movement? You take Pepto-Bismol when you have the runs!"

"Darrell!" Rosie yelled.

He was laughing so much he rolled over backward. That's when he farted. I don't know if he did it on purpose or if it just came out, but there's something about farts. Even when you're feeling real serious, it's hard not to laugh at them.

I started to grin but bit my lip because Rosie wasn't laughing. She stood up and stomped her foot. "Darrell Dunlop, you ruined everything! It would've worked if it hadn't been for you!"

He could hardly talk through his laughing. "OK, I'll leave so you can go on with your stupid spirit calling." He let one more rip before getting up and walking off, still chuckling.

"It's too late now!" Rosie yelled after him. "No spirit is going to come to this place tonight, thanks to you!" She grabbed the Ouija board and stormed after him, her beads slapping back and forth.

I didn't feel like laughing then because there I was, all alone by Daddy's headstone. I touched the smooth, glossy surface of the black-flecked granite.

FRANCIS STEWART PORTER,
LOVING HUSBAND OF BETTY ANN PORTER

FATHER OF FREDERICK STEWART PORTER

—— AND JOHN BROWN PORTER ——

FEBRUARY 11, 1933—JUNE 28, 1972

And I knew then that there was nothing Daddy could do anymore. I was the one in charge. So I told him again, "You can count on me."

Chapter Four
Darrell's Idea

I hardly slept that night, and early the next morning I was staring into the kitchen cabinet, my hands hanging onto the doors, groaning. With a jolt, I realized I was doing exactly what Daddy did on mornings after he'd worked late or was out playing poker until all hours. So I did what he always did. I fished around for his NASCAR mug, which Mama hid in the back because she said it was chipped and we should throw it out, grabbed the jar of Nescafé, and put the small pot on the stove with just a little water in it so it'd heat up fast. And I put the lid on the pot, which Daddy said was the trick to having it heat even faster. While the water heated I put a spoonful of instant coffee and two spoonfuls of sugar in the mug, stirring up the brown and white granules until they were mixed together. The water was already hot by then. I realized too late that I'd only heated enough to fill the mug halfway, so I filled the rest up with milk.

It tasted a little like melted coffee ice cream, which isn't as good as mint chocolate chip but isn't bad. After a few sips,

I noticed that it had an after bite. The taste stayed with you, almost like the coffee had turned back into little grains and attached themselves to your tongue and the insides of your cheeks, and even if you tried to suck them off they stayed put. "Man, Daddy," I muttered, "no wonder your breath smelled like coffee all morning."

"Are you talking to Daddy again?" J stood in the doorway in his red briefs and matching undershirt.

I almost spilled my coffee. "Of course not. I'm just muttering."

"What's for breakfast?"

"Beats me," I said, taking another sip of coffee. Mama hadn't cooked since Daddy died, and J was a real picky eater, which didn't help.

J grabbed his plastic Flintstones bowl from the drain board and slammed it on the counter. He'd gone back to using his baby plates all the time now. "I'm starving!"

"There's cereal," I said.

"I don't like milk!" He slammed his bowl again. No wonder Daddy called him Bamm-Bamm after that noisy kid in *The Flintstones*.

"How about oatmeal?"

"Ew!"

"Then have some toast."

"I don't want toast!"

"You're pretty picky for someone who's starving."

Rosie knocked on the screen door to the kitchen, and J ran over to whine at her. He wasn't the least bit embarrassed for her to see him in his underwear. "Red won't fix me anything to eat!"

"I will, too, you just don't want anything!" I sounded as ornery as J.

Rosie came inside and smiled at J, bending down so she could look him in the eye. "What do you like to eat in the mornings?"

"Pie!"

Rosie bit her lip and flashed me a look.

"Come on, J, you know Mama hasn't made pie since Daddy . . ." I couldn't bring myself to say it. Mama used to bake pies all the time to sell at the What-U-Want. People came from all over for those pies for birthdays, holidays, funerals, any special occasion. Now folks didn't come by as much, since there were no pies and no Daddy to fix cars.

J stuck his bottom lip out. "I miss those pies."

Rosie gave him a hug. "Everyone does, honey. What else can we get you, huh?"

"I dunno. Sump'in special."

I saw the bananas on the counter and remembered what Daddy used to make for us. "Hey, J, how about some bananas in orange juice?"

"Yeah!" J said, jumping up and down.

Rosie smiled at me, which went a long way toward putting me in a good mood. I took another swig from my mug and her eyes settled on it.

"You're drinking coffee now?"

"Yep."

She thought about that for a moment and then nodded like it made total sense.

I couldn't help smiling as I sliced the bananas.

J ran circles around the kitchen table, making hot-rod

noises so loud that Rosie was able to get away with whispering, "I'm sorry the séance didn't work."

I shrugged. "That's OK."

J ran into the counter next to me, pretending to crash, just as I dropped the pointy end of the banana out of its skin into his Flintstones bowl.

He just about flipped. "I'm not eating banana poop!"

"J, there's no such thing as banana poop."

"Yuh-huh, there is, too! It's that black stuff at the bottom of the banana." He picked the banana piece out of his bowl and showed me the tiny bit of black at the pointy end. "See? That's where it poops."

Rosie giggled.

It wasn't worth arguing with J, so I took the poopy end and put it in my bowl.

"Ew!" He hopped in circles around the kitchen, yelling, "Red eats banana poop! Red eats banana poop!"

I swear, it was hard trying to be nice to J. I splashed some orange juice in his bowl. "Come on," I said to Rosie, "let's get out of here."

Rosie was still giggling, but as soon as we left the kitchen steps and crunched our shoes onto the gravel, she turned serious. "Darrell wants to see you."

"Darrell?"

"Yes." She folded her arms and looked over at the row of pines that ran from our shop to her shed. "He says he has a better idea than a stupid old séance." She was pushing her lips together the way she did when she didn't want the crying to come out.

"It wasn't stupid, Rosie. It just didn't work out is all."

She gave me her little smile, and I followed her along the path of scrubby pitch pines that stretched in a line from our shop to the Dunlops' shed, except where it broke for the narrow bit of creek. Unlike the stupid pine tree stuck to my window, I always thought that this line of pines was something good, like a lifeline. Except for one thing: I loved our shop just as much as Rosie hated their shed. It was the place her daddy beat Darrell. Without that rope of pines connecting them, our places were about as far apart as heaven and h-e-double matchsticks.

We jumped the creek because it was nothing but a trickle, and I looked at the shed as we walked past. "Did Darrell . . . have to go to the shed?"

She shook her head.

Just then, I heard a scraping sound from inside the shed, and I jerked back.

"It's Daddy," Rosie whispered. "He's still going through the boxes of Civil War stuff he got from Granddaddy at Easter time."

"Well," I said, giving her a grin, "he better watch out for those raccoons."

She laughed out loud, now that the shed was far enough behind us. "It's just old papers, anyway. He wanted guns."

Darrell jumped out from behind a tree, and I couldn't help but flinch.

He smirked, glanced down the row of pines to our shop, and looked at me. "I know how to stop your mama from selling."

My heart lifted, even though it was Darrell talking. "How?"

He grinned so evil his dark face looked like his daddy's. "No one will buy a place that's destroyed."

My heart sank again. "I'm not destroying the shop, Darrell. I want to keep it."

"Not real destroying, stupid, just things that's easily fixed but make it look ugly. You know how a place can look bad because, say, it ain't been painted in a while or a screen is hanging off the window?"

I nodded, wondering if he was talking about his own house, because it sure was a sorry-looking place.

"Well, you just need to trash it up a bit."

I thought for a minute and suddenly Darrell's idea didn't sound so bad. "Yeah," I said, "Mama's been doing some painting, trying to fix up the house. Maybe it's time for me to do some painting of my own."

"Naw, Red, you don't want to go fixing the place up —"

"I'm not saying that. I'm thinking . . . spray paint."

Darrell got his evil grin again. "We got lots of spray paint in our shed." He hitched up his jeans around his beanpole waist. "And I got me some experience."

I kept expecting Rosie to jump in and stop us, but she only chewed her lip.

Darrell spit like he always did to look cool. "You should come by Kenny's. Meet me and my gang there tonight. We'll help you with the plan."

He'd never invited me to Kenny's Pizza & Pool with him and his buddies, so I was quick to say yes.

"Eight o'clock tonight, squirt. Be there." He pointed his finger at me and clicked, like he was holding a gun and cocking it. Then he turned and swaggered off as if he was Clint Eastwood in *Dirty Harry.*

"Come on," said Rosie, grabbing my arm, "I want to go to your store and get a Hershey's bar for Mama as a little treat before Daddy leaves. He's going hunting and won't be back until tomorrow night because he's sick of — because Mama's sick. It's a strain on him, her being sickly all the time. He never gets away. He deserves a break."

A break? It wasn't like he did anything. Rosie was the one who took care of her mama. Why was she always covering up for him?

I listened to the slapping of her Dr. Scholl's sandals as we walked down the path. I couldn't help looking at her because she seemed, I don't know, a little different. Maybe older? Or maybe it wasn't her looks. Maybe it was something else. That was it! "You smell, Rosie!"

Her sandals quit slapping, and she turned to stare at me.

"I-I mean, have you been making lemonade or something?"

Her open mouth quickly turned into her little heart smile. "Ohhh, it's Love."

I felt my face get hot, and I knew it was already pink, going on red.

Rosie laughed. "Love's Fresh Lemon, silly. It's the brand of shampoo and talcum powder I'm using now." She held her wrist up to my nose. "Doesn't it smell nice?"

"Y-yeah," I said, even though I was backing away.

Rosie rolled her eyes but not in a mean way. In fact, she looked real pretty when she did it.

My face was still burning when we'd almost reached the What-U-Want and I noticed the silver Chevelle. It was Thomas's granddaddy's. He didn't stop by the store as much now that me and Thomas didn't hang out. And then I realized Thomas might be with him.

I ran up the steps of the What-U-Want and burst inside. Thomas was handing a shopping bag across the counter to Beau, which was weird because it should've been the other way around.

"Hey, Thomas," I said.

He flinched, like he'd been caught, but he turned to face me. He looked as if he'd grown taller and thinner just since June. He was wearing his new clothes — a peace-symbol T-shirt and jeans — and the MIA bracelet he got to support a missing soldier in Vietnam. It wasn't anyone he knew, but it was a black soldier who was a CWO, some kind of technical specialist, like Barney in *Mission: Impossible*, and Thomas said he wanted to honor him.

Rosie had caught up with me and stood real close. "Hi, Thomas," she said, crossing her arms. "I haven't seen you in a long time." She said it the way a teacher would talk to a kid who'd been skipping school. She even raised her eyebrows at Thomas like she expected an answer.

Thomas's granddaddy stepped up to the counter with some Life cereal and milk. "Oh, that's because young Thomas here has his bags packed already even though he doesn't leave until next week. Now that he's fourteen, he thinks Stony Gap is an ignorant little town not worth visiting anymore, don't you, Thomas?"

Thomas hung his head, but his hands were on his hips,

kind of like he was split between feeling bad and feeling angry.

Mr. Jefferson sighed and his voice was softer. "There are ignorant people everywhere, Thomas. Sure, we got our share, but most people here wouldn't . . . aren't like that."

Beau tugged at his hair, and Rosie looked at the floor. We all knew what he was talking about. It was the reason Thomas quit hanging out with me. Someone had tried to burn a cross in the Jeffersons' front yard just because they happen to be black.

Sheriff Scott called it an "isolated incident," which meant it was some crazy person and it wasn't going to happen again. But it was like someone told Thomas we couldn't be friends anymore, since I was white and he was black. Mama said she didn't blame him for being unsettled and that she'd want to move her entire family away if that happened to us. But that was Mama for you.

Thomas raised his head and looked his grandfather square in the eye. "I'm still going to find out who did it."

I watched Mr. Jefferson's face turn hard. When he spoke, it sounded like his teeth were clenched. "It's time to go, Thomas."

" 'Bye, Thomas," Beau said. "Don't be a stranger, OK? I sure do miss your laugh."

Thomas gave him a nod and followed his grandfather out of the store. I stared at the back of his head, noticing that his hair was longer than it used to be, like one of those new styled Afros that Reverend Benson said were the slippery slope to crime. Thomas said everyone had Afros in the city. He said he could do anything he wanted there and nobody stopped him just because he was black. We'd argued about Stony Gap, Virginia, versus Washington, DC, but he said I wouldn't understand because I was white. I reminded him that we'd done that Black Power salute together for years. He said I really didn't get what it meant.

I wasn't ignorant. And Stony Gap wasn't an ignorant town. Sure, there were a few folks like Mr. Dunlop and Reverend Benson. But not us Porters. That's why I was still mad that Thomas wouldn't be friends with me.

Beau walked over to me with the shopping bag. "Thomas brought this for you."

I took the bag and looked inside. It was our Rock'Em Sock'Em Robots game.

"Thomas said you might could play it with J," Beau said. "Hey, Rosie," he added, "how are you today?"

"I'm fine, thanks. How about you? And your mama?"

"Oh, she's not too good . . ."

I only half heard their conversation about how sick their mamas were because I was busy staring into the bag. It was his year to have the game. Now he was giving it back? Did that mean he was too old for it now or that he never wanted to be my friend again?

Rosie waved the Hershey's bar she bought for her mama in my face and smiled, but when she looked in the bag, her lips drooped. "You and Thomas used to play that nonstop."

I shrugged. "It's a kids' game." But as I looked in the bag, a part of me sure wished Thomas would hang out and go another round of Rock'Em Sock'Em Robots with me. Why did he have to change so much?

Chapter Five
The Lawyer

I watched Rosie crunch her way through the gravel over to our shop, then disappear behind the pines as she turned onto the path that led to the Dunlops' shed. I put the Robots in my closet, hiding them from J. I didn't care what Thomas said, I wasn't playing with J. Thomas was two years older than me and he didn't want to hang out with me anymore. What made him think I'd want to play with J, who was more than four years younger than me? I gave the bag a kick to send it to the back of the closet, and also because I felt like it. I went back to the What-U-Want to help Beau stock the shelves, but not before I heard Mr. Dunlop yelling at Rosie, which made my heart start pounding and my feet start wishing I could go over and kick Mr. Dunlop.

While I was putting the cans on the shelf, I thought about the only times I saw Daddy's temper flare. It was at Mr. Dunlop. Once it was about Mr. Dunlop shooting his rifle off willy-nilly when he knew me and Thomas were playing *Mission: Impossible* in the woods. Once it was because Mr. Dunlop was saying nasty things about Miss Georgia, and Daddy couldn't abide anyone poor-mouthing Miss Georgia. But the third time was around Easter this year, and it was the maddest I ever saw Daddy.

Daddy and Mr. Dunlop were talking to each other across the creek, so I didn't catch everything they said, what with the gurgling water and my hanging back, since I wasn't supposed to be spying on them, but it was something to do with land and great-granddaddies. Daddy raised his voice after a time, saying Mr. Dunlop didn't know what the h-e-double matchsticks he was talking about, and Mr. Dunlop, a sly look on his face, actually walked into the creek so he could hand Daddy an old brown piece of paper. "Now that's what I call history!" I hated the smirk on Mr. Dunlop's face, and when he turned his back on Daddy I wanted to yell at him and at Daddy to go after him. But Daddy just stood there a long time, staring at the piece of paper with his mouth hanging open. Finally he slowly folded it into thirds and marched home with his jaw muscles bulging.

The next morning Daddy wasn't in the shop like he usually was. Beau was tugging at his hair with both hands and said Daddy had headed up north along the creek. I had a feeling I knew exactly where: the same place he and Mr. Dunlop had that argument.

I ran up there, and Daddy was standing, hands on his hips, gazing across the creek at the Dunlops' property. His eyes were all squinty and fixed above the horizon, so I could tell he wasn't really looking at anything. His jaw was clenching and unclenching, and sometimes he'd flinch, like he was seeing some kind of horror movie in his head.

I didn't want to scare him, so I tried to make a lot of noise with my feet and my breath as I walked up beside him. "Daddy, what's wrong?"

He didn't move but kept gazing across the creek toward the Dunlops' land. "There's a lot wrong out there, Red."

"Well, can I help?"

It seemed like it took awhile for my words to sink in. Slowly he turned to me, eyeing me like he'd been away somewhere. His face crinkled into a smile, but his eyes were still sad. I remember how the red sunrise shone off of them. "Maybe you should, son." He put a hand on my shoulder and took a deep breath.

I stood up tall, because I could feel that he was about to say something real important, when we heard a shot and Mr. Dunlop's rebel yell.

"Take that, you dang coon!"

Daddy's jaw tightened, and his face screwed up so he looked like he might be sick. He clutched my shoulder hard and even grabbed his stomach with his other hand. I thought he was going to puke.

"Are you OK, Daddy?"

He looked across the creek, his face still all clenched. "Let's get to the shop. We've got a lot of work to do."

As we walked in silence, I was mad at Mr. Dunlop for ruining the moment. I looked at the sign on the shop as we walked in, PORTER'S: WE FIX IT RIGHT, and I wondered if I'd be able to fix whatever Daddy was feeling so sick about. I tried bringing it up a couple of times that day, but the first time Beau walked in and interrupted us, and the second time

Daddy didn't even answer, just looked across to the Dunlops', clenching his jaw. Soon after that, Daddy was gone.

Now I'll never know what it was. And that made me madder than ever at Mr. Dunlop. Because it must've been serious. Daddy even said *should. Maybe you should, son.* Not *maybe you could* or *if you want to.* He said, *Maybe you should.*

I heard a car drive up outside, but it didn't really register because I was still thinking about Daddy and what I *should* be doing. When the engine made a last rev before cutting off, I thought about me and Daddy identifying cars by their sounds. By the time the car door shut, I dropped the cans of soup I was stacking because I knew that it was a high-performance car. I ran to the front porch of the What-U-Want and, sure enough, I was right.

It was a brand-new '73 red Mustang convertible. I didn't even know those convertibles were out yet. Sometimes we got lucky and rich folks came for a drive in the country, and we got to see some pretty cool cars. Until now, I'd seen this Mustang only in *Motor Trend*, but here was the real thing. Right in front of me. Live. The engine still hot. All shiny red and gleaming chrome, looking like it could eat up the road in one fell swoop. Daddy would've loved it. It was the most beautiful thing I'd seen in my entire life.

What was weird was the guy who stepped out of the Mustang. He looked like the Poindexter nerd in that dumb Barbie game Rosie made me play when we were little, even the red hair on top of his thin milk-carton head. He was so skinny that Miss Georgia would say if you saw him from the side, you might miss him altogether.

Mr. Harrison drove up, too, but I hardly noticed him. I was too busy gawking at the Mustang and wondering why a nerdy guy like Poindexter had such a cool car. Until Mr. Harrison pointed at my open mouth and said, "Watch out, or the bugs will fly in!" and laughed like he was funnier than Maxwell Smart.

Mr. Ha-ha Harrison headed on over to our house, and I shut my mouth but I kept looking at the Mustang. I heard Mr. Harrison, though.

"Betty, your house is looking lovely, as always. I'm sure we'll get you a buyer in no time. In fact, I believe I might have one snagged already!"

What? I felt myself gritting my teeth, but what I heard from Poindexter, inside the store, made me even madder.

"So all this property is for sale? The store, too?"

I whipped my head around and was in the What-U-Want before Beau had a chance to speak. "Who wants to know?" Was Poindexter the buyer Mr. Harrison had snagged?

Beau's eyes went wide. "Wh-what he meant to say, sir, is he'd like to know your name. I-I'm Beau, and this here is Red."

Poindexter held his hand out to Beau, who touched the bill of his Quaker State cap with one hand and shook with his other.

"I'm Bill Reynolds. From Richmond." He puffed out his chest. "I'm a lawyer."

Right then I knew I didn't like him. I remembered what Daddy said about the only thing slimier than Mr. Harrison was a big-city lawyer, so I squinted my eyes at Mr. Reynolds from Richmond. "Why do you want to know about our land?" I scared him, too, because he stepped back and stuttered. I realized that he was pretty young, at least for a lawyer.

"I-I'm inquiring on behalf of a *client*." He emphasized the word *client* like that made him the most important guy in the world. I'd seen *Perry Mason* on TV. I knew a client was just someone who hired a lawyer. So if Poindexter wasn't the buyer, who was?

"Well," I said, "I don't think any *cli-ent* of yours would be interested."

"Oh?" said Poindexter, looking at Beau, who was tugging his hair and staring at me wide-eyed.

"Yeah," I said slowly, giving myself time to think of a good reason. "Yeah, we got termites and wood rot. Everywhere."

Beau looked at me, shaking his head. "I don't think —"

"And," I said, talking over Beau, "it's too dangerous for another reason. You see, Mr. Dunlop — he lives behind us — he doesn't take kindly to folks who are strangers to these parts. Heck, he doesn't even take kindly to us, and we've lived here for thousands of years."

Beau coughed.

"Well, hundreds of years, anyway."

"I'm aware of Mr. Dunlop," Mr. Reynolds said.

How did he know about Mr. Dunlop? "Well," I said, "are you *aware* that he'd just as soon shoot you as look at you?"

Mr. Reynolds flinched, and Beau was tugging his hair with both hands now.

"I see. Where, exactly, is his house?"

I pointed behind the store. "Right back there. Shotgun distance."

His Poindexter face went even paler. "Well, thanks for that information," he said, heading for the door.

I figured I'd gotten rid of him for good.

He took a deep breath and said, almost to himself, "I'll have to go pay Mr. Dunlop a visit."

What? It took me until he got in the Mustang before I remembered what Rosie had said and found my voice. I ran out to the steps. "Mr. Dunlop's gone hunting and won't be home for two days!"

"Thank you," he said, giving me a wave, "I'll be back."

Maybe, I thought, *but when you get here you won't like what you see because our shop is going to be a spray-painted mess and your client won't be wanting this place anymore!*

Chapter Six
Kenny's

Through the pool-hall window I could hear Kris Kristofferson's voice singing "Help Me Make It Through the Night," and I felt like he was singing for me. Kenny's stank like beer and sweat and maybe something else but I don't know what. Looking through the glass door was like staring at a smoky bad dream. All I could think about was how Daddy always told me not to come here.

I could barely make out Darrell and his gang over by the rack of pool cues. They wore cool clothes, like Grateful Dead tank tops or black T-shirts with rolled-up sleeves. I looked down at my own clothes and wished I wasn't wearing my striped T-shirt and too-short jeans. I tugged at my jeans, trying to make them stretch down to my sneakers, but it was no use. I looked like that kid Opie from *The Andy Griffith Show.*

I yanked open the door and stepped inside like I belonged there. I looked around quickly to see if Kenny was in the main room and breathed a sigh when I realized he must be in the kitchen. Daddy said Kenny was all right, unless you hurt him or his property and then you were a goner, but Kenny kind of scared me. He was the size of Beau but as hard as Beau was soft.

"Quit gawking like a little kid," Darrell hissed in my ear.

I hadn't even seen him walk up to me.

"Follow me," he said.

I tried to walk with a swagger like Darrell did, but my legs felt more like a couple of loose pistons slapping. When I finally made it over to the group by the pool table I was glad to slink against the wall even though the stucco poked my back like a bunch of tacks. I didn't much like how the smoke was stinging my eyes, but I appreciated the fog it made so I could hide in it.

Darrell was standing across the table from me, at the edge of the group of guys, all high schoolers. If he didn't feel out of place, he sure looked it. The other boys seemed cooler than Darrell without even trying. While they were talking quietly, Darrell would laugh real loud all of a sudden and they'd all look at each other or shake their heads, but Darrell didn't seem to notice. Even when he slapped Glen on the back, Darrell didn't see the dirty look Glen gave him.

Glen Connor wasn't the kind of guy you should slap on the back, especially if you were Darrell. His daddy was some local politician, I couldn't remember what, and Glen was the spitting image of him, only not as wide. He even had the same slicked-down blond hair and stuck-up voice. He and his daddy came by our house at election time and Daddy had said, in a nice way, that they were wasting their time because we were dyed-in-the-wool Democrats. Mr. Connor had grinned, but it was the kind of grit-your-teeth grin that you do when you want to stop some bad words from coming out. Glen didn't bother to even fake a smile. I didn't care for them much, but Daddy said to watch myself because Mr. Connor had a lot of power. Judging by how the guys in Kenny's were flocking around Glen, he seemed to have power, too, even though he hadn't been elected to anything.

The other guy I knew was Larry, who just happened to be both Kenny's and Mr. Harrison's nephew. Right now, I didn't feel too kindly toward him because of Mr. Harrison. Other than that, Larry was OK. The rest of the guys I'd seen in and out of the What-U-Want, but I didn't really know them.

But I sure knew the guy who yanked the glass door open and hesitated for a moment, just like I had, before stepping into Kenny's like it was the principal's office. Thomas! The line between his eyebrows as he stared at Darrell's gang reminded me of that same look of concentration when we played Rock'Em Sock'Em Robots. Even though I was mad at him I was still relieved to see him. He was the best friend I had in that place.

"Hey, Thomas."

He did a double take when he saw me. All the guys stopped talking, too, and stared at Thomas, then at me, like they were noticing me for the first time.

"What," Thomas said, his face grim, "are you doing here?" He was talking to me like he was the daddy and I was the little kid!

I guess the gang agreed, because they snickered and one of them said, "He don't belong here."

I felt my fists clench. I jerked my head in Darrell's direction and made my voice tough. "Meeting my boys."

The gang laughed more at that, which made me even madder.

Thomas shook his head. "You're just a kid, Red. You shouldn't —"

"I'm the man of the house now!" I said, drawing myself up as tall as I could.

"The man of the house, huh?" Thomas looked at the gang and walked over to me, lowering his voice. "Hanging out here with Darrell?" He shook his head and almost sneered at me before turning and reaching for a pool cue from the rack. "Yeah, Big Red, your daddy'd be *real* proud of you right now."

Something like fireworks went off inside of me, and I'd punched him before I even realized what I did. All I knew was that my right knuckles hurt, Thomas was doubled over clutching his stomach, and the whole rack of pool cues was clattering to the floor like a bunch of giant pickup sticks.

I heard the chanting, "Fight! Fight! Fight!" but overtop of that I heard Kenny's voice boom, "Stop right now!" and I looked at the ground.

"What are you thinking, boy?" Kenny said.

"Sorry," Thomas breathed.

I jerked my head up and tried to say it was me who started the fight, but Glen was already talking — and pointing at Thomas. "He shouldn't be in this establishment, Kenny."

Kenny's left eye twitched because you didn't tell Kenny Rae Campbell how to run his place. I was slowly taking in the fact that the gang had been talking about Thomas, not me, as the one who didn't belong.

Kenny held his snake-tattooed arm out to Thomas. "Let me see your money, boy."

Thomas sighed, and I saw his shoulders slump before he pulled his wallet out of the back pocket of his jeans. He hesitated, but Kenny snapped his fingers, still staring at Glen. Thomas pulled a five-dollar bill out and slapped it in Kenny's hand, harder than I would've dared.

Kenny didn't flinch. He held the note up to the flickering fluorescent light and squinted at it. "Yep, it's genuine American money." He looked at Thomas, who was putting his wallet back in his pocket. "You planning on causing trouble, boy?"

"No," said Thomas. I noticed he didn't say "sir."

"You planning on paying for your sodas?" Kenny asked.

"Of course."

I held my breath because Thomas sounded almost like he was sassing.

Glen Connor folded his arms and lifted his chin.

Kenny gave the five bucks back to Thomas. "That's all I care about."

I don't know who was more surprised — Thomas or Glen, who glared at Kenny and then at Kenny's nephew. Larry was too busy gawking at Kenny, so Glen had to elbow him.

"Oh, yeah," said Larry. "Uncle Kenny, my boys here wanted —"

"To play pool?" Kenny interrupted him. "Play darts? Drink you some Cokes? Well, that's fine."

Glen looked hard at Larry, who opened his mouth again. "But we —"

"But," Kenny went on, "any one of you boys mess with my property? I will personally throw you out of here so hard your hiney will have skid marks."

Darrell was the only one who laughed.

"And then I'll call the sheriff," Kenny said, "and maybe all y'all's mamas and daddies, too." His narrowed eyes swept across all of us. "Are you hearing me?"

Some of the gang nodded or murmured yes, but Glen didn't blink and his face was stony. Kenny noticed and put his hands on his hips, staring Glen down. The room was so quiet all you could hear was the buzzing of the fluorescent light.

I was real surprised when Darrell cleared his throat and said, "Hey, Thomas. How about a game of pool?"

Kenny switched his gaze to Darrell, who looked everywhere around the room except at Kenny, or at Thomas for that matter. He bent down and picked up the fallen pool cues, setting them all against the wall except one. He chalked the head of that thing until it was raining blue dust.

Thomas brushed past me, saying softly, "Go on home, Red."

"But . . . I didn't mean . . . I —"

"Forget it," Thomas said, looking over at the door. "Someone's waiting for you."

I saw the Quaker State cap through the smoky haze.

49

Beau knocked on the glass door and waved. I looked back at Thomas, but he was ignoring me, racking up the balls on the pool table, so I went on outside.

"What do you want, Beau?"

"You to come home."

"How did you know where I was?"

"Sometimes things just pop in my head. When they do I know they must be right because they ain't had a chance to run around my brain and get stupid."

"You're not stupid, Beau."

"How come you here, Red? Your daddy told me never to go inside this place. Didn't he never tell you that?"

I squirmed on the inside but cleared my throat like Clint Eastwood. "I had some business to take care of."

Beau tilted his head like he was sloshing all his brains to one side. "Business?"

"With Darrell and his gang — I mean, his buddies."

Beau's mouth fell open like the hinge busted. "Darrell? Darrell Dunlop?"

"Well, of course, Darrell Dunlop. What other Darrell is there?"

Beau reached a hand up to tug his hair. "Darrell and his buddies was the ones who threw rocks at Miss Georgia's house last winter, even broke two of her windows."

Oh, yeah. I'd forgotten about that. It was hard to keep up with everything Darrell did.

"Just because Miss Georgia's brown," Beau said.

"You mean black."

He shook his head. "No. I don't know why people say

that because I ain't seen anyone with black skin. There's dark brown and medium brown, like Miss Georgia, and light brown and even lighter brown, and then there's this darkish tan color and —"

"OK, Beau. I get it. Anyway, sometimes Darrell can be useful."

"Yeah?" Beau stopped tugging his hair and looked at me like a little kid. "How?"

"Never mind. We'd best be getting home, huh?"

I kicked every stick and stone out of my path as I headed back. I was mad for a lot of reasons. I was mad at Beau for chasing me down at Kenny's. And I didn't like the way Glen seemed to have it in for Thomas. What had Thomas done except come by to play a little pool? But I was also mad at Thomas. It was like the first day I met him, when I realized he understood more about the store than I did because he could read, even though it was my store. Now did he understand more about Kenny's, about Darrell's gang, than I did, even though this was my own town?

I felt bad for punching Thomas, but I didn't like him saying what Daddy would think of me, either. What I hated most was that when I thought about what Thomas said, I saw Daddy's face, the hurt-disappointed face that he hardly ever gave me because when he did I felt so bad I swore I'd never let him show it to me again. It only happened a few times in my whole entire life. But it was happening now. So I started getting mad at Darrell for talking me into going to a place that would make me see Daddy's face that way. And on top of everything, he never even talked to his gang about how to destroy things just enough that no one would buy our place, so we could stay right here in Stony Gap.

When I got home, that stupid For Sale sign was staring me in the face like it had won. I was so mad I kicked that dang sign and it tilted just a little, but enough to give me an idea. I decided to pull it clear out of the ground. Maybe next time old Poindexter drove by in his hot red Mustang he wouldn't feel so hot.

But it was harder than I thought. I had to go into the shop and get a shovel. Once I dug around it, though, the soil being pretty loose since Mr. Harrison had put it in recently, I hauled it out of the earth and dragged that thing behind the shop. I dug a hole back there, which was also hard work, except the hole didn't have to be very deep because I laid the sign down flat. I said a few words over it that weren't exactly a prayer.

Who would know that it could actually feel good to bury something?

Chapter Seven
Miss Georgia

I must've been tired from my work of burying that sign because I slept later than usual. I woke up and Mama was on the phone to Mr. Harrison, asking him for another For Sale sign. Shoot.

I walked through the kitchen without stopping.

"Good morning, Red," Mama said. "I don't suppose you know anything about —"

"No, ma'am," I said as I scurried out the door. I figured if I didn't hear the whole question, then saying no wasn't really a lie. Besides, I didn't much feel like talking to Mama lately. All she wanted to do was explain why moving to Ohio was such a good idea. "You have cousins there," she'd said, except none of them were my age, and the one who was closest was even more annoying than J. "You have two uncles there who care about you very much," as if two uncles added up to one daddy. She wouldn't listen to any of my reasons why we should stay, like how much Daddy loved this place and how our family heritage was here in Virginia. She'd put her hands on her hips and said, "Red, half of your ancestors come from Ohio." But the ancestor I was named for came from right here. And so did Daddy. Everything the Porters stood for came from right here. Nothing Mama said about Ohio could make me want to leave this place. Ever.

I wandered over to the shop, where I heard Beau talking, and looked inside.

". . . a new alternator. It'll cost a couple hundred dollars, Miss Georgia, ma'am."

"I don't have no two hundred dollars, Beau." Miss Georgia was ricketier than her old car. I thought she might crumble on the spot. She always wore a navy blue sweater over her dress, even when it was hot out. Lately she was using a cane.

"Yes, ma'am," Beau said. "I'm afraid even one from a junkyard will cost at least a hundred by the time it's pulled out and brought to the shop."

"Don't have no one hundred dollars, neither. Not two hundred, not one hundred."

Poor Beau looked about to cry. He said he'd do the work for free, but just getting the part to the shop would cost more than Miss Georgia could pay. Daddy always did the work for Miss Georgia for free. Sometimes he'd pay for the parts, too, or at least most of it. But we couldn't afford a hundred dollars any more than Miss Georgia could. Not now. Not with Mama thinking there was no way we could keep our businesses running. I backed away from the door and stood on the side of the shop in the shadows.

Miss Georgia heaved a big sigh. "I need my car, Beau. I need my car."

Miss Georgia always said things twice, probably on account of her coming up back when folks didn't listen to what a black person said. Not the first time, anyway. Maybe by the second time they might. And if they hadn't by then, there wasn't any use wasting her breath for a third time.

She sighed and walked slowly out of the shop. I stayed in the shadows because it felt too bad to see her pain. Beau walked out of the shop looking as sad as she did, maybe sadder.

I stared at the Rambler sitting inside. There had to be something we could do. Daddy said that Rambler was her freedom, even though she hardly ever drove it. He never would've let Miss Georgia walk away all hopeless like that. He said sometimes hope is the only thing that keeps us going.

It was all that kept Daddy going as church deacon, trying to get Miss Georgia invited to our church. Daddy said the name itself — Open Doors Baptist Church — kind of begged to let everyone in, but the other deacons all agreed with Reverend Benson. I heard them talking after Easter service. "It's time to do what's right," Daddy said. "In fact, it's past time."

Reverend Benson had drawn himself up to his full six foot three and looked down on Daddy like he was just a little puppy who didn't understand the world. "Now, Frank, you got to understand that they're happier with their own kind and, besides, they got their own church to go to."

"Her own church is thirty-five miles away," Daddy shot right back, "and I think she'd be the one to say where she's comfortable, don't you?"

Mr. Harrison, Sheriff Scott, and the other deacons all looked away like they didn't want to be associated with Daddy.

"Oh!" said Reverend Benson, like he'd just thought of something, "I meant to ask you all about paying for new music for the choir. My wife is bound and determined to do Handel's *Messiah*, and she says, given the skill of this choir, they need to start practicing now."

Daddy looked around at each one of the men, but they jumped right into the church-music conversation like it was as exciting as talking about the baseball players' strike and what that might do to the World Series.

Except for the sheriff, who was chewing on a toothpick and still staring into the distance. When Daddy finally caught his eye, Sheriff Scott made the tiniest bit of a grimace, lifted one shoulder into a shrug, pursed his lips around that toothpick, and gave the slow sucking sound he made when he wasn't happy about something. Darrell called it the Kiss of Death. I guess it was, since that's what happened to Daddy's idea for Miss Georgia.

I lay down on the creeper that Daddy used to roll under cars before he got the hydraulic jack, putting my feet off the edge onto the floor so I could roll myself back and forth. It felt kind of like being on a porch swing. I used to roll on the creeper a lot, helping him fix cars. He'd say, "Get me a filter for this F-250, would you, Boy Wonder?" Or, "Boy Wonder, what's wrong with this here drive train?" This time I asked him, "So what's wrong with Miss Georgia's car? Come on, I know you want to help her. You said she was like a grandmother to you." And to me, too, I thought.

Me and Thomas used to go over to Miss Georgia's all summer long. She froze Kool-Aid in ice-cube trays for us. When I was little she'd wrap the ice cube in a paper napkin so I could hold it and suck on it. The first time she gave me a whole ice cube to put in my mouth I thought I would die. It stuck to my tongue and the roof of my mouth. I didn't want to open my mouth because I might rip the skin off. I didn't know how you would stop bleeding in your mouth. Band-Aids wouldn't stay stuck. I tried to keep my mouth shut and breathe through my nose while I waited for the ice cube to melt. The whole time, Miss Georgia was talking away and I was acting polite, nodding and trying hard not to look like a chipmunk, even though Thomas was laughing, so it was almost impossible not to laugh myself. I never knew it was so much work to melt an ice cube. Water came out of my eyes faster than it came off the ice cube. That made Miss Georgia stop and look at me hard. "You ain't crying, is you?" I shook my head because I still couldn't talk. "Speak up, Red." It was like being at the dentist when his hand is in your mouth and he wants you to tell him all about school. Then she said, "Cat got your tongue?" "No, ma'am," I finally managed to sputter, "ice coog got it." She and Thomas laughed so hard they couldn't talk.

Then I heard it. Daddy's voice. "Brushes."

It wasn't like you see in the movies. He wasn't standing there in the shop looking at me and talking like he was alive. I just heard his voice.

"Brushes?" I said it out loud and, shoot, that chased his voice away. Brushes? What kind of an answer was that? I thought about toothbrushes and hairbrushes and bottle-brushes, but I still didn't see how that could help me fix Miss Georgia's car.

Maybe I heard wrong. Maybe it wasn't "brushes." Rushes? Crushes? Those didn't sound right, either. I shook my head. What did brushes have to do with Miss Georgia and her Rambler and the bum alternator — hey!

I jumped up so fast the creeper wheeled across the shop and crashed into the door. I kicked it out of the way and ran over to the What-U-Want and yelled, "Brushes!"

Beau looked at me as confused as I must have looked when Daddy first told me.

"Miss Georgia's car! Brushes!"

Beau tilted his head and squinted at me. "You want I should wash her car, Red?"

"No, I mean alternator brushes!"

Beau's grin crawled across his face like a possum crossing the road. "That's why your daddy called you the Boy Wonder."

I couldn't help grinning. "Actually, Daddy's the one who told me."

He nodded like that made sense.

We both ran over to the shop, found the page in the American Motors parts book that had alternator brushes and how much they cost, and grinned at each other.

Chapter Eight
Freedom's Folly

I hightailed it all the way to Miss Georgia's. She was just climbing the steps to her porch, jerking herself up there like the hydraulic lift when it's not working right.

"Hey, Miss Georgia!" I caught my breath while she turned herself around. "You got ninety-five cents?" Then I winked.

She leaned on the porch rail, raised one eyebrow, and smiled, while I explained that just replacing a tiny part of the alternator, the brushes, would fix the problem. "You is your daddy's boy, Red, yes, you is. Just like him."

I grinned a big one.

"You have a seat while I get you some of your favorite ice cream, all right?"

I sat down on the top step of Miss Georgia's front porch and started picking away at the peeling paint like I always did. And I ran my finger over the IMF, for "Impossible Missions Force," that me and Thomas had carved into her porch railing years before. She wasn't happy about it at first, but when we told her it was so she'd always have protection from us, Barney and Willy, the *Mission: Impossible* team, she didn't seem to mind as much. It felt like old times. Except that everything was different. No Daddy. No Thomas. No home, if Mama got her way.

Miss Georgia's screen door creaked open, and she appeared with my bowl in one hand and her iced tea in the other. I jumped up to get the bowl from her because her hand was shaking the way some old people's do.

I took a bite of the mint chocolate chip ice cream and felt it go down the inside of my chest, the chill feeling like the creek running over hot swollen feet. I sat back down on the top step and leaned against the porch railing.

Miss Georgia lowered herself into her green metal glider and squeaked slowly backward and forward. I remembered that sound from the time I was a little kid. Miss Georgia used to babysit me — and J, once he came along. We'd play on the porch and smell the sausages and eggs she'd fry up in the kitchen. I always liked the way she made breakfast for supper. More than once after supper I'd fallen asleep right there on the porch, listening to the squeaking of the glider and sometimes Miss Georgia talking to her dead husband, James, when she thought I was already asleep.

I wasn't sitting on her porch long before I blurted out what was on my mind. "Mama's trying to sell our place and some stupid lawyer from Richmond is trying to buy it" — I put on a stuck-up voice — "for his *cli-ent.*"

The squeak of the glider stopped. "I like me some of them white lawyers from Richmond."

"What?"

"Uh-huh, even got one of their photographs up on my wall. You've seen it."

She was right. I'd seen it, but I'd never known who that guy was next to Martin Luther King Jr. and Jesus. "He's a lawyer?"

"Uh-huh, Mr. Howard Carwile. He got my land back for me."

"What land?"

"The land you sittin' on right now."

"What are you talking about, Miss Georgia?"

She swept her hand that wasn't holding the iced tea out toward the vegetable garden beyond her porch. "I'm talkin' about this land. This house. This porch. This was my grand-daddy's homeplace, but after his church burned down and he died, my grandmother took my daddy and the other kids and moved away. Still, it was our land. Should've been our land. When my daddy moved us back and rebuilt the house, we weren't here very long before the sheriff came and told us to get on out because the land wasn't ours no more."

"That wasn't right."

"Lot of things happened that weren't right, Red, you know that. And seeing as how the sheriff back then was part of the Ku Klux Klan . . ." She shook her head. "So we moved way on out of here, clear to Atlanta, Georgia. I missed this place, though, I always did." She smiled. "Then I met James, and Atlanta didn't seem so bad."

I decided to make my point about how Mama shouldn't think this place was so bad, either, since it was where she moved when she married Daddy. "Georgia was pretty good to you, wasn't it? I mean, it even made you a beauty queen."

She stared at me like I hadn't washed in two weeks. "How do you figure that?"

"Well," I said, starting to feel my face getting pink, "before you become Miss America, you have to be Miss Some-State-or-Other, like Miss Virginia. So if you're Miss Georgia, weren't you the beauty queen of Georgia?"

She laughed so hard that every time she started talking she busted out laughing again. All I could make out was "imagine," and "black woman," and "oh, child!"

Now my face was all the way red, and I wished I'd just kept my mouth shut. "Well, shoot, Miss Georgia, it's not like your name is Georgia. It's Fannie Mae Freeman Jones. I know because I heard my daddy say it lots of times. And you lived in Georgia when you were beauty-queen age, so what was I supposed to think?"

She wiped her eyes and finally quit laughing. "I like your thinkin', Red, I really do. But I wasn't no beauty queen."

"Then how come you're called Miss Georgia?"

"My daddy's name was George, and I followed him around and copied whatever he did from the time I was a toddler. Didn't matter how tough or dirty the task was, I wanted to be right in there with him. Guess I was a tomboy, closest thing to a son he had, what with three daughters. So my nickname became Georgia, after my daddy, George. Nobody ever used my real name. I was always Georgia. Your mama and daddy brought you up right, which is why you call me Miss Georgia and ma'am." She gave a little laugh. "No, sir, Georgia wouldn't a seen fit to make me no beauty queen."

"Atlanta's a big city, though. Wasn't it better in a big city instead of the country?" I'd seen pictures on the news of big cities like Washington, DC, and there were a lot of black people there with jobs and houses and everything. I knew Thomas's parents both worked and they had their own house.

"You mean, better for my kind?"

I kind of shrank down into the porch, because that was exactly what I meant but I hadn't wanted to come right out and say it.

Her voice went all grumbly, and I knew what that meant. She had stuff she wanted to say, but she figured people weren't going to listen, so she kind of mumbled it. But she said it loud enough for you to hear in case you might be inclined. "Big cities. Huh. Big don't mean smarter, and big don't mean better. Big only means there's more of it."

I tried to turn the subject back to Mama and the move. "But you stayed in Atlanta for a long time."

"I stayed until I couldn't run the bakery no more all by myself after my James passed."

"Didn't your son want to stay in Atlanta?"

"George was grown by then. He was makin' his own way, didn't want nothing to do with this country life." She shook her head. "Now, my granddaughter, Carolyn, she might want to move down here some day. I keep tellin' her this'd be a better place to raise up Anthony, especially now that she a widow. Don't know why she'd want to live in Washington, DC."

"It's the nation's capital, Miss Georgia. Thomas says it's a really cool place to live."

"You ever see young Thomas anymore?"

I looked away. "No, ma'am. Mama says he got too old for me." I didn't mention the real reason. She probably knew, anyway.

"You boys were like two peas in a pod. Remember how you'd try to trick me when I gave you cookies? You'd say, 'Nu-uh, Miss Georgia, you didn't give me none, you only gave some to Thomas,' and when I gave you some more, Thomas would say, 'Miss Georgia, you forgot about me,' and then the two of you'd be gigglin' like you really thought I was fallin' for it."

"That was when we were little kids, Miss Georgia."

"Right," she said, "like last year."

"It was not!"

"I'm just teasin' you." She started chuckling. "Remember when you screamed like to raise the dead 'cause your raft was sinkin' and you thought you'd drown? And the creek wasn't more than two feet deep? I could hear you all the way from this porch."

"We were really little when that happened, Miss Georgia!"

"Oh," she said, trying not to smile, "I thought that was last year, too."

I tried to raise one eyebrow at her, the way she always did, but I never could do it and it made her laugh, as usual.

"I sure do miss having Thomas around, though," I said.

"I know what you mean. I miss my granddaughter, and Anthony's my only great-grandchild. We need some young folk here. I won't be around much longer, and I don't want my history buried along with me. But don't seem like anybody wants to know about history."

"That's 'cause history's boring and stupid." I didn't mind reading and I liked science, but history class was always boring — and pointless, because it had all happened already, so there was nothing you could do about it.

"Stupid, huh? Do you know what this area used to be called?"

I shook my head.

"Oh, I see. You don't even know what your own homeplace was called, but it's history that's the stupid one, huh?"

If I weren't so respectful I'd have given Miss Georgia a nasty look.

"My granddaddy's church was named the Freedom Church. And this area was called Freedom's Folly. You got any idea what a folly is?"

"No."

"It's a mistake. Folks said it was a mistake for him to try to build a church here for black folk." She sighed. "But I had hope, just like my granddaddy. I wanted to go back to my childhood home, Like your mama does."

"Mama's got a home and a business and a family here. She's got no reason to leave. Daddy wouldn't have liked this one bit. It's shameful."

"Don't you go poor-mouthin' your mama. She's a fine lady, yes she is. She always been more than kind to me. Does some shoppin' for me, takes me to the doctor when I need to go, used to take me to church when I could make that long trip. She a good woman."

And then it hit me, another thing that was wrong with our moving. Who was going to help out Miss Georgia if

Mama wasn't around? And who would be Rosie's best friend if I was gone? And where would Beau work? Daddy was the only one in Stony Gap who would give him a job. What would happen to Beau?

"You got to be patient with your mama. She come all the way from Ohio to be your daddy's bride. It's been hard for her to live here as an outsider, but she stuck it out."

"Outsider? It's not like Ohio is a different country."

She chuckled and shook her head. "Child, it might as well be another planet. It's hard breakin' into a community. You always the outsider." She looked across her vegetable garden and toward our house. "Always the outsider."

I shook my head and let out a groan.

I guess Miss Georgia thought I was sassing her because she said, "You be careful or I'ma start singin'."

I couldn't help cracking a smile.

"You know what I'm talkin' about."

It was the song Daddy sang in the What-U-Want. "I know," I said, "R-E-S-P-E-C-T."

"Uh-huh, that Aretha Franklin, she know what she's talkin' about. So did your daddy. And I *expect*" — and she lingered on *expect* the way a teacher would — "you do, too. Right?"

"Yes, ma'am." I grinned up at her. "Especially if it'll stop you from singing."

She raised one eyebrow back at me and tried to make a stern face, but her lips turned up and the lines around her eyes crinkled as she tried not to smile.

Chapter Nine
Spray-Painting

When I got home, I helped Beau pull the alternator out of Miss Georgia's Rambler so we'd be ready to put in the new brushes when they arrived. We also did a couple of oil changes, which was about all anyone brought their cars in for anymore. I guess they all thought Daddy was the only one who fixed their cars. It was mostly him, but there was a lot me and Beau could do, too.

Finally it was suppertime and I was starving, so I headed into the house. J was in his underwear again, like a baby, whining about being hungry, and Mama was sitting at the dining-room table with her forehead in her hands, her pretty blond hair all messed up like she'd been pulling at it. Daddy's accounting books were spread in front of her. I knew what that meant. She was putting in the receipts and invoices, figuring out who owed us what and who we owed money to. From the mess of papers spread across the table it didn't look like she had any idea what she was doing.

Daddy always took care of everything. If he needed

Beau's help in the shop, they hung a sign at the What-U-Want telling folks to call at the house, and Mama would go take care of things. But Daddy said Mama was a better cook than Betty Crocker and Julia Child combined, made a home look finer than *Southern Living* magazine, and kept J and me in line, which was more than enough jobs for any one person. Except now Mama wasn't cooking at all, and it seemed like I was the one taking care of J.

Mama looked at the piles of papers in front of her on the dining-room table and sighed. "I'm trying to figure this out, baby." Mama's voice was as slumped as her shoulders. "Can you just pick something out?"

J groaned. "How come you never make us anything anymore, Mama?"

"How come you never wear clothes anymore?" I asked him.

"Leave me alone!" J said.

Mama rubbed her temples. "I'm just not inspired to cook lately."

"But I'm hungry."

"There's food in the fridge," she said.

"I don't want any of that icky stuff!"

"How about a sandwich?" she asked.

"I'm sick of sandwiches! And I'm thirsty. We don't have anything good to drink. How come you never let us get sodas from the What-U-Want anymore, huh? Daddy always let us have a Coke. Now we're like poor people!"

Mama slapped her hand down on the table and stood up real sudden. I stepped out of the doorway so she could march past me into the kitchen. From her face I couldn't tell if she was going to start yelling or bawling.

With a shaky hand she grabbed J's Flintstone's glass from the cabinet, opened the fridge, and poured him some milk. "Here," she said, sticking it in his hand so hard some milk sloshed over his wrist. "I need to drive Beau home, and I'll figure out what to feed you when I get back."

The screen door slapped behind her while J stared at the glass in his hand. "I don't drink milk," he said in a small voice. He stared at the screen door. "Don't you remember, Mama?" He looked at me, his bottom lip shaking. "Doesn't she remember?"

I didn't want him to start bawling, so I quickly took the glass from him. "It's OK, I'll make you a sandwich."

"But I don't *want* —"

"A special sandwich. Out of special stuff. Like Daddy used to make, remember?"

He was still pouty but he'd raised his eyebrows, so I knew he was curious. "With potato chips inside?"

"Maybe."

"With mayonnaise and peppermints inside?"

"Let's see what we got."

Peanut butter was about all we had and we were both sick of it, but I opened the fridge slowly and dramatically to give me a chance to think. I played up rubbing my chin and hemming and hawing and saying, "Oh, my," like an old granny enough times that I got a little smile out of J.

"Why, yes, young man, I believe I've found something that will take care of your thirst and your hunger at the same time . . . a pickle-peanut-butter sandwich!

J frowned.

I looked past him to the kitchen table with the lazy

Susan on it. And the sugar bowl. "With a heap of cinnamon sugar inside."

He finally nodded.

I made him sit at the kitchen table and I did, too. The sandwiches weren't bad — it's amazing what you can add to peanut butter and it still tastes good — and I wolfed two of them down while J was still on the first half of his.

"You shouldn't eat so fast," he said.

I laughed. "Who are you? Mama?"

"No, but Mama said after supper we're supposed to clear out our rooms."

I felt the peanut butter stick in my throat. "What?"

"We have to collect old clothes and books and toys so we can give them away to charity." He pointed to a bunch of brown paper bags in the corner of the dining room that I could see from the kitchen. I hadn't noticed them before. The bags had high-heel shoes and purses coming out of the tops. "See?" J said, "That's her old stuff, and she says she doesn't want to pay to move any of our old stuff, either."

"I'm not moving anything."

J's eyes went big. "You're giving it all to charity?"

"I'm not planning on moving."

"But Mr. Harrison said he's bringing somebody by to see the house, so Mama says we have to."

I slammed the table with my fist. "I don't care what Mama says!"

J jerked back in his chair and stared at me.

I pushed away from the table and headed for the door.

"Where are you going?"

"Nowhere." I slammed the screen door behind me and jumped down the steps.

"Can I come with you?"

"No!" I called over my shoulder.

"How come, Red? You're supposed to babysit me when Mama's not here! I'm telling! I wanna . . ."

But I let the sound of my footsteps in the gravel drown him out.

I decided pretty quick that I didn't need Darrell's gang to help me spray-paint. Maybe I didn't have any experience, but how much did you need? You just made a mess when no one was watching. All I had to do was wait until it got pitch-dark. Then, when Mr. Harrison came by to show off our place to whoever it was, it sure wouldn't look good.

I found myself over at Rosie's and heard Mr. Dunlop yelling foul words at Mrs. Dunlop. I also heard a sweeter, softer sound, like a bird. It was getting dark, so it took me a moment to realize it was Rosie singing, and another moment before I saw where she was. She was sitting in our climbing tree, on that branch that was level with the bushes by the side of the Dunlops' house. When we were little, Darrell used to dare us to jump off that branch and over the bushes, landing in the dirt of their front yard. It was a big leap back then, but now we were taller than the branch.

Rosie had her back against the tree trunk with her legs stretched out along the branch like she was lounging on a sofa. She had her eyes closed, the ear jack of her transistor radio in one ear, a finger plugging her other ear, while she sang along to that Helen Reddy song that was always on the radio, "I Am Woman." I guess she was blocking out her daddy. She looked sweet and peaceful, and I decided to just watch her for a minute instead of bother her. I wanted to tell her what I was about to do, but I figured it might be better if she had no idea. Then no one could blame her for not stopping me or for lying about it afterward.

Since it was almost dark, I headed down the path to our place. I crept as softly as I could across the gravel, opened the door of the shop, and grabbed the can of spray paint from when Daddy sprayed the wrought iron railings around the front porch. Inside the shop, I talked softly to Daddy, almost like a little prayer. "I'm sorry to do this, Daddy. I know it's not what you'd expect from the Boy Wonder, but it's for a good cause. Remember when you took my slingshot away from me because I hit Bobby Benson? Even though he hit me first — and a lot of times? And I got just one tiny bruise on him? And Reverend Benson never took Bobby's slingshot away? You said it was for my own good. I was mad at you, but now I understand, sort of. You gave it back to me in the summer, when you said I'd grown up enough. So I'm really messing up the shop for your own good, and I promise I'll get it back in shape once Mama decides not to sell."

I ignored the voice in my head that said, "*If* Mama decides not to sell."

When I came back outside, I noticed the new For Sale sign Mr. Harrison had put up. In concrete, so I couldn't pull it out again. I practiced my spray-painting on it until it was black. Then I stared at the shop for a long time. Because I didn't know what I should spray on it.

Darrell always used that Nazi cross when he spray-painted, but Daddy hated it with a passion, so I wasn't going to do that. Rosie sometimes drew little vampire symbols on her arms, but I didn't know how to make them. Besides, other people might not know what they meant, either, and I wanted to make my message loud and clear.

Then it came to me, like genius inspiration. I would use the kind of word that meant filth and would make everyone want to stay away from my shop. That old Poindexter lawyer wouldn't be able to get anyone interested in our place by the time I was done with it.

I popped the lid off the can and started to spray. I picked the part without the window so nothing would get in the way of my word. It was hard to see how well it was working, but my hand sure felt shaky, more shaky the longer I held the spray nozzle down, because that thing is hard to press. I got all the way through it and held it down extra long at the end to be sure I made my point.

When I lifted my finger off of the nozzle, it didn't stop. For some dumb reason, I turned the can toward me and sprayed myself in the face. I dropped the can real quick, but it started jerking all around, spraying black, like one of those firecracker snakes. I was trying to dodge it and grab it at the same time, and ended up tripping over it, slamming my knee into the gravel.

"Ow!"

The light went on in Mama's bedroom.

I lay there frozen for a second. I grabbed the can that had finally quit spraying, jumped up quick, and hightailed it to my window. I scraped past the tree and fell inside, shoved the can under my bed, and, with the light from the hall, saw the paint on my hands. Oh, man! And there was probably paint on my face, too! There was nothing for it but to make a wild leap for the bathroom. I heard Mama in the kitchen, opening the screen door, as I slammed and locked the bathroom door behind me.

I looked in the mirror and it was worse than I thought. So bad, I let out a loud moan. I quickly turned on the faucets and started scraping soap onto a towel to scrub down my face.

The bathroom door shook as someone banged on it.

"What?" I screamed.

"Red, is that you?" It was Mama.

"Yes!"

"Are you all right?"

"Yeah, I just have to go to the bathroom, OK?"

"I thought I heard something outside."

"Well, it wasn't me. I-I'm in here. See?"

"Are you sure you're all right?"

I was scrubbing my face now. "I'm fine."

"You sound a little funny."

"Well . . . that's because you don't usually talk to me when I'm trying to use the bathroom."

"OK," she said slowly, like she wasn't quite convinced. "If you need anything, you just let me know."

"I won't." I could feel her still standing there on the other side of the door. "I mean, I won't need anything."

It took me awhile to get myself cleaned up, and awhile

longer to feel safe enough to come out of the bathroom. I finally shut the light off and could see around the cracks of the door that the hallway outside was dark. When I opened the door, I saw that Mama's light was off, too.

I crept softly across the hall but not quietly enough.

"Good night, Red," Mama called from her room.

"Yeah, good night," I said, and made a beeline for my bed so I could scramble under the covers before she saw I was still in my clothes.

Chapter Ten
What Would Daddy Say?

The next morning, I woke up to the screen door slapping and the sound of footsteps across the gravel. I was out of bed in a flash and jumped to the window, even though I knew I couldn't see the front of the shop from my bedroom.

I couldn't see Mama, either, but I heard her. "What in the world is that?"

I ran to the kitchen, where J looked up from eating his bananas in orange juice. "What?"

I remembered to play it cool and did a fake yawn. "Oh . . . sounds like Mama found something strange outside," I said, and shrugged.

J was out of the screen door like a bolt of lightning. I wanted to fly out of there faster than J, but I managed to walk. I stared at the ground to keep from running. When I looked up, I saw Mama and J staring at the front of the shop, Mama with her head cocked and J with his nose all scrunched up like he was trying to smell the word. I was torn between laughing and cheering, but I knew I couldn't do either one.

I took a deep breath before looking at the shop myself. When I saw it, my mouth fell open and I felt like someone punched the breath right out of my stomach.

J read the letters out loud. "S-h-i-p. Why does it say *ship*? Somebody don't know how to spell. Shop is s-h-*o*-p."

I couldn't believe it. I never was any good at cursive, but how could it have gone so wrong? I stared at the *p* that wasn't supposed to be, and I realized that I should've taken my finger off the trigger before I tried to cross the *t*, because I'd ended up making a loop. Then I figured out my other mistake. I held the trigger too long at the end and all the extra paint had run down to make a long drip that turned into the bottom of the *p*. *Ship*.

Mama picked up the black plastic cap of the spray can that I forgot about. *Shoot*. "Spray paint," she said, "like we have in the shop."

J pointed at my jeans. "What's that black stuff?"

I looked down and saw what that snakish spray-paint can had done to me. Even though I'd stashed the blackened shirt under my bed, my jeans were giving me away. I lost my voice for a second, but then managed to say, "It's just dirt."

"You're gonna get in trouble for making such a mess of yourself," J said.

I knew J was just mad because I didn't take him with me yesterday. I was more worried about Mama. I could feel her staring at me even though I was looking at the ground. I knew she was going to have a fit, I just didn't know exactly what she'd do.

"Well," she said, her voice calm, "I'm sure it won't happen again. Will it, Red?"

I looked up, and she was squeezing the cap of the spray can between her fingers.

"No, ma'am," I mumbled.

She was staring at me, her eyes narrowed down to real tough. "I think I'll let you paint the shop, Red. And while you're at it, why don't you start cleaning it out so you can paint the inside, too? We'll need to get rid of all that junk before we move."

I gritted my teeth. "It's not junk, Mama."

"Well, there's nothing in there that'll be any use to us in Ohio."

"There's Old Man Porter's desk — my desk."

She raised her eyebrows, either because she didn't know that Daddy had promised it to me or because she'd always thought "Old Man Porter" was a rude way to talk, even though Daddy said it was a mark of respect. Old Man Porter was the boss of Stony Gap.

"Daddy said I'd inherit Great-Great-Granddaddy Porter's desk. It's got my name on it. And there's no way I'm leaving it behind."

"Red, it's just an old desk, and it's too big —"

"It is not just an old desk! It's all I'll have left of Daddy if you're taking me away from here! Maybe you don't care about him anymore, but I do!"

Mama's hands went to her hips and her eyes flashed daggers at me. Her foot started tapping the gravel like a jackhammer. "I am not," she said, pointing at the shop, "lugging that huge thing with us all the way to Ohio!"

"Well, I am!"

"You don't have the money to move that monstrosity, so it's staying right there."

I narrowed my eyes down to hateful.

She turned and marched back inside like she'd won the battle. But she hadn't won the war.

The whole time I was painting the shop, J rode his bike back and forth, saying, "Are you having fun, Red?" and "Is this better than what you did yesterday?" and "That's what you get for being mean." I tried to ignore him, but the hotter it got, the harder it was to pretend he wasn't bothering me.

When Mr. Harrison drove up, I saw my chance. I called J over. "Hey, J, do you want to do something fun?"

He scrunched his face up. "I ain't painting the shop. I know that trick already. Daddy read us *Tom Sawyer*, remember?"

"Do you want to be a spy, like James Bond, double-o-seven?"

That got him. He skidded his bike to a stop beside me. "What do I do?"

I whispered so he'd get the idea it was something sly. "Go spy on Mama and Mr. Harrison and see if you can hear what they're saying."

He frowned. "That doesn't sound very fun."

"It's real important, though."

"If I do, will you buy me a Coke? Mama says we can't take them from the What-U-Want anymore."

"And where am I going to get the money? Come on, J."

He twisted his mouth up, trying to think of another deal. "Can we play Rock'Em Sock'Em Robots?"

"No!" I was as surprised as J at how loud I said it. But it

belonged to me and Thomas. I guess I still hoped that we'd play it again.

"Then forget it," J said, getting back on his bike.

"Wait! You can play with my Hot Wheels. I'll even help you set up my track in your room."

"Will you help me play, too? It ain't as much fun by myself."

"It *isn't* as much fun," I corrected him, like Daddy used to.

"I know it, so will you play, too?"

"Sure."

"Promise?"

"Yes, now go spy on them."

J was stuck to the side of the house like a tick on a dog, listening through the screen door. It didn't take him long to get tired of being a spy, though, and wander off.

"J!" I called.

"What?"

I looked from side to side like I had a big secret and motioned him over to me.

He came running. "What?"

I bent down and whispered to him. "What did Mr. Harrison say?"

"Aw, is that all? Shoot, I thought you had something good."

"What did he say?"

"Nothing. Just boring stuff."

"Did he say anything about Mr. Reynolds?"

"Who?"

"How about a buyer?"

"A what?"

"Somebody buying the house and shop."

"Oh, that. He said there's plenty of rich people wanting summer places."

"What else?"

He shrugged.

"Go back and listen some more."

"I don't wanna. It's boring."

"Then I'm not playing Hot Wheels with you."

"You promised!"

"Not if you don't hold up your side of the bargain."

J grabbed a fistful of gravel and threw the wad where I'd just painted. A mess of dirt and grit spread across the wall, sticking itself in the wet paint.

"J, I swear, you're paying for that!"

"You ca-ain't get me!" he taunted, running off behind the shop.

"Oh, yeah?" I raced the other way and was almost on him before he noticed and ran hollering toward the house. For some dumb reason I skidded and fell, which gave J time to reach the pitch pine outside my window and begin climbing. The problem is, those branches are so close together and the pine needles are so prickly, it's about the worst getaway tree you could pick, so I was on him in seconds, pulling him down. He fought back pretty well for a little kid, so I had to hit him and he started screaming.

So did Mama. Even Mr. Harrison felt like he should get in on the yelling, shouting, "Stop it now, boys!"

I let go of J, and he ran crying to Mama, as usual, so I'd get in trouble instead of him.

Mr. Harrison shook his head at me before getting in his

car. He called out the window to Mama, "'Bye, Betty, I'm always here to help," as he drove off.

Mama was ready to spit nails, so I figured I'd better defend myself while I had the chance.

"J started it! He's been pestering me all day. He just threw gravel —"

"Red! You're twelve years old now! J is only seven."

"I know, but —"

"You're his big brother. You're supposed to be helping him."

"I'm trying, but he won't listen to me! You don't know what that's like!"

Mama was silent for a long moment, clenching her teeth together. Finally she said, "Oh, yes, I think I do, Red," and glared at me.

I wasn't going to let her make me feel guilty. I had a good reason for not listening to her. Ohio.

"My knee hurts," J said in a crybaby voice, hanging on to Mama.

Mama looked down at the tiny little trickle of blood and gasped. "See, Red?"

When she looked over at me, J lost his pained look and started grinning.

I shook my head. "He's faking —"

"Honestly, Red!" Mama put her hand on her hip. "I know you're upset about your daddy, but what do you think Daddy would say if he were here now?" She stared at me, her eyes turning pink and watery.

I looked away because I didn't want to hear what she was going to say. But she said it anyway.

"Writing foul language on his shop? Running after your little brother, hurting him and then trying to blame him, a seven-year-old, for starting it all? And treating me like I don't even exist?" Her voice was shaky now, and she took a raspy breath. "What would your daddy say?" She choked up, spun around, and marched to the house. "Come on inside, J," she said, without turning her head, "I'll fix you up."

As soon as the door slammed behind her, J started his teasing. "Ha-ha, you got in trou-ble."

When I looked at him I was surprised at how blurry he was and how croaky and quiet my "shut up" came out. Then I realized I was all choked up, but it was too late to hide it from J. I turned my back on him, waiting for a stream of name-calling and meanness. Not that I cared. Nothing would make me feel worse than I already did, because I knew what else Daddy would say. He said it anytime he left, anytime there was a problem, anytime he needed my help.

I know I can count on you, son.

When I wiped my eyes and turned to stare at him, J wasn't grinning. His mouth was drooped open and his dark eyes looked kind of scared. I guess he'd never seen me almost crying before, at least not without a lot of blood coming out of me.

"What?" I said.

He shrugged, stuffed his hands in the pockets of his shorts, and looked at the ground, pushing some gravel around with his Keds. Finally he turned and walked toward the house, but he kept looking back at me over his shoulder.

Chapter Eleven
The Sheriff

The next day, Mr. Harrison came by with another For Sale sign since I'd spray-painted the last one. He was hopping mad because he had to dig the whole wad of cement out of the ground to get the old sign out. I was in my room because I was grounded, but he kept yelling over to my window stuff like, "Boy, you want to come over here and help with this?" and "I don't own a lumberyard, you know!" and "Sheriff Scott might like to know about this kind of vandalism!"

I didn't mind at all, though, because I also heard Mr. Harrison tell Mama that the buyer he thought he'd snagged had gotten away. In fact, I thought the whole thing was downright funny until the sheriff came by that afternoon.

Every kid in town had been scared of Sheriff Scott since the day he shot his gun off in my first-grade classroom. I'll never forget it. He started out real nice, about how police-men and sheriffs are your friends. He slowly pulled out his gun, which is what we boys had been waiting for, and we all oohed and aahed. He said, "Y'all like this gun, huh? You want to see how much fun it is?" and suddenly his face went all mad and red, and he let out a blood-curdling war whoop, swung his gun around, and fired a bullet right through the open window. It was such a thundering noise that it sent the birds screaming from their trees and us screaming under our desks. Mama was beside herself when she found out. Daddy said Sheriff Scott did it because he'd seen too many kids get hurt by guns and he wanted to show us once and for all that it wasn't a toy to be played with. It worked. After that whenever I saw the sheriff I felt queasy, because all I could see was his red face hollering as he shot that powerful gun off right in front of me.

I could hear my own heart pounding when Mama called me into the living room. You don't know how much you make a floor creak until people are hushed and staring at you. It felt like the time everyone came over after the funeral. Only quieter. At least then, some of them were talking softly. Now it was dead still. Mama was real pale and wavering like she was about to drop. Sheriff Scott was sticking his lips out, making that long, slow kissing noise.

The Kiss of Death.

I couldn't look straight at him. I was too busy looking at the floor. But out of the corner of my eye I could see his boots, his legs, and all the way up to his holster, with that gun.

I saw a hand move to his belt. "What were you up to last night, Red?"

"N-nothing. Much." I swallowed hard, and it felt like someone clapped their hands inside my head.

"You weren't over at the graveyard, were you?"

I let out my breath because I knew I was safe on that one. I even looked up. "No, sir, nowhere close."

The sheriff looked over at Mama.

"He went straight to bed after painting the shop. As . . . as far as I know."

Sheriff Scott made another Kiss of Death. "Seems like a lot of spray-painting going on lately." He stared at me, took a deep breath, and put his other hand on his belt. The gun side. "This your new hobby?"

I shook my head.

"I don't think this is what your daddy had in mind for you. You got anything to say?"

I didn't know what I could say.

Mama spoke real slow, almost like she was taking a breath between each word. "Frederick Stewart Porter, did you spray-paint those headstones at the graveyard last night?"

I stared at her. "Headstones? Someone spray-painted headstones? Daddy's? Did someone paint Daddy's?"

Neither of them answered. They just stood there like headstones themselves.

I bolted out of the house and ran all the way to the graveyard without stopping, even though my lungs felt fit to burst. I was almost there when I saw Rosie sitting on the grass in the corner of the graveyard, crying. I wanted to check on Daddy's headstone, but I couldn't exactly walk right past her.

"What's wrong, Rosie?"

"I don't want to be around when Daddy gets his hands on Darrell."

"Oh. Yeah." I should've known Darrell was responsible. I looked around and there was more than just spray-painted headstones. One was even busted. It was a Dunlop's. I looked over toward where Daddy's headstone was.

"It's OK," said Rosie, "I didn't let them do anything to your daddy's." She sniffed.

I still craned my neck, trying to see if there was any damage. The mayonnaise jar was broken and the roses on the ground. I stormed over there and carefully brushed the glass away from Daddy's grave. I propped the roses up against his headstone, like the blossoms were leaning on Daddy.

When I heard Rosie sniffling some more I looked around. She was looking back toward her house, or more likely, her shed.

I walked over to her. "Maybe the sheriff won't find out it was Darrell."

Her big dark eyes looked at me like I was slower than a possum. She took a deep breath and let it out. "At least school starts in a week and a half, so Darrell won't be getting in as much trouble."

"What?"

"OK, he gets in trouble at school, too, but they don't always tell Daddy, so —"

"No, I mean, school starts in a week and a half? Are you sure?"

"Next Monday is Labor Day, Red. You know school always starts the day after Labor Day."

How did it get to be almost Labor Day already? Without me even noticing?

I sat down next to her. "Shoot. How am I going to stop Mama from selling our place if I'm stuck in school all day? Who cares about stupid English and stupid history and stupid math?"

She didn't have a chance to answer because we heard the distant slam of a door, and we both knew it was the Dunlops' shed. Rosie looked at me, her eyes pleading, like she wanted me to help but there was nothing I could do. Me and Thomas had tried. But it hadn't worked. She flinched when we heard Darrell scream the first time. After that, we just sat there, as still as the graveyard.

It's weird how when you want to cover up an awful noise like that you can't think of anything to say or do and you just sit there stupidly in the stillness that you don't want. Rosie squeezed her lips together hard, but it looked like the crying was going to come out of her eyes anyway.

I don't know what made me do it, but I reached out and put my hand over hers. Her hand was so soft and fragile. She looked at me, and if she hadn't been about to bust out crying, I swear she would've smiled. It was almost like holding hands. And it helped while we waited, trying to tune out the smacking sound and Darrell's crying. I wished Mr. Dunlop wouldn't do it. Couldn't he see that it didn't stop Darrell? If anything, it made Darrell worse.

Finally Rosie whispered, "He's done."

I gave her hand a little squeeze, and we both let out our breaths. It was over. For now.

Chapter Twelve
The Brotherhood

Darrell came to see me the next day. I tried to pretend that he wasn't walking funny. I guess his backside still hurt from the beating his daddy gave him.

"We're meeting in the woods behind Kenny's tonight," he said.

"Who?"

"The gang, dingbat! Do you want our help or not?"

"It didn't work so well last time."

"That was Kenny's fault. And Thomas's."

"Thomas didn't do anything!"

Darrell shrugged. "Glen said to bring you up the mountain behind Kenny's, because tonight's the Brotherhood's big night."

"The Brotherhood?"

"That's the name of the gang." Darrell looked at me like he was so smart and I was an idiot.

How was I supposed to know the gang's name? "Why's it called the Brotherhood?"

Now Darrell didn't look so smart. "It's the name Glen picked, OK?"

"Is he the boss?"

"He's not a boss, he's a chieftain."

I guess Darrell didn't like the face I made. "Fine, you don't have to come."

"I'll come if you think the gang — the Brotherhood — can help me."

"Of course we can. You have to show you're worth it, though."

"How?"

"Glen will tell you."

I got the feeling that Darrell didn't have a clue. In fact, I wasn't convinced he was even a real member of the gang. Still I was desperate. "All right, I'll come."

He pointed his finger in my face. "I'm sticking my neck out for you, pipsqueak, so you'd better behave." He turned on his boot heels and walked awkwardly back home.

• • • • • •

Late that night Larry led us up the hill with his flashlight held low to the ground, "so Uncle Kenny don't see us," he whispered, as if Kenny could hear us all the way up the mountain.

I heard the gang's voices before I could see them, talking softly and occasionally laughing. When we got close, Larry's flashlight lit up the faces of half a dozen guys. They were mostly the guys from Kenny's earlier that week. Every one of them had a black cross drawn on his right cheek, except Glen, who had a big black smudge on his puffed-up cheek and what looked like the beginnings of a black eye. He also had a white scarf thrown around his neck, which was weird, considering how warm it was.

He raised his arm to cover the banged-up side of his face. "Cut the dang light!"

Larry turned it off and we were in darkness.

"What's with the crosses?" I whispered to Darrell.

"Nobody told me," he said, and swore under his breath.

"Password?" Glen demanded.

I looked at Darrell.

Darrell looked at Larry, who looked back at him. "You," Larry said.

"Brotherhood?" Darrell asked.

"Figures," a deep voice to the right of us said. "That must be Dunlop."

Glen sighed. "Brotherhood is our name, stupid. The password is 'Burn 'em all.'"

"What's a kid doing here?" the deep voice said.

I looked into the darkness and could barely make out the figure, standing off to the right of the gang, leaning against a tree. When I stared harder, I saw it was actually two figures, one much bigger than the other.

"It's all right, Joe," Glen called over to the tree. "Porter needs help. And it's just the type of problem the Brotherhood is here to take care of. Come on over here."

Me and Darrell both started walking until Glen barked, "Not you, Dunlop! Porter."

I felt a little bad for Darrell as I left his side and stood next to Glen.

Larry somehow knew to turn the flashlight on low, aimed at Glen's feet, and Glen warmed up to it. He cleared his throat and tugged on the white scarf around his neck. "Porter, your family has owned that land almost as long as my family has owned ours. You deserve to stay here. And we don't want any outsiders moving in, if you know what I mean."

I didn't know what he meant, but I didn't want anyone buying our place so I nodded.

"That's right. Do you think your great-great-grandfather took care of this land for *them*?"

I didn't know exactly who *them* was, but Glen was staring at me for an answer.

"No," I said, "he was taking care of it for us Porters."

"Exactly." Glen put his arm around my shoulders like I'd seen his daddy do to people a hundred times. "We don't need any of them moving in on our land, do we?"

"No."

"That's right, Porter."

"So," I said, "how are you going to stop it?"

He gave that politician chuckle. "You mean, how are *we* going to stop it? First you need to be a part of the Brotherhood. Are you in?"

I looked at Glen's swollen face. "I — I guess so."

"Oh, you need to be a little more enthusiastic, young Porter." Glen talked like he was as grown up as his daddy. "Virginia passed a law this spring allowing *anyone* to buy property. Do you know what that means?" He explained that *anyone* meant blacks, too. Only he didn't say blacks. He used a bunch of names that Daddy said would get our mouths washed out with soap if he ever heard such language.

"I know you agree, don't you, Porter?"

"I don't want anyone buying my land," I said. "I don't care who it is."

"Well, we can stop that for you. We have friends in high places." Then he talked on and on about keeping our land white and the importance of our heritage and the legacy of our founding fathers, sounding like a politician. I knew he was being a bigot, which I didn't care for, but I needed the Brotherhood's help to stop the sale.

Finally Glen took his arm from my shoulder and rubbed his hands together. "Now, we'll do a purification ceremony. That's your initiation. Are you ready to join the Brotherhood?"

I felt queasy, but the idea of losing my home felt even worse. So I nodded.

"Good. Larry, give me that flashlight." The shaft of light wobbled along with Larry as he crunched through the leaves.

"You," said Glen, aiming the beam at a small clearing, "are going to set that on fire."

I followed the beam of light. A yardstick was stuck in the dirt. About a foot down from the top, a ruler was attached to it with wire horizontally. It was a cross.

I knew what it meant to set fire to a cross. The only folks who did that were the Ku Klux Klan. Or the folks who tried to do that in Thomas's grandparents' front yard. They did it to be hateful. I swallowed hard to keep the queasiness in my stomach from coming up. "A cross? Why?"

Glen flashed the light on the faces of the gang members as they squinted from the brightness. "See those crosses? That's why."

That didn't really answer the question.

"It's for the Brotherhood," he added. "You do it for the Brotherhood and you're one of us."

"But burning a cross? You can't do that. That's like —"

"It's just a symbol," Glen said.

Over by the tree Joe muttered something.

Glen held a lighter out to me.

I realized something, and my throat went dry. "Did — were you —" I coughed.

"Spit it out, Porter," Glen said, his voice weary.

"Did you guys . . ." I wanted to ask if they were the ones who put the cross in Thomas's grandparents' front yard. But as I looked at the gang of boys with crosses on their grim faces I lost my nerve.

Glen shook his head like he couldn't believe me. "We're Christian, OK? It's not like we're the KKK!" His voice turned calm and soothing. "Don't worry, Porter. It's OK. It's only three feet high. Like I said, it's just a symbol. Besides, no one will see you."

I thought about what he said, and he was right. No black person would see, anyway, and that was all that mattered. But I couldn't help feeling a little sick.

I took the lighter and walked over to the cross, kneeling in front of it. The sharp smell of kerosene hit my nose, and I noticed the cross was wet with it. The ground was cleared of leaves and sticks in about a ten foot circle, for safety, I figured.

It took me a few tries to flick the lighter on because my hand was shaking, but I finally got it started. The yardstick caught fire right away. I stepped back.

Yellow flames shot up, and the thick black smoke stung my eyes. The fire spread out across the ruler and it looked just like a cross, a burning cross. We were all quiet, staring at it, until Larry spoke.

"I sure hope Uncle Kenny don't see this. You better put it out!"

"Quit worrying," Glen said.

Still I fell on my knees real quick and threw handfuls of dirt on it. It felt good to put it out. "OK," I said, standing up, "now can we talk about how to stop the sale?"

"Just one more thing to prove you're worthy of the Brotherhood," Glen said.

"But I just —"

He held up his hand, his face losing its friendliness. "It's a privilege being in this group with all its power. It's a small price to pay to show your loyalty to the Brotherhood. Bring him over, Joe."

At first I thought they were talking about me because they pushed me around until I was standing as part of a circle of guys around the burned-out cross. But when I heard a scuffling over at the tree, I looked behind me, trying to make out the two figures in the blackness. Joe was the big guy with the low voice. The other was smaller and skinnier.

When Glen flashed the light on the tree I saw who the other person was. Thomas. My mouth dropped open and my legs about dropped to the ground.

He had a cut on his brow that was bleeding down his cheek. I couldn't see all of his face because there was a gag over his mouth. And he wasn't just standing by the tree; he was tied to it. I heard myself gasp.

With his busted up face, Thomas must've been the one who got in a fight with Glen, and that was bad news. What were they going to do to him? When Joe untied him from the tree, I saw that Thomas's hands were tied behind his back. I thought I was going to throw up.

I looked around fast. Darrell was on my left, the far side of where Glen stood. "It's Thomas!" I whispered.

"Shut up," he hissed.

"But it's Thomas!"

He shrugged, but his eyes were as stricken as the times Mr. Dunlop ordered him to the shed, which got me even more scared.

I turned, and Thomas was staring at me with something between disbelief and disgust, like I was part of the Brotherhood. And I started shaking then, because I realized that he'd been here the whole time. He'd seen everything. Me, going along with Glen. Me, burning the cross. Walking right over and lighting one on fire. Just like those people tried to do to him. It was all there in his eyes.

I had to look away.

I heard Joe bring him into the circle with the burned cross. When I had the guts to look at Thomas, I saw his gag was off but he stood with his lips clamped shut and his jaw stuck out. His hands were still tied behind his back.

"What's going on?" I said, but my voice came out as a whisper.

The light was shining full on Thomas.

"Welcome to the trial," Glen said in an important voice, "of the so-called Thomas Jefferson, impersonator of our founding father and author of the Declaration of Independence."

The Brotherhood laughed and sneered, repeating, "Thomas Jefferson."

I cringed, remembering how I'd laughed at Thomas when I'd learned about the president Thomas Jefferson, because I thought it was funny that a kid would have the same name. I hoped Thomas didn't remember that.

"How dare you impersonate a president?" Glen demanded.

"It's just his name," I said quietly.

"Shut up, unless you want to join him, Porter!" Glen snapped, flashing the light on me.

I flinched because suddenly he didn't seem so fond of me.

The light went back to Thomas. "The accused is also guilty of attacking a member of the Brotherhood." In the darkness I could see Glen's hand go up to his right cheek, touching it gingerly. "In return you will feel the wrath of the Brotherhood. You need to learn a thing or two."

"What are they going to do?" I hissed at Darrell.

"They're just messing with his head."

The flashlight shone on me and Darrell, and Glen cleared his throat, loudly. "Is there something you want to say, Porter?"

I looked at the ground and shut up fast.

Glen turned the light back on Thomas. "We need to show him what happens when his kind gets uppity. Larry!"

The light swung to Larry, who was standing opposite me. His eyes were wide, even though the flashlight was in his face. He looked around like he was hoping there was another Larry in the group.

"Well," said Glen, "go on. Kick him."

Larry shrugged and gave Thomas a little kick in the shin.

"Not like that!" Glen said. "Like this." He kicked Thomas hard in the stomach, and Thomas bent over, his eyes squeezed shut. I winced, too, because that was exactly where I'd punched Thomas that night at Kenny's.

"Stop it, guys," I said, my voice much weaker than I wanted it to sound, but I was shaking because I'd never been so scared in my life.

"Shut up, kid," Joe said next to me, as he kicked Thomas in the back.

Thomas let out a cry before clamping his mouth shut again.

"Stop it," I said, louder this time.

"It's your turn," Glen said.

"I-I'm not kicking him."

"Just give him a little kick," Darrell murmured.

"No!"

Darrell grabbed my arm, hissing in my ear, "Play along so it'll be over!"

"Come on," said one of the guys I didn't know, "let's get it over with."

"See?" Darrell whispered.

Thomas wasn't looking at me. Even when I took a step toward him, he stared at the ground. I hesitated, then raised my leg and pushed it against his hip, more of a nudge than a kick. Even so, he stumbled backward like I'd punched him.

"A real kick, Porter," Glen said, his voice rising, "The Brotherhood is waiting!"

Thomas raised his head to look at me, and his eyes told me everything: anger, sadness, resentment, disappointment.

Betrayal. As hard as it was to look at him, his eyes gave me the strength to do what I did next.

I stepped back from the circle, shaking my head. "I don't want to be in the Brotherhood anymore."

Glen and Joe grinned at each other before Glen looked back at me. "Oh, it's too late for that, Porter. You're already in deep."

"Why?"

He tilted his head. "Because you're the one who lit a fire on Kenny Rae Campbell's property. And not just any fire . . . a cross!"

I felt that sick feeling in my stomach again.

"So kick him."

I shook my head.

"Joe!" Glen yelled.

Joe was on me in a flash, one arm crushing my back against his chest, the other wrenching my right arm behind me. "Stop!" I cried, and heard, at the same time.

Only my "stop!" came out all screamy because my arm hurt real bad. The other "stop!" was so loud and commanding it even made Joe loosen his grip on my arm. I looked to where the sound came from and I realized it was Thomas.

He stood in the spotlight looking taller and stronger than he had a minute ago. There was no fear anymore. The blood on his face only made him look tougher.

"Leave him alone," Thomas said, his teeth gritted and his voice shaking in anger.

It was weird how everyone froze and did what he said, for a moment at least. He was the one with his hands tied. And there were ten guys against him.

"Who's your friend, Porter?" Glen finally said. "You one of them?"

That seemed to wake Joe up, and he twisted my arm until I heard my shoulder pop out of its socket and I screamed again.

"I said, leave him alone!" Thomas's voice ended like the howl of a dog left out in the cold too long. He rushed toward us until two guys grabbed him and threw him on the ground.

A second later I was thrown into the circle, too. My right cheek hit the burned cross as I went down, and I could smell the charred wood and kerosene. It was still warm. I lifted my head and turned it, facing Thomas. His eyes flashed at my cheek and stared at me for a moment before looking away. And I knew from the darkness in his eyes that I had a black mark on my right cheek, just like the Brotherhood.

"Well, Porter," said Glen, "since you broke the circle and we couldn't finish the punishment, now we have to up the ante."

Something landed with a thud between Thomas and me, spraying dirt in my eye. It took me a moment of blinking before I could see what it was.

A rope. With a noose. Right in front of Thomas's face. He was staring at it like it was alive, like maybe if he didn't move, didn't breathe, it wouldn't kill him.

I looked up and saw Darrell at the edge of the flashlight beam. I stared at him, my eyes saying, *Do something, Darrell! Stop them!*

He stared back. I think he'd gone whiter than me, and his eyes were shouting even louder, *Do something, Red!*

At that moment, I got more mad than scared. Darrell was the one who brought me here. This was supposed to be his gang, his people. And he was three years older than me. And now, here he was, staring at me like a useless person. How in the name of heaven was I supposed to stop this thing? By myself?

I had to try something, anything. "The cops wouldn't like this!" I said.

But Glen only laughed. "What wouldn't the cops like? The fact that this boy attacked me? The fact that me and my buddies are just trying to tell him how to behave?"

"Ten against one?" I said. "With his hands tied?"

"Oh, we'd untie him, and there's only a couple of us here, right, boys? The rest will slip off into the night."

"Well, Thomas can tell the real story." I looked at Thomas, hoping to see redemption in his eyes, but he looked back at me like I was so ignorant he pitied me. If he hadn't been too scared to move, I bet he would've been shaking his head at me.

I swallowed hard and realized it was up to me. "And — and I'd tell them, too."

"Who's going to believe a little brat?" Glen said, his voice turning cold. "Especially if his mama or his baby brother might get hurt if he opens his mouth."

What? I tried to say, but it didn't come out because I was stunned. Was he threatening to do something to Mama or J? To cover up his lie? Hurt innocent people so he could keep his stupid Brotherhood going? When I looked at the ugly smile on his face I knew the answer was yes.

Darrell laughed an awkward laugh. "Come on, he's just a dumb kid."

"Shut up, Dunlop," Glen said, losing his smile. "Joe?"

Joe grabbed the noose and Thomas, lifting them both.

"No!" I yelled, scrambling to my feet.

Joe shoved me to the ground.

Larry stepped forward. "Hey, guys, I thought we were just scaring him. You can't" — he looked at the noose in Joe's hand — "you know . . . not on my uncle Kenny's property."

But Joe kept dragging Thomas to the tree where he'd been tied up. I tried to run after him, but someone was on top of me. "*NO!*" I screamed.

"Leave the kid alone," I heard Larry say.

"Someone shut the kid up!" Glen yelled, and the guy holding me down put his arm in front of my mouth.

"Aw, come on, man," Darrell said, "let him go." I saw Darrell's boots next to me and felt pushed and pulled around the dirt. The whole time I was trying to scream and get my head in a position where I could see Thomas. I saw Larry running after Joe, tugging on his shoulder. Glen, his white scarf falling off, shoved Larry away and joined the group of guys heading to the tree with Joe and Thomas. As I struggled and tried to choke out my screams, Thomas was blurring and I realized the screaming was coming out of my eyes.

A gunshot split the night and everyone froze.

"What are you punks doing on my property? Who set that fire?" It was Kenny, crashing through the leaves behind me. "What the —" and the anger drained out of his booming voice until he sounded almost like a little kid. "What's going on here?""

Everything happened at once. The flashlight went out, the guy holding me down jumped off me, Glen shouted, "Get the rope, Joe!" and there was a scurrying in every direction.

Darrell grabbed my arm that was still out of its socket, and I screamed.

"Well, get up!" he hissed.

"You boys get back here!" Kenny shouted, turning on a flashlight and waving it around. He ran past me, swearing, and headed to the tree.

I saw Thomas, his hands still tied behind his back, slumped against the tree trunk, and I screamed again. "No!"

"They didn't do it, dingbat. Now get up!"

And I saw Darrell was right. Thomas was leaning against the tree, breathing heavily, but there was no rope around his neck.

"Keep your mouth shut!" Darrell said, dragging me into the darkness, but not before I saw Kenny untying the rope from Thomas's hands, and Thomas looking at me like I was lower than a whole line of Dunlops.

Chapter Thirteen

Thomas

The next morning I woke up late, with the feeling that something had woken me. When I remembered the night before, I felt sick. When I heard the voices in the kitchen, I felt worse.

The sheriff. And Mama. By her reaction, he was filling her in on what happened.

There was a knock at my door and Mama's voice. "Red? Are you up?"

When I didn't answer, she opened the door. I tried to pretend I was still asleep.

"Red, honey, get up! Something awful happened to Thomas — he's OK, but you should hear this. Put some clothes on and come in the kitchen. Sheriff Scott is here."

At least Mama didn't know I was involved. When I got to the kitchen, I saw Beau was there, too, standing by the sink, next to Mama. The sheriff was blocking the light from the door. I hovered in the dining room doorway opposite him, rubbing my sore shoulder. All the while I kept my eyes on the kitchen wallpaper, staring hard at the little blue coffeepots and pink flowers. I couldn't look the sheriff in the eye, but what I could see of his face didn't look surprised at that. In fact, he was staring at me like he knew I was guilty.

Mama was too busy to notice, asking him about any injuries and how could something like this happen and what was going to be done about those boys. I glanced at Beau because something about him felt different. I realized that he wasn't tugging his hair where it stuck out beneath his cap, like he normally would. He'd taken his cap off, clutching it in front of his chest, his head bowed like he was at a funeral. When he began to raise his head, I turned away quick because I didn't want to have to look him in the eye, either.

"Red!" I flinched at Mama's sharp voice as she stared at me. "They were even threatening to lynch him. Can you believe it? In this day and age!" She turned back to the sheriff. "Are the Jeffersons going to press charges?"

The sheriff seemed to get real interested in his big brown hat, turning it around and around as he stared at the gold braid. "Well," he finally said, "seems like the ringleader was the Connor boy."

"Oh," said Mama. "I see. So nothing will be done."

"I'm looking into it," he said quickly. "Kenny Rae got Larry to tell me who all the boys were."

I felt myself stiffen.

"And I talked with Thomas about it, too." The sheriff gave his Kiss of Death. "Apparently the boys also lit a cross."

Mama gasped. Beau moaned. I cringed.

"Kenny saw the fire. That's why he went up to check it out. You know what a burning cross means." I saw the sheriff's boots turn so he was directly facing me, but I didn't look up. "Thomas didn't want to talk about that. If anyone has information, though, I'd like to hear it."

I felt his eyes still on me, but I kept my eyes on the floor.

"Well, good day, Betty, Beau." He paused as he put his hat on. "Red."

I listened to the sheriff's patrol car start up, crunch over the gravel, and drive down the road. We all stood in silence until J ran into the kitchen, slamming the door behind him. I swear we all jumped.

"How come the sheriff was here? Did Red get in trouble again?"

"Of course not," Mama said.

Beau let out a little moan like he knew I'd done wrong. "J, you want to come see the new toys in the Cracker Jack boxes?"

"Yeah!"

Beau put his hat back on and left with J.

Mama grabbed the phone receiver and yanked the dial over and over like she was going to rip it off the wall, muttering, "I'm calling Lily. This is just awful."

Lily was Thomas's grandmother. I backed up against the stove in the corner.

"Lily? It's Betty Porter. I just found out what happened to Thomas last night and I am so sorry. Is he all right?"

As the pause stretched longer and longer I couldn't look at Mama's face, but I heard a little gasp come out of her and saw her body slump against the wall next to the phone. Her hand went up to her forehead like she was checking for a fever. "I had no idea." Her voice was real quiet. "Yes, I'm surprised, too. And — and sorry. I'm very sorry. Good-bye."

Mama hung up the phone slowly and turned to me.

I wish I hadn't glanced up. The look on her face was like, well, like she was staring at a rabid fox corned in the kitchen and she didn't know whether to turn and run or back away real quiet and hope it would disappear. She started to speak, but no words came out until she cleared her throat several times. "What were you doing up there, Red?"

"I just went along with Darrell. I had no idea what they were going to do."

"You know better than to go anywhere with Darrell Dunlop! Why didn't you leave? Run get help?"

"It all happened so fast! Plus, I was scared to leave Thomas there. I didn't know what they might do if I left."

"But as soon as you saw him and how those boys were acting, you must've known something bad was going to happen."

"I didn't even know Thomas was there for most of the time!"

"How could you not have seen him?"

"They had him tied to a tree and gagged."

"What?" Any color she had left drained out of her face. She shook her head and her eyes filled up.

After a few long minutes, Mama turned to the phone again, her voice slow and croaky. "You need to talk to Thomas."

"I don't know what to say."

"Well," she said, her voice gaining speed and power, "you'd better think fast."

It hurt to see Mama dialing their number again and not just because I didn't want to talk to Thomas. It hurt because, like me, she knew the number by heart. For years we'd called back and forth. This kind of thing shouldn't happen with someone whose number you know by heart.

"Lily? It's Betty again. I'm sorry to bother you, but Red would like to speak to Thomas so he can explain —"

Mama swallowed hard and went even paler, if that was possible. Again she tried to talk without any sound and had to clear her throat. "Of course. I can understand that. I-I'm sorry."

She hung up slowly. "Thomas doesn't want to talk to you."

At first I was relieved because I really didn't know what to say, but then it hit me what that meant. Thomas didn't want to talk to me? *Me?* I wasn't one of the Brotherhood guys. Is that what he thought? That I was one of them now? A Porter would never be one of them.

Mama's arms were crossed and her foot was hammering the floor. "If Thomas doesn't want to see you or talk to you — and I can certainly understand why — then you need to write him a letter, a very long letter to explain, if that's possible, what in heaven's name you were doing up on that mountain." She marched out of the kitchen and returned with a pen and several sheets of paper, thrusting them at me.

I took them and headed for the kitchen door.

"Where do you think you're going?"

"To the shop."

"Oh, no, you don't! You are writing Thomas a letter right —"

"I know. I'm going to sit at my desk and write it."

It was almost like Mama took my words in her mouth and was chewing on them before she finally spit out, "Fine."

Even the shop's oil and dirt smell didn't make me feel better. I trudged up the stairs in the back, slumped down on the chair, and put the paper on the desk. I got as far as "Dear Thomas," and then I was stuck. I couldn't even talk to Daddy because I felt like he was staring at me with his hurt-disappointed look. Even the hymn he wrote out and put on the wall by the desk seemed to be staring at me.

Buried in sorrow and in sin . . . I closed my eyes and put my head down on Old Man Porter's desk. I sure felt buried in sorrow and sin.

I thought about the day of Daddy's funeral. Thomas and his grandparents came to the burial. I guess they knew better than to try to come to the service at our church. Thomas had tried to give me a hug, but I didn't feel like hugging anyone except Daddy that day, and I was kind of mad at Thomas for not being my friend anymore and never coming over, especially when he and Daddy got along so well. It was like me and Daddy had both lost a friend. So I hadn't even talked to Thomas. Mama snapped at me afterward. She said Thomas had been crying during the burial and he thought the world of Daddy and I should've shown him a little more kindness, for Daddy's sake, at least. I felt bad after that, but it wasn't like we hung out anymore and I could talk to him. And now I'd probably never talk to him again.

The shop door jiggled and light came in from outside. I lifted my head and saw Rosie marching across the shop floor toward me and up the stairs, her Dr. Scholl's sandals clomping and her bangle bracelets clacking.

She stopped by the desk and looked down at me. "Darrell told me what happened. Why would you do that, Red?"

"I don't know. I-I didn't really know what was happening until it was too late."

Her hands were on her hips now. "You didn't know you were burning a cross?"

"Well, yeah, but I didn't mean, you know, what it really means to burn a cross. And I didn't know Thomas was there. I never would've done it if I'd known Thomas was right there!"

Rosie didn't say anything, which almost made it worse. It made my excuse sound stupid. I knew it wasn't OK to do something like that, even if no black person actually saw you do it. The Brotherhood was there. And it made it look like I was one of them. And Thomas saw me.

She shook her head like when Mama was annoyed with us. "I don't understand."

"Me, neither," I muttered.

"I know those boys," she said. "Some of them are real nice. I can't see them doing that."

She looked away and I stared at her so hard my eyes stung because I was waiting for her to say that I was one of those boys who was real nice. But she never did. She just shook her head again, clomped down the steps, and walked out the door. The slapping of her Dr. Scholl's had never sounded so hollow.

Chapter Fourteen
School

I had to mail Thomas's letter to Washington, DC, because he left Stony Gap the day after "the incident," as Mama called it. I told him that I hadn't known what kind of group the Brotherhood was or what they were going to do. I told him I was just trying to stop Mama from selling and that's why I was stupid enough to follow Darrell and burn a cross, even though I should've known better. And I told him I was sorry. I said he was the best friend I ever had and I wished it hadn't ended this way. And that I hoped, maybe, some day, we could be friends again. I wasn't sure that last part would ever happen, but I still wanted to say it because I meant it.

I thought about Thomas a lot, and not just because Mama told me to. I couldn't help it. I listened to both the albums he'd given me: James Brown's *Say It Loud — I'm Black and I'm Proud* and Edwin Starr's *War & Peace*. I pushed the buttons on our Rock'Em Sock'Em Robots, but it wasn't the kind of game you could play real well by yourself. Even when I got one robot to knock the other's block off, it didn't feel like much of a victory. I still didn't want J to play it, though, or he'd probably bust it, and Rosie refused to do any kind of fighting game, including fake fighting like this one. Even trying to get her to play G.I. Joe had never worked. She always brought Barbie over to lecture me and G.I. Joe about making peace not war.

Making peace not war is easier than it sounds. I tried to figure out how everything had happened up on the mountain behind Kenny's and what I could've done about it. It had all gone so fast yet slow at the same time, like being in that accident with the Plymouth Belvedere before we got the Chevy. We were driving home from a church supper and it was dark and raining. An eighteen-wheeler was coming down the mountain toward us, and Daddy had just said a truck that size had no business being on a little country road when the truck skidded and crossed into our lane. I remember seeing those huge headlights coming straight for us and hearing Mama scream, "Frank!" and Daddy swear, and even though we were in that ditch in seconds, it also felt like it went on forever, because I remember thinking, "Oh, man, we're going to crash," and "If my legs get broken I won't be able to ride my new bike," and "Should I wake up J, or is it better for him to sleep through this?" It was weird to have enough time to sit there pondering the terrible thing that was about to happen, feeling like you were trapped because it was going to happen anyway. That's what it felt like on the mountain behind Kenny's, only worse.

When school started, I didn't even care because I figured it'd take my mind off things. J was real excited to get on the bus and pushed ahead of me to make sure he was first. I climbed up the rubber-treaded steps and was hit by the smell of the Pine-Sol cleaner the bus driver always used. I turned into the rows of faces and remembered how long it had been since I'd seen all these kids. They seemed to remember, too, because some of them quit talking and most of them stared at me. Or maybe they'd heard about what happened on the mountain behind Kenny's. Only Lou Anne Atkins said hey. I mumbled a hey back and slid into an empty seat, putting my lunch bag beside me, hoping no one would sit there. I looked through the scratched-up window at the disappearing shop as the bus pulled away.

I didn't want to look at the kids because they reminded me of when Daddy died. A lot of them came to the funeral, and their mamas and daddies told them they had to be nice to me. They called me up or even stopped by for the first couple of weeks, but seems after that they felt like I should've gotten over it, sort of like I had a bad case of the flu. The thing is, when you get over the flu, everything goes back to normal. When your daddy dies, nothing is ever going to be normal again. Riding on the bus felt familiar and strange at the same time, like being in school and finding a substitute teacher. The classroom might be the same but it felt different, like you were in the wrong place.

I felt like I was in the wrong place in Miss Miller's class, too. Sure, she was pretty, like Mary Tyler Moore on Mama's favorite TV show. She had bouncy brown hair that flipped up at her shoulders, big green eyes, and a happy smile, but that was just the fake outside. Inside she was a teacher like any other. She might've had a peace-symbol necklace and a flower-power book bag, but her speech about working hard was just like a regular teacher.

"This year is going to be full of new and exciting challenges! We're going to learn how to question and how to think. We're going to work hard to find our place in this world."

It's always dangerous when a teacher says "we." "We are going to work hard" really means, "You are going to work hard, and I'm going to mark it all up with my big red pen."

Miss Miller told us we'd learn all about history, and recent history. She wanted us to watch the news or read the paper every day. She called it "living history."

I groaned and slumped down in my desk. Every teacher has a pet subject she loves so much she can't shut up about it. With Miss Miller, just my luck, it was history. How could people get so excited about history? It was all old and gone and you couldn't do anything about it, anyway, so what was the point?

"Young man, what's your name?"

I didn't realize Miss Miller was talking to me until I heard the giggling and then Bobby Benson say, "That's Red Porter, ma'am. He's a little touched in the head." Then he whispered, "He talks to dead people, retards, and Negroes!"

I sat up fast and glared at Bobby.

"Red, are you not feeling well today?"

Everyone was staring at me. Some kids were snickering. I was getting nervous and didn't want to stare right in Miss Miller's eyes, so I looked at the blackboard behind her. She'd written in blue chalk: *The truth will set you free.*

It was like a sign. I decided to tell the truth. "I'm fine, ma'am. I just don't like history."

Everyone's eyes got bigger, even Miss Miller's. And there was no more snickering, either.

Miss Miller folded her arms and all eyes were on her. She said, in kind of a friendly way, "I love history. Why is it that you don't like it?"

All eyes were on me again. "Well . . . because . . . who cares?"

There were a few gasps from around the room as everyone looked back at Miss Miller. I thought maybe I'd gone too far, so I tried to make up for it a little. "I mean, it's all happened already and there's nothing you can do about it, so it's kind of a waste of time." There were more gasps, and I realized that I'd probably made things worse, so I added, "Isn't it?"

Miss Miller sucked in her lips till they were all gone. She stared at me and there was no happiness in her eyes anymore. I slid down in my seat some more as she started pacing back and forth in front of the room. All you could hear were her high heels clicking on the linoleum.

Finally she stopped. "Red, let me ask you something."

I swallowed.

"Have you ever made a mistake?"

I wondered if she'd heard about the Thomas incident. "Yes, ma'am."

"Have you ever learned from any of those mistakes?"

"Yes, ma'am."

"Have you ever heard the expression 'history repeats itself'?"

"I don't think so." I had no idea where she was going with this.

"If we don't learn what has happened in the past, do you think we might make the same mistakes again?"

I hated those kinds of questions. I never knew if the teacher wanted a yes or a no. I tried to hedge my bets. "If you say so."

There were a couple of gasps and oohs, and Miss Miller stared at me, her eyes narrowing.

I guess it sounded like sassing, but I hadn't meant it that way. She decided I could stay in at recess and help the janitor "pack up some history" in the boxes he was shipping to the county office building and maybe I could "learn a little something." As if that weren't enough, she made me switch desks with Emma Jean so I was at the head of the middle row, right in front of Miss Miller's desk. I don't know which one of us was more upset, me or Emma Jean, who had claimed a front center seat ever since first grade.

• • • • • •

It was dark in the school basement, and it smelled of bleach. The janitor got up from a desk in the corner where he was eating a sandwich and wiped his hands on a napkin. "Can I help you?"

"Miss Miller says I need to help clean up."

He raised his eyebrows. "Oh. I see." He handed me a broom. "What else did Miss Miller say?"

I looked around the basement. "She says I might learn a little history of this place."

"Well, I've been coming here for close to forty years." He picked up a box and stacked it on top of another one.

"You mean, you went to school here?"

"Oh, no, I didn't go to this school. I went down the road a piece."

There was a shack overgrown with vines that folks called the "rows in wall" school, which always made me think of rows of desks attached to the walls, where black kids used to go. It was falling apart now. "The rows-in-wall school?"

"It's Ros-en-wald. He's the man who put up the seed money to build the school and we matched it."

"Why'd he make you build your own school?"

"He didn't make us. It was a gift. Got a lot better schools that way than what the county would give us."

"But you wouldn't have had to pay for it."

"Oh, we were paying for it —" He gave his head a little shake. "Where are my manners? I'm Philip Walter." He held his hand out and gave a little bow.

I shook his hand. "I'm Red Porter, sir." Daddy said we had to say sir or ma'am to grown-ups, even if they were black.

Mr. Walter smiled. "I know." His smile faded as he said, "I was surprised you were involved in that . . . event with young Thomas. I thought you boys were friends."

I felt my face going red. "We were — we are." I looked at my feet. "We were."

"You don't want to be hanging out with those boys, son."

"I know. I — It was really dumb." I couldn't look at him because what if he knew the part about me burning the cross? Thomas hadn't told the sheriff, but maybe he'd told others.

"I heard you got roughed up by those boys pretty good yourself, so I suspect you learned something."

"Yes, sir," I whispered.

"Well, we all make stupid mistakes, especially when we're young. As a matter of fact," he said, his voice sounding less serious, "I seem to recall your daddy being in the same position you are right now."

I looked up. "You knew my daddy?"

"I told you, I been here a long time."

"What'd he do?"

"Got in a fight with another boy."

I thought about that for maybe two seconds. "Mr. Dunlop?"

He chuckled. "Yup, Baby Ray."

"Baby Ray? Is that what they called him?"

"Now don't you go repeating that."

"I won't. So was he a crybaby?"

Mr. Walter's eyes widened. "He was a bully, but he turned into a crybaby as soon as any teacher was around. I think we were all ready for that boy to be laid out. It was hard for me to have to carry out any punishment on your daddy."

"What'd you make him do?"

He tilted his head toward the corner where his desk was. "Sat him right over there and made him keep me company while we ate MoonPies."

I guess he saw the look on my face.

"Well, my wife had packed me two and I didn't see why I should have to suffer through both of them." He winked at me.

The rest of the time I was sweeping and then helping

Mr. Walter stack boxes of files, I kept looking at the corner, picturing Daddy at my age eating a MoonPie while he laughed with Mr. Walter. It made me want to laugh, too, except that I couldn't help thinking of the difference between us. He'd gotten in trouble for fighting a Dunlop. I'd gone off with a Dunlop and acted as nasty as they were.

All I could picture of the grown-up Daddy was him staring at me and shaking his head, and it hurt to see the disappointment in his eyes.

Chapter Fifteen
Why Don't You Paint Miss Georgia's?

I got off the bus and walked to the house but stopped before opening the kitchen screen door. Rosie was wearing one of Mama's skirts, and Mama was kneeling on the floor next to her, a couple of pins held between her lips, pinning up the hem to make it much shorter.

"I hope you don't mind cutting off the bottom and making this into a miniskirt, Mrs. Porter."

Mama took the pins out of her mouth and put them in the skirt. "I'm just glad you've grown enough that you can use these," she said, nodding at several bags of clothes on the floor.

"Hey, Red," Rosie said, finally noticing me. "How do you like Miss Miller? Isn't she cool?"

"Oh, that's right," said Mama, smiling up at Rosie, "you had her last year."

"Just for a little while, as a student teacher, but I loved her," Rosie said.

"Well, I sure don't," I said, opening the screen door and banging my books down on the kitchen table.

They both flinched.

"Why not?" Rosie asked.

"For one thing, she says we have to watch the news every night and discuss it the next day, and she's giving us homework already!"

"Imagine that," Mama said with a hint of a smile, "a teacher giving homework. What will they think of next?"

Rosie giggled and the two of them looked at each other, then looked at me, like I was some dumb little kid. I didn't like it one bit, not them sharing smiles together and not Rosie looking at me like I was a little kid.

I slammed the door behind me and went to the What-U-Want to find Beau.

He stood up from stacking bags of kitty litter. "Hey, Red! How was your first day of school?"

"Miss Miller hates me just because I don't like history."

"Aw, I'm sure she don't hate you. I bet she's just trying get y'all to learn a lot. You're real lucky, Red, 'cause you're smart and you can learn."

Beau didn't understand. Like Mama saying how lucky I was to have a brother. I could see why Thomas said that, what with being an only child and all, plus he didn't have to live with J. Mama should know better.

I propped my elbow on the edge of the counter and leaned on it, thinking about Thomas. "I just wish it were summer."

Beau grinned. "Boys always like summer better than school." He lost his grin and looked at me carefully. "Are you ever going to hang out with Thomas again?"

My elbow fell off the counter because it was weird how

Beau was thinking of Thomas at the same time I was. "I don't know," I said, as I backed out of the What-U-Want.

I decided to go over to Miss Georgia's. I saw her sitting on her glider looking at something on her lap. When I noticed the box of tissues next to her I knew what it was. A photo album. She always got sad when she looked at the photos of her family and friends because most of the people were dead and the others hardly came to visit. When I got to her porch I saw that she also had the black album that was full of old news clippings, the one she never let me look at. I'd only seen it once when I was little and she snatched it away from me, all upset.

I guess I startled her when I said, "Hey, Miss Georgia," because she jerked and the black album fell off her lap. I picked it up and she took it from me quickly, sandwiching it between two of her flowered family albums. After she blew her nose and wiped her eyes, she launched right back into talking about the Thomas incident even though I thought we'd already talked it through. I sat hunched on her porch feeling small.

"I still don't understand why you didn't run for help," she said, leaning so far forward on her glider that I thought she might fall on top of me. "I know you can run fast."

"I didn't know it was going to get so bad. And when they got the rope, that's when their big goon sat on top of me." I shifted against the porch post and rubbed my shoulder that was still a little sore from having my arm pulled out of its socket.

She shook her head. "Next time, you get on out of there and get help."

"Next time?" I snorted. "There's not going to be any next time."

"Not with Darrell Dunlop and his gang, maybe, but there'll always be a next time."

I swallowed hard, feeling like I might throw up.

"Oh, it may not be like the other night. But you'll see more ugliness, that's for sure."

"Well, I'm not going to turn and run every time I do. That's not what a Porter does."

Miss Georgia opened her mouth to say something but closed it again, working the sour words around like she'd just had a big swallow of milk that'd gone bad. I knew what the words were, though. *Oh, and hangin' out with Darrell Dunlop's gang is what a Porter does?*

We were quiet for a while as I let the words she didn't say sink in. I sure hoped Thomas hadn't told her about the cross burning. Part of me wanted to apologize for it, but part of me wanted to pretend it never happened. I stared out at her Rambler that was back in front of her place, now that Beau had fixed it, just like Daddy would've wanted.

"I bet Daddy could've talked them out of it," I said softly. "He would've stopped them."

"Maybe," Miss Georgia said with a sigh. "But you ain't your daddy, not yet. I know you tryin'. He'd be proud of you for that."

I didn't think Daddy would be proud of me at all. I bet he would've asked why I'd gone to a Dunlop with a problem in the first place. And I didn't have a real good answer for that.

"Well," said Miss Georgia, shakily pushing herself up

from her glider with one hand and leaning on her cane with the other, "I need to make me a tuna fish sandwich for supper. Why don't you come on in and tell me about school."

She put some bread and honey out for me because she knew I didn't like tuna fish.

"Thanks, Miss Georgia, but I don't feel like eating."

She tapped the tin sign above her stove that used to hang in her bakery in Atlanta: GEORGIA'S BEST: YOU WON'T LEAVE HUNGRY! "You need to have somethin' in front of you if you're sittin' at my table."

All I wanted was to complain about Miss Miller, but Miss Georgia didn't want to listen.

"Did you hear that Thomas is going to Gonzaga?" she asked.

"Where's that?"

"It a real good high school in Washington, DC, a real good school. It's run by Jesuits, the kind of religious folk who think education should be open to everyone. That boy is going to go far, uh-huh, he sure is." She took a sip of iced tea. "So how about you, Red? What are you doing with yourself at school?"

When I told her about being sent to the janitor, she raised one eyebrow at me and shook her head. "Don't be sassin' your teacher like that."

"I wasn't, or I didn't mean to, anyway. The janitor was real nice, though."

"That's young Philip, right?"

"Young? Miss Georgia, he's old!"

"To you, maybe. To me he'll always be young Philip." She took a bite of her tuna fish sandwich.

"Did you go to that Rosenwald school with him?"

She laughed so hard she started choking on her sandwich. I got up and filled up her iced tea glass, adding three spoons of sugar the way she liked it.

She wiped her mouth on her napkin. "That was way after my time, Red! My son and grandkids weren't around to use it, neither." She took a sip of tea. "But I gave money to help build that school, yes, I did."

"How come?"

"If you'd seen where those children were tryin' to learn, you'd a given money, too."

"Shoot, it's just school. Nobody wants to be there, anyway."

She looked up at the ceiling. "James, you see what I have to put up with down here? Now nobody wants to go to school."

"Well, I don't want to."

"Then what you gonna do with your life?" She coughed and picked up her glass again.

I looked around to give myself time to think of something to say. My eyes settled on the three pictures above her fireplace: Jesus, Martin Luther King Jr., and that lawyer from Richmond. I pointed at the photo of Martin Luther King Jr. "He was a minister, and Bobby Benson said he never even got a high school diploma." I figured she couldn't argue her way out of that one.

She put her glass down with a slap. "Red, you best stay in school because right now you showin' your ignorance. It's true that he didn't get a regular high school diploma, but you know why?" She looked up at Martin Luther King Jr.'s picture like she was talking to him. "He skipped two years of high school and went on to college at fifteen years old. After he got his college degree he went on to divinity school and got a degree there." She glared at me. "What do you say to that?"

I sank down in my chair. What could I say to that? "Oh?"

She stared at me, but all the anger seemed to drain out of her and she laughed. "*Oh?* That's all you got to say?"

I nodded and smiled, kind of embarrassed. "Oh."

Pretty soon she was saying "oh" in all kinds of funny voices, and I couldn't help but laugh.

"Hey, guess what else, Miss Georgia? I know what Mr. Dunlop's nickname was in school — Baby Ray."

She raised her eyebrow at me again.

"I know, I'm not going to say it in public, but I figured you already knew it."

"You right about that. I heard it from your daddy, matter of fact. He and Ray never got along."

I told her all about the fight Mr. Walter told me about, including the MoonPies afterward. "Do you know about any other fights they had?"

"I'll tell you one story from when they were a little older than you are." She sat back in her chair. "Your grandmother used to send your daddy up here to help me out, pullin' weeds in the summer, rakin' leaves in the fall, shovelin' snow in the winter. I didn't have no money to pay him but I baked him cookies."

Just the word *cookies* made me realize all of a sudden that I was hungry, and I tore into my bread and honey while I listened.

"Well, I didn't know this, but your daddy acted like he was gettin' somethin' real good, like money, which made Ray all jealous. So when my house needed paintin', your daddy said he'd allow Ray to do it and Ray worked real hard. When he was done and came to the door, I gave him a whole bag of cookies. His face fell down to the floor. I said, 'What's wrong, Ray? You don't like chocolate chip?' His face went all red. 'I can make you some oatmeal raisin if you like them better.' But he was fit to be tied. He ran off so fast he didn't even take the cookies. I heard later that he and your daddy got into a real big fistfight over it. After that your daddy would tease him, sayin', 'Why don't you go paint Miss Georgia's?'"

I laughed, and Miss Georgia was smiling but she shook her head. "Yeah, it's a little bit funny but a little bit sad, too. You see, Ray always felt like he was bein' made fun of. Ray's spent his whole life fightin' back, even when no one's fightin' him."

"You're not blaming Daddy for making him mean, are you?"

"No. Ray was never a nice boy. But his daddy was never kind to him, either, and I think that's what turned him from the beginnin'. Ray never learned kindness. Ray's granddaddy beat his daddy, his daddy beat him —" She sighed.

"And now he beats Darrell," I finished for her.

"They're a long line of angry, fightin' folks. That Ray is still fightin'."

"I sure wish they didn't live right next to us."

"You and Rosie are good friends."

I shrugged. "The rest of them I could do without. I hate Mr. Dunlop, and Mrs. Dunlop stays in her bed all the time —"

"Now, Red, she's sickly."

"Yeah, sickly of Mr. Dunlop."

She gave a little snort of laughter but tried to make her face serious. "Some women ain't as strong as your mama."

"Mama? She's not —"

A phone rang, and I about jumped out of my chair because I didn't think Miss Georgia had a phone.

She put her hands on the table and pushed herself up. "Excuse me. That's my son. Again."

I wasn't trying to listen, but the phone was on the wall just inside Miss Georgia's bedroom, and there were only three rooms in the house — the kitchen and living area were one room, the bathroom was behind the kitchen, and the door to her bedroom was right by the living-room fireplace. I wasn't but ten feet away.

"I'm fine, George. I was fine yesterday, and I'm still fine today. Probably be fine tomorrow, too. When you comin' to visit?" There was a long pause. "Uh-huh, I thought so. Well, you give my best to my granddaughter and her boy. Is she keepin' him out of trouble?" There was another pause. "Well, if she'd raise him up in the country she wouldn't have those city problems." She glanced over at me then looked away. "'Course we have our own type of problems here. But I'd sure like to have them close-by. You tell her that. Uh-huh, yes, Mama. I'm sure you will. All right, well I got young Red sittin' here at the kitchen table, so I better go keep him company. I love you. You're an ornery old thing, but I do love you."

Miss Georgia stretched the phone cord out of her bedroom and held up a pink receiver pinched between her thumb and forefinger. "Look at this! George had it installed because he says, 'Mama, you all alone in the middle of nowhere.' Huh. It ain't exactly the middle a nowhere. Plus, you mean to tell me he just noticed I live by myself? James, what am I going to do with that boy of yours, huh?"

"It's good to have a phone, Miss Georgia." Daddy had always been worried about Miss Georgia living on her own without a phone.

"It's called a Princess phone. Do I look like a princess?" She held it in front of her face, turning it around and scrunching up her nose at it like she was eyeing a rotten melon. "Fool thing only fit for a teenage girl. I told him I didn't want no phone, but he's as stubborn as I am. I'd rip it out except he's taken to callin' me every day, and he'd just have them come put in another one." She glared at the phone. "Might be a tiara on that Princess, so I better quit while I'm ahead."

She shook her head and hung the phone up right inside her bedroom door. "'Centrally located,' he said. I told him I don't care how *centrally located* it is. If I fall in the kitchen I'm not goin' to be able to reach it here, or if I'm outside —" She stopped herself. "Shoot, I suppose I just don't want to admit I'm gettin' old."

I guess my face showed what I was thinking, because she laughed and said, "OK, you right, I'm already old! Well, how about you carry the dishes to the sink for this old lady, huh?

Then she might just have the energy to scoop out a couple of bowls of mint chocolate chip ice cream."

We sat out on the porch eating our ice cream when we heard Mr. Dunlop's rebel yell, screeching and hollering at something.

Miss Georgia rolled her eyes. "Oh, Lordy."

"I hate when he does that," I said.

"You and me both."

I started picking at the paint on her porch like I always did. There was something satisfying about getting a whole strip of paint chip, like peeling a long strip of orange rind.

She scraped the last drips of ice cream out of her bowl. "Why you always doin' that?"

"Doing what?"

"Peelin' the paint off my porch?" She roughed up my hair. "I'ma make you paint it someday, seein' as how you're the one who made it look this way."

"I wouldn't mind," I said. "What color do you want? Psychedelic pink?"

She chuckled as I lay down on the porch and looked up at its ceiling. "I could paint you a giant peace sign up there."

"I don't care what you put up there, long as you keep it sky blue."

"How come?"

"Because I want to look up and see the sky. Free and open. Makes me feel like anythin' can happen." She nodded at the distance. "Makes me feel like I can see Freedom Church."

Just then, Mr. Dunlop let out another yell and we both groaned.

Chapter Sixteen
The New Plan

After school, I was in the shop, lying down on the creeper, rolling back and forth, thinking about the TV news now that I had to watch it all the time because of Miss Miller. Walter Cronkite was Mama's favorite news guy, so that's who we always watched. He said a larger voter turnout was expected for the presidential election in November, seeing as how the Twenty-Sixth Amendment had passed last year, moving the voting age from twenty-one to eighteen. I remembered when that happened. Daddy had said, "Imagine, Red, you'll be able to vote in seven years, when you're still a teenager."

Earlier this summer, while he was fixing the timing of a Dodge Dart's engine, he'd said, "I wish you could vote now, Red."

"How come?" I'd asked.

He turned on the timing light. "I don't trust that Nixon. I'd vote for Shirley Chisholm before I'd vote for Nixon."

"Who's she?"

I watched the frantic flickering of the timing light, mesmerized, as Daddy told me she was this black congresswoman who didn't take any guff from anyone.

"So why don't you vote for her?"

"She won't make it as a candidate."

"Why not?"

He turned off the light and chuckled. "Red, weren't you listening? I said she's a black woman. Do you think this country is ready to vote for a black or a woman, never mind both together? Maybe in your lifetime, son, but not in mine."

A week later he was dead.

I rolled around on the creeper, listening for Daddy's voice, missing him more than ever. "Why did you have to leave now, Daddy, when everything's so confusing? I'm finally old enough to understand the news, and now I can't ask you about the election or Vietnam or —"

The shop door jiggled, and Rosie's face appeared. She looked like an angel in the shadow.

"Hey, Red."

"Hey, Rosie." I sat up on the creeper.

She shut the door behind her and smiled. "How are you liking Miss Miller now?"

"About the same."

Her smile turned down a little. "I think she'll grow on you. You do think she's pretty, don't you?"

"Well, sure, but —"

"That Mr. Reynolds thinks so, too."

"The lawyer?"

She tilted her head and gave a sly smile. "Uh-huh. Wouldn't they make a cute couple?"

"No."

"I think they would."

"Why would she want a slimy lawyer, anyway?"

"He's not slimy!"

"All lawyers are."

She shook her head. "He's real nice, Red."

"How do you know?"

"He's been over at our house."

"What was he doing at your house?"

"He was there with Mr. Harrison."

"Why?"

Her little heart mouth exploded into a grin. "Because Daddy's talking about buying the shop!"

"What?" I stood up, the creeper flying out from under me. "He can't do that!"

Her grin disappeared. "Why not?"

"I'm not having your daddy take over my shop!"

"But, Red —"

"This is my daddy's special place, and he worked hard to make it what it is. Your daddy would ruin everything!"

She grabbed my arm. "But don't you see? If Daddy buys the shop, then you don't have to sell the house. We'd run the shop, and you all could still live here. I want you to stay, Red!"

I wanted to stay, too, but I looked around the shop and pictured Mr. Dunlop spitting tobacco and kicking things and talking mean to Beau — Rosie was tugging at my arm again because I guess I'd quit listening to her.

"Mama said it'd be great work for Darrell to have and might keep him out of trouble. I think so, too, and Darrell said he'd like doing that kind of job."

"What job?"

"Fixing cars, silly."

"Darrell doesn't know how to fix cars!"

"Well, not yet, but he could learn."

"All Darrell's good at is messing things up!"

"That's not true!" She let go of my arm and took a step back. "Maybe no one ever gave him a chance to try putting things together."

"Sorry, Rosie, but I'll die before I let your daddy take over our shop."

Her eyes flashed. "We were just trying to do you a favor!"

A favor? To have Mr. Dunlop take over my shop? "Don't do us any favors. And don't go destroying the shop, either, thinking you're doing us a favor."

"That was your idea, Red!"

"Just spray-painting is all, and I don't even want that anymore!"

"Well, I don't go around spray-painting things!"

"Oh, like you don't go around spray-painting gravestones?"

"That wasn't me! That was Darrell and his gang!"

"But you were there. You had to be. How else could you have stopped them from painting my daddy's gravestone if you weren't right there?"

I knew I was right because she didn't have an answer. Plus, she looked a little scared.

"I'm through doing you any favors, Red!" She turned and ran, slamming the door so hard the hinges cried.

"Good!" I hollered after her.

After she left I had a chance to think through what she

said. Mr. Reynolds. And Mr. Harrison. Together. Talking with Mr. Dunlop about buying our property. So Mr. Dunlop was the client? I knew Mr. Reynolds was as slimy as Mr. Harrison! Well, there was no way I was letting him buy our property for Mr. Dunlop. Not in a million years. I'd keep their nastiness off of our land if it was the last thing I did.

"Nobody's taking our shop!" I yelled. I paced around the shop, banging the metal shelves that held all the tools. It felt good to hear those mad thoughts coming out, and I banged and kicked until there was so much noise that you wouldn't think you could hear anything.

Except I did. I swear I heard Daddy say, *I hear ya, son.* It made me stop all my noisemaking and stand still so I could hear him again. But the shop was silent.

I stood there for a long time, trying to figure out what he meant. He always said, "I hear ya, son," when I was spouting off about something. He'd never give me the answer, but he'd ask some questions and eventually I'd come up with what to do. So I asked myself questions until it finally hit me.

Mama didn't think we could handle the shop and store so we had to move. Sure, I'd told her that me and Beau could handle it, but, just like a mama, she wouldn't believe it. I had to show her. I had to show her that it was no big deal keeping everything going, even without Daddy. Sure, Daddy could fix any car problem and with lightning speed, and there were only certain things me and Beau could fix, but still, we could handle some business. After school and on weekends there were three of us — what with Beau and me and Mama — and when I was at school, they could put a sign on the What-U-Want to say go to the shop or go to the house if you needed help. Maybe I didn't have such a big problem after all.

Except the bookkeeping part, which was the money stuff that Daddy always did and Mama hated. She spent all day Sunday, after church, working on the books and by suppertime she was spitting nails. But it wasn't something Beau or I could do. Yet.

So I came up with a plan. First, show Mama that me and Beau could handle the shop and the store ourselves. Second, do real good in math so I could take over the books for Mama.

Chapter Seventeen
Miss Miller

In math the next day, I realized pretty quick that Miss Miller's word problems weren't going to help me one bit with our accounts. What use was it to find out how long it'd take sixty protesters to get to Washington, DC, if their bus went forty-five miles per hour and they had one hundred and fifty miles to go?

"Now," Miss Miller said, "we're going to talk about how songs are like poetry and do our own writing!"

We all groaned, except Emma Jean, because she was a teacher's pet from way back. "That sounds like fun, ma'am," she said, all perky.

Miss Miller gave her a tired smile. "Some might question why a teacher is assigning her students rock songs for homework."

That made all of us sit up as perky as Emma Jean.

Miss Miller opened up her flower-power bag and it was full of albums, the kind of albums you'd expect in a flower-power bag. We'd never had a teacher play real music before.

Sure, we'd listened to stupid little kid songs in first grade, and one time in fifth grade Mrs. Riley made us listen to *The Wartime Speeches of Winston Churchill*, but this was different.

Holding up an album cover, Miss Miller put the record on the turntable and lifted the record player arm. The whole class hushed while we waited to hear Marvin Gaye sing "What's Going On." So when Miss Miller couldn't get the record player working, we all groaned.

"Get the monkey to fix it!" Bobby said.

Miss Miller looked puzzled. "What monkey?"

"The janitor," Emma Jean explained. "He can fix anything."

Miss Miller's head jerked and she stared at Bobby. "What did you call him?" She didn't wait for him to answer. "How could you be so disrespectful?"

"Well?" he said, shrugging. "I forget his name."

"Then you'd best learn it."

Miss Miller was still smoldering when Mr. Walter came into the room and fiddled with the record player cord. I saw him raise his eyebrows at the Marvin Gaye album. I bet he was as surprised as us that we were listening to cool stuff.

In just a couple of minutes, he had the record player working.

Miss Miller smiled. "Class, this is Mr. Walter. I'm not sure if you've ever been properly introduced. I'm sure there's something you'd like to say to him."

We looked at each other, then at Bobby. Did she want Bobby to apologize for calling him a monkey?

Emma Jean raised her hand. "Thank you?" she said, looking at Miss Miller for approval.

Miss Miller only gave a half smile back and said, "You'd address *him* and say, 'Thank you, sir,' or 'Thank you, Mr. Walter.' Shall we try that again, class?"

I bet not a one of them had ever said *sir* to a black man or a janitor before. But most everyone did now. Some kids rolled their eyes or looked away or made faces. I don't think Miss Miller noticed because she was too busy smiling at Mr. Walter. I know Mr. Walter saw, though. I slunk down in my seat because I felt embarrassed for him that he had to see that. But he didn't act embarrassed. He said, "You're welcome," nodding at me and then at Miss Miller, and walked out of the classroom with his head held high, even with kids still making faces at him.

Miss Miller turned to us. "How many of you can fix a record player in two minutes?" She looked at Bobby. "How many of you can get up at five o'clock in the morning and work all day cleaning up behind children who call you names?" Still looking at Bobby, she added, "In a town where even some of those children's parents call them names?"

Bobby was looking down at his desk.

It seemed quiet for a long while before Miss Miller started playing the Marvin Gaye song.

After it was over, Miss Miller asked, "What's the subtext?"

What was she talking about?

"I mean, what's he really saying? What's the bigger story behind this song, hmm? Why is he saying too many of his brothers are dying?"

We stared at her blankly.

She explained that Marvin Gaye was really talking about guys, especially black guys, coming back from Vietnam and nothing had changed for them. There was still prejudice, even after these guys had risked their lives for freedom and democracy. That's why he was asking, "What's going on?" It made me think of Thomas's MIA bracelet and why he decided to wear it.

At least the homework Miss Miller gave us was OK: pick a song and write what it was really saying underneath the words. I already knew what mine was going to be — from the Edwin Starr album Thomas gave me, *War & Peace*.

Class got boring again when Miss Miller pulled a paperback book out of her flower-power bag, acting as if she were Santa Claus. "This is one of my favorite, favorite books, and I want to read it out loud to you."

I looked at the cover. It looked like a baby book with a goofy barnyard on the front. It was called *Animal Farm*.

Bobby Benson screwed his face up at it. "I'm beyond talking-animal books."

"You can't judge a book by its cover," Miss Miller said with a smile.

I tuned her out while she read and looked at the posters around the classroom. There was one of John F. Kennedy with the quote Daddy loved. *Ask not what your country can do for you; ask what you can do for your country.*

Miss Miller had put up a picture of Harriet Tubman, that Underground Railroad conductor, and handwritten a quote by her. *Always remember, you have within you the strength, the patience, and the passion to reach for the stars to change the world.*

The one I liked best was by Martin Luther King Jr., because it was short but said a lot. *The time is always right to do what is right.*

Which is exactly what I was going to do to make sure we stayed in Stony Gap. By the time history rolled around, I was figuring out a schedule for me and Beau to cover both the shop and the What-U-Want. I was wondering why I was even wasting my time in school because I could be working at home when I heard Miss Miller say, "Then the property has to be preserved just the way it is. That's what the National Register of Historic Places is all about. They can't be changed or destroyed. So if a site has historic importance —"

I shot my hand up in the air even though I hadn't really been listening to the whole story.

"Is something wrong, Red?"

"Does that mean you can't sell the property?"

"Well, there certainly would be restrictions on a sale —"

"Restrictions?" That was all I needed to hear. "So how do you get on that register thing?"

"Well, you'd start by contacting your local historical society —"

My hand shot up again. "Do we have a local historical society?"

She looked at me like I was fooling with her. Me. Historical society. It did seem kind of strange. "I'll talk with you at recess, Red."

When recess came, I explained about getting our shop

and the What-U-Want on the historic register. She explained that those weren't exactly the kind of buildings they usually preserved, but she took me to the office with her to make a call to the historical society people, just in case.

By the time she hung up I knew it was bad news. "I'm sorry, Red. They're focusing on preserving stately homes. Besides, it sounds like there's already an older store in the county."

It sure would've been nice if someone else, like a historical society, could've told Mama we had to keep our place just the way it was. I followed Miss Miller back to the classroom because I didn't feel like being outside with a bunch of yelling, happy kids.

She sat down and motioned me over to her desk. "Red, why is your mama wanting to sell?" Miss Miller was tilting her head at me. Not mean, but concerned. I noticed then that she started off in the mornings like a jumpy Chihuahua but later in the day she looked like a droopy basset hound. I guess we tired her out. Maybe her basset hound look was why I spilled my guts. I told her all about Mama trying to sell our place and me trying to stop her, without the parts about the For Sale signs and spray-painting.

"I see," she murmured, twisting her necklace in her fingers. "That explains a lot."

"And Mr. Reynolds is part of the problem." I figured she should know what he was really like so she'd quit thinking he was so wonderful.

She stopped fiddling with her necklace. "Why do you say that?"

"Because he's trying to sell my place, that's why! And he's trying to sell it to our neighbor, who comes from a whole line of bad blood." I told her all about what Mr. Dunlop was like, giving her example after example, because there were a lot of them.

Miss Miller was leaning back in her chair and I realized I was bent forward and practically spitting on her, so I stepped back. She cleared her throat. "I-I wouldn't necessarily believe that Mr. Reynolds is involved in something so . . . so . . ."

"Slimy?" I said. "He's a lawyer, Miss Miller. No offense, but you can't trust them."

She blushed and smiled just enough for me to see her dimples. "I think I know this one pretty well. And I don't think you need to worry about him."

"You mean, you think you can stop him from selling my place to Mr. Dunlop?"

She sighed. "Red, sometimes change is mysterious and complicated but it can be good. Change is just a new chapter in your life." She twisted her peace necklace and looked at the Marvin Gaye album on her desk. "Change can be a very good thing."

I stared at her as the bell rang and kids came back inside the classroom and took their seats. *Change*, Miss Miller? I guess change could be a good thing. Because I thought of a big change I could make, and it was a very good thing.

Chapter Eighteen
Change

On Monday morning I made the change that I wanted. Mama went to town early, before the bus came, so she could take care of something about Daddy's will at the courthouse. I skipped school. I had to. Mama didn't think we could handle the whole business, both the shop and the What-U-Want. But if I stayed home, at least sometimes, we could hack it.

I told J that I was getting a ride to school and he was just as happy that his stupid brother wasn't going to be riding his bus. Then I put on Daddy's work shirt, the one with his name on it in red, even though the sleeve was torn, because it made me look official.

When I walked into the What-U-Want, Beau tilted his head at me and I don't think he quite believed my story that it was a teacher workday. "How come J's in school, Red?"

"Uh . . . this is just a special day for the sixth-grade teachers. Something about getting us ready for junior high, I think."

"Oh." Beau scrunched his nose up like he was still confused, but he didn't say anything to Mama.

He didn't have to. Miss Miller called her up and ratted on me.

When Mama asked me why I skipped school, I think she was surprised that I didn't look scared. I didn't feel scared. Just ornery. "You want to yank me out of this school and start me in a new one somewhere else, anyway."

She didn't know what to say to that. Before I went to bed, though, she told me she didn't expect it to happen again and she'd better see a change in my behavior.

Well, like Miss Miller said, sometimes change is mysterious and complicated, so I stayed home again the next day. This time I hid in the shop because I didn't feel like answering Beau's questions. I sat at Old Man Porter's desk. *My* desk. I'd inherited it just like Old Man Porter's name, even his nickname. He'd had red hair, too, and Daddy said the Porter way was for it to skip a generation but when it came out it was "a shock of red." Old Man Porter had red hair, then my granddaddy, and now me. Frederick Stewart Porter.

I didn't care what Mama said, there was no way I was leaving my desk behind. She'd taped a PLEASE MOVE note on the bookcases in the living room that looked built-in but weren't. She didn't want to forget to tell the movers, when they came, that those bookshelves were coming with us.

I looked through the drawers of the desk until I found a blank piece of paper and a marker and wrote in big letters, ON PAIN OF DEATH THIS DESK HAS TO BE MOVED! and taped the paper to the top of the desk. "There," I said. If Mama had her way and we really did move, at least I'd have my way and take the desk with me. It was my legacy.

When Miss Miller called that night, Mama was spitting nails. "Do you want this on your permanent record, Red? That you're a truant?"

Truant sounded like such a bad word I figured it must mean a kid like Darrell, and I wasn't doing anything that bad. "I'm not causing any damage."

"Just to yourself, Red. Think about it."

I had to think about it for maybe two seconds. Manning the store was something that Daddy would call "productive," not like what I did on the mountain behind Kenny's. I had to go to school the next day, though, because Mama decided the courthouse stuff could wait and she'd best be hanging around the house for a while.

At school Miss Miller said, "We're glad to have you back with us, Red."

I doubted she was really glad. I sure wasn't, and I don't think any of the kids cared if I was there or not. And I got a D+ on my Edwin Starr paper, which said, "The subtext of '*War*' is that war is bad," so it didn't take very long for me to be sick of school.

A couple of days later Mama went back to the courthouse and I put on Daddy's shirt and skipped school again. Beau tried to talk me out of it. He even talked to Daddy about it. I heard him out back while I was loading boxes of TV dinners into the freezer.

"I tried, Mr. Porter, honest, but he won't listen." There was a pause as he let out a little moan, and I could just picture him tugging on his hair. "I'm sure it's on account of how much he misses you but Miz Porter's gonna be real upset, I just know it."

I was still distracted by Beau when I heard the bell on the door jangle and a stuttery voice call out, "H-hello?" Mr. Reynolds. What was Poindexter doing back here again?

I was about to go to the front of the store when Beau blocked my path. He motioned me to lay low and whispered, "You shouldn't let a *lawyer* see you out of school."

Beau lumbered to the front. "Well, good morning, Mr. Reynolds. How is the *law* business today?" I rolled my eyes because I wasn't scared of old Poindexter. Being a lawyer didn't exactly mean you were the law.

I heard Beau and Poindexter talking as I kept stacking the freezer, and then Beau raised his voice, saying, "Well, good morning, Sheriff! How is the *law* business today?"

"Beg your pardon?" Poindexter said.

Poor Beau. He was trying so hard to scare me into being good, but the bell hadn't even jangled on the door, so I knew the sheriff wasn't there.

I stepped into the aisle and called out, "Nice try, Beau," just as the bell on the door jangled, the boots stepped inside, and I heard the Kiss of Death.

Sheriff Scott stared at me. "You was just on your way to school, wasn't you, Red?"

"Uh — yes, sir," I said, tripping over my own feet as I headed for the door.

"Get in the patrol car. I'm driving you."

My voice was as high as a little girl's. "That's OK. I can walk."

"Didn't you hear me, boy?"

I nodded and wobbled all the way over to the patrol car like the gravel had turned into slippery marbles.

I swear, as fast as the sheriff drove, it must've taken all of ten minutes to get the ten miles to school, even with all the twists and turns. It still seemed like forever.

Every time Sheriff Scott took the toothpick out of his mouth he'd take a deep breath, and I was sure he was about to holler at me. It smelled like sweat in the patrol car, and I was sticking to the vinyl in the backseat, wondering if all criminals felt like jumping out of their skin and throwing up at the same time.

When we peeled into the school parking lot, I tried to open the back door before he even stopped. When I realized he had me locked in I almost wet my pants.

He turned around in his seat and gave me a stare that just about melted me. "Tell me you ain't gonna be skipping school again."

I still had that baby girl voice. "No sir, never." And I meant it. I'd have to find another way.

Chapter Nineteen
Retribution

On Monday morning I had to meet with Miss Miller before class so she could tell me what my punishment was going to be for skipping school. Mama drove me in early, telling me all the way how disappointed she was in me and asking me what Daddy would say, reminding me how he always said he could depend on me. I'd rather have had ten rides to school with the sheriff than one ride like that one.

I stood slumped in front of Miss Miller's desk and got ready for a long lecture from her, too. She was taking her sweet time writing stuff down while I sweated. I stared behind her at the quote she put on the top of the chalkboard the first day of school and still hadn't erased. *The truth will set you free.*

"I don't condone what you did," she said, finally, her head still bent over her papers, "but I do admire your persistence. It's very important to you to preserve your heritage, isn't it, Red?"

I tried to be truthful like the quote said, but I wasn't sure

I understood her. "I guess, if that's what you mean by my house and the shop and the What-U-Want."

"That's exactly what I mean." She smiled and looked up at me. "That's your history, and you don't want to lose it. In fact, you've given me a wonderful idea for a class project!" She held up a piece of paper that said FOXFIRE: STONY GAP, and it had a lot more words but she laid the paper down again. "There's a high school teacher who published some articles in a magazine about his students interviewing people in their Appalachian community so they can preserve their heritage. The articles are so popular, they're being made into a book called *The Foxfire Book*. And we're going to do the same thing — record and preserve the history of this community. It'll be a class project that'll go on all year! And it's all thanks to you."

I groaned inside, and I could already hear the groans of the whole class, too. "You won't tell anyone it's all my fault, will you?"

She rolled her eyes like a teenager. "Don't worry, your secret's safe with me."

"Thank you, ma'am." I turned to leave, but she cleared her throat real loud and I turned back around.

"There's also the matter of punishment for skipping school. Your mama and I discussed it, and we've decided retribution here at school would be best."

I found out that retribution is just another word for punishment or, as Miss Miller put it, "paying back to your community." Lucky for me, the paying back was helping Mr. Walter rake leaves for three hours after school the next day. I tried hard not to smile.

Miss Miller read to us some more from her *Animal Farm* book. It turned out, there was a lot more to it than a bunch of talking farm animals. She explained that the book was criticizing how societies tell people what to do and how to think.

When we reached her favorite part Miss Miller slowed down and looked around the room at us before she said, "All animals are equal, but some animals are more equal than others."

I thought it was a pretty dumb line because equal meant exactly the same. How could some animals be *more* equal if they're all exactly the same?

Lou Anne laughed out loud. "That doesn't make any sense!"

"Excellent, Lou Anne!" Miss Miller's smile was so proud as she gazed at Lou Anne that I wished I'd said it first.

After that we talked about our society and our rules, in the Miss Miller way, which meant we could mostly shout out our answers without raising our hands.

"We had to pass a law to have equality," Lou Anne said, "because women and minorities weren't allowed to do the same jobs as men."

Bobby Benson snorted. "Where'd you hear that?"

"It was on the news. You know, that TV show we're supposed to watch for homework," Lou Anne said with a smirk. I had to smile myself because it shut Bobby up. "The president signed the law this year that says women and minorities have to be treated just the same as men."

Some of the boys had stuff to say about that, and Miss Miller smiled and even laughed about our "lively discussion" until the door opened and the principal walked in, her lips puckered up so tight I swear a Kiss of Death was about to come out.

"What is going on in here? I can hear you all the way down the hall!" Mrs. Pugh's nostrils flared as she looked at Miss Miller and then at all of us. I noticed Miss Miller slide her copy of *Animal Farm* under a folder on her desk before the principal looked back at her for an answer.

Miss Miller twisted her peace necklace. "We're talking about democracy, Mrs. Pugh."

"And equality for women and minorities!" Lou Anne said, but shut up quick when the principal narrowed her eyes at her.

Still looking at Lou Anne, Mrs. Pugh said, "Miss Miller, I never hear disruption from other classrooms. You need to learn to control these children. I'll see you in my office after school." And she slammed the door.

The class was real quiet. Miss Miller's face was pink. When the bell rang at three o'clock, she headed for the principal's office and I knew her punishment was going to be a whole lot worse than staying after school one day and raking leaves.

Chapter Twenty
Catch-22

Mr. Walter looked like he was about to bust out laughing when I walked over to him in front of the school, dragging a rake. He tightened up his face enough to say, "To what do I owe the pleasure of your company today, Red?" even though his eyes were still smiling.

I grinned. "I skipped school. Three times!"

I swear he looked like I'd punched him in the stomach. He bent over a little and his eyes lost any hint of a smile. He didn't say a thing, just raked for a while in the same place, over and over, long after the leaves were off that patch. I was watching him because if he raked any more he'd pull up what little grass was left.

Finally he stopped, took a wallet from his back pocket, and pulled out a photo.

"You in sixth grade, right?"

I nodded and he handed me the photo.

"This is my grandson when he was about your age."

I looked at the school picture of a boy in a jacket and tie, smiling.

"He was a lot like you — real smart and had some spunk. He knew what he wanted." Mr. Walter took the photo and stuck it back in his wallet. " 'Course what he wanted was to get an education. We all figured he'd be a teacher or a lawyer or maybe even a doctor for sure."

I started raking alongside Mr. Walter because it sounded like he was on a roll.

"Yep, smart as a whip, that Leroy."

I kind of tuned out and just raked until I heard him say, "Stopped going to school right before sixth grade."

I stopped raking. "He quit?"

"I didn't say he quit."

"What happened?"

"Oh, there was a time . . . you were just a baby . . . when schools closed for years."

"What?"

"Well, for some folks. Like my grandson."

"Where was this? 'Cause if my mama's going to make us move, I'd like to move there!" I was joking, but he didn't even smile.

He gave his head a nod to one side. "Farmville area. Over toward Richmond. They didn't want him in a white school."

Then I understood. It was because his grandson was black. Mr. Walter raked the long line of leaves we'd been gathering over toward the woods where he always dumped them.

I followed him. "Didn't they have one of those Rosenwald schools?"

"It was shut down back in '58 or '59."

"How come?"

"Because the Supreme Court said there wasn't supposed to be separate schools, so the state didn't have to provide teachers or anything for the Rosenwald school."

I stopped raking again. "But they wouldn't let him go to a white school."

Mr. Walter nodded and kept raking. "Catch-22."

"Catch-22?" I said. "Isn't that a movie?"

"Sure is."

I remembered Daddy telling me about it. This World War II pilot pretends to be crazy because he doesn't want to fly any more missions, knowing he'll get shot down. But they told him, if you know it'd be crazy to fly those missions then you must be sane, and since you're sane, you can't get out of it.

Mr. Walter gave a little laugh, but he wasn't smiling. "Caught between a rock and a hard place."

"So what happened to Leroy?"

"Oh, the government got involved and finally made the states open the schools to black kids or the schools wouldn't get any money at all. Took years."

"How could it take that long?"

"With all deliberate speed. That's how fast they had to integrate."

"What does that even mean?"

He shook his head. "Exactly, Red. Exactly."

We raked a little more before I asked him, "Did he go back again — Leroy — once they finally let him in?"

"Well, if you were sixteen, would you like to join a class of sixth graders?"

"No. That's crazy."

"I guess that's how he felt." He paused and looked at me. "Do you know what he is now?"

I figured it was going to be one of those stories like Martin Luther King Jr. Maybe he skipped high school and went right on to college. "What?"

"A janitor."

"Just a janitor?" As soon as the words came out of my mouth I knew they weren't real respectful, considering that's what Mr. Walter was.

"Just a janitor," Mr. Walter repeated.

"There's nothing wrong with being a janitor," I said quickly.

"No, there's nothing wrong with being a janitor." He stopped raking and looked over at the front door of the school. "What's wrong is not having a choice."

The breeze picked up and there was a chill in the air as we finished raking in silence. When he shook out his rake for the last time he bent down and picked something out that was caught between the tines. "See this?" He held it out to me, and I opened my hand. I barely felt the acorn fall onto my palm.

"You know what that can become, right?"

"Sure. An oak tree."

"Not all of them, though. Some of them get left on the ground." He took the rake from my other hand and eyeballed me. "Thank you, young man, although I hope you won't be needing to help me out again anytime soon. You understand me?"

I rolled the acorn between my thumb and fingers. "Yes, sir, Mr. Walter."

• • • • • •

It was getting dark as I sat on the front steps of the school, waiting for Mama to pick me up. I heard the door open behind me and looked around to see Miss Miller, her flower-power bag loaded up with papers and her suede purse slung over her shoulder. She surprised me by sitting down on the step next to me. "Are you waiting for your ride?"

"Yes, ma'am." It was weird having a teacher sit right next to me. It felt like we were a couple of teenagers or something.

She smiled. "How did it go with Mr. Walter?"

"Fine." I was still twirling the acorn around in my hand.

I guess my "fine" didn't sound too fine because she said, "What's up?"

"Nothing. I was just thinking . . ."

"That is like music to my ears, Red." She put her purse down next to her flowered bag and leaned over, resting her elbows on her knees and her chin on one hand. " 'Just thinking' is about the best thing anyone can do." She turned her head toward me and rested her head on her palm. "Do you want to let me in on what you're just thinking about?"

I shrugged. "Those kids — black kids — who weren't allowed to go to school for four or five years. How could that happen?"

She lost her smile and didn't sound like a teenager anymore. "I wish I had a good answer for that."

"I don't see how people could get away with it. I mean, not here. Not this country. Not in Virginia."

She looked down at her nails, clenching her fingers into a fist. "Virginia was one of the worst states. It was a Virginia senator who introduced the Southern Manifesto."

"The what?"

"It was all about the different ways to keep schools from integrating. Senator Byrd and his buddies in other southern states wanted to keep blacks out of the schools."

"You mean it wasn't just in Farmville?"

"Farmville — Prince Edward County — was the worst, but it happened other places. Lots of other places." She stared at the steps.

I shook my head. "That's just crazy."

She was still staring at the steps, like she didn't hear me. "How come I never heard of it before?"

She turned her head and stared at me like she'd just realized something. "That's a very good question." She was making me uncomfortable the way she kept staring at me. I was glad when her ride showed up, until I saw that it was Mr. Reynolds and how big they smiled at each other.

Chapter Twenty-One
A Boy Like You

A couple of days later, Miss Miller made an announcement. "Class, I have a surprise for you." She was smiling, almost giggling, and her face was pink. "A guest speaker." She nodded at the little window in the door to someone out in the hall, and the door opened.

I don't know if I was expecting Marvin Gaye to come in, or what, but I sure was shocked to see who did walk through that door. Mr. Reynolds! Poindexter himself!

"Class, Mr. Reynolds graduated from Harvard Law School, the finest law school in the country." She paused to let that sink in, but it seemed like the two people most impressed were Miss Miller and Mr. Reynolds. She cleared her throat. "Also, Mr. Reynolds has studied the civil rights movement and has agreed to talk to us about it, so I want you to give him your undivided attention."

I crossed my arms, sank down in my desk, and glared at him.

Poindexter went pink and stuttered, "H-hello . . . students." He stared at us like we were a pack of wild dogs and took a few deep breaths before talking about boring court cases until the whole class was about asleep. Even Miss Miller was twirling her necklace and jiggling one of her feet, I swear just to stay awake.

Bobby Benson saved us by catapulting an eraser off his ruler so perfectly that it hit a thumbtack holding up the map of the world with such a bang that the map flopped down kitty-corner, held up by one thumbtack in Alaska. Miss Miller gave us her mean-teacher look as we busted out laughing, but at least it got her to make old Poindexter hurry along to another topic, which she whispered to him.

"Oh, that's right!" he said, like she'd told him that already but he'd forgotten. He started talking about Massive Resistance, which was what Miss Miller had told me about on the steps. Schools were supposed to be for white and black kids, but white people kept coming up with ways to block black kids from going to school — even throwing rotten tomatoes at the kids! Just when it was getting interesting, Bobby made a loud yawn.

"Miss Miller jumped out of her chair like she was a lion going after prey. "This is an important part of our history, class!"

"No offense, Miss Miller," Bobby said, "but what does a bunch of black kids not going to school a long time ago have to do with us?"

Mr. Reynolds held his hand up to stop Miss Miller and looked at the ceiling. "What state is it, again, that you all live in?"

There were some giggles and a few kids called out, "Virginia."

"That's what I thought," he said, rubbing his chin. "And were any of you alive in 1964?"

More laughter. "That was only eight years ago," someone said. "Of course we were all alive!"

Mr. Reynolds quit playing dumb and stared at us hard. "Well, I guess it does concern you, then, doesn't it? This is your world. What are you going to do about it?"

Nobody was laughing after that. Because he talked about some other things that happened — not in Virginia, but he pointed out that it did happen in the United States, and, last time he checked, Virginia was part of the United States. He told us about buses getting blown up and civil rights workers in Mississippi being kidnapped and found dead. Mr. Reynolds was pacing around the room and got so heated up he took his suit jacket off. "Now I'll tell you about a boy named Emmett Till."

Miss Miller sat up straight in her chair and opened her mouth like she was going to say something, but Mr. Reynolds was on a roll.

"He was a kid. About your age. A boy like you. He was beaten, cut, mutilated —"

Miss Miller's eyes went wide and she stood up from her desk, her chair making a sharp scrape on the floor. Mr. Reynolds didn't notice, though, because Emma Jean and some other girls were too busy going, "Ew!" and "Gross!"

"Do you know what else they did?" His face was red and his eyes were big.

Miss Miller rushed toward him, her mouth open to say something, when he threw his jacket behind him. It would've hit Miss Miller in the face if she hadn't put her hands up so fast to catch it. He didn't seem to hear the snickering, his face was so sweaty and angry.

The door opened and Mrs. Pugh stood there, breathing fire. That's how I realized that Mr. Reynolds, for all I didn't like him, was a pretty good storyteller because normally I couldn't miss the hammering of Mrs. Pugh's high heels coming down the hall, even with the door closed.

"May I speak with you, Miss Miller?" Only it came out more like a command than a question.

Miss Miller, still holding Mr. Reynolds's jacket, slunk to the door and closed it behind her, but not before we heard Mrs. Pugh hiss, "I don't remember giving permission for a guest speaker!"

Most of the kids were looking at the door, but I couldn't help getting caught up in the Emmett Till story. Something about it seemed almost familiar, although I was sure I'd remember a story like this, so I couldn't have heard it before. While most of the other kids strained to hear what was going on in the hallway, I listened hard to Mr. Reynolds.

"Imagine. Imagine having just turned fourteen, you're away from home, visiting relatives."

I swallowed hard, as I saw Thomas's face in my mind. He was fourteen. He was away from home, visiting relatives.

"People say you made a smart-aleck remark," Mr. Reynolds went on. "Maybe you did, maybe you didn't, but several men come to your relatives' house in the middle of the night, demanding that you be handed over to them and threatening your relatives with death if they call the police.

They grab you, throw you in a pickup truck, and take you to a barn, where they interrogate you and pistol-whip you until you cry for mercy."

"No," Miss Miller said from the hallway, in a small voice, and I flinched.

"Did they lynch him?" Bobby Benson asked.

My heart started pounding harder than it already was, and my breathing got real fast.

Mr. Reynolds shook his head. "It wasn't that painless. The horror was just beginning. Imagine being thrown, bleeding and crying, into the back of the pickup, to a shed."

"You need to learn a thing or two!" Mrs. Pugh's voice cut in from the hallway.

I cringed. She sounded exactly like Glen Connor.

"They drag you into the shed —" Now Mr. Reynolds was acting out the role of one of the bullies, picking up an imaginary Emmett Till and throwing him on the ground, giving him a kick, picking him up again, and throwing him right in front of my desk, then stomping so hard in front of my desk that I jerked. I could almost feel it, and I looked down at where Emmett Till would be, seeing Thomas.

"No!" I didn't even know it was me until after the word came out.

"Imagine," Mr. Reynolds said, looking at me, "three grown men grabbing you, kicking you, beating you, maybe putting a gun to your head."

"No," I breathed, shaking my head, trying to stop him. "No."

"Then," Mr. Reynolds went on, "they load your bleeding

body into the pickup yet again and drive you to another shed, where they do the same thing, until you're in such pain and fear you're calling, begging, for your mama. And people outside can even hear you." He looked down.

"Someone stopped to help him," Lou Anne said, her voice high, "right?"

Mr. Reynolds shook his head slowly. "They're scared. They feel helpless. They walk on past."

"That's terrible!" Lou Anne cried.

I was mad at those people, like Lou Anne was. But I also understood them. Because I was one of them.

I looked down at the floor and remembered seeing Thomas lying helpless next to me, the blood streaming down his face. In slow motion I saw the rope fall between us and the terror in his eyes. And then they were dragging him to the tree. *Stop it, guys!* I don't know if I thought it or said it, but I jerked when the door opened.

Miss Miller came back inside the room, gently closing the door behind her. Mr. Reynolds went on talking but it seemed to take a moment for Miss Miller to hear. I didn't hear him anymore, either. I was just staring at the floor, seeing Thomas, seeing the horror on his face, feeling his heart beating a mile a minute just like mine was, and wishing, wishing so hard that I could help him, that I could stop what was happening.

"And then they gouged his eye out while he was still alive!"

"Stop!" Miss Miller screamed at the same time I did.

My heart was beating so hard I was panting and my

forehead was wet with sweat like I'd sprinted all the way up the mountain behind Kenny's.

"That's enough, Bill," she said, her voice quieter now, but firm, like you'd talk to a little kid who was having a tantrum.

It was like someone had shaken Mr. Reynolds and he realized where he was.

"They're children," Miss Miller whispered.

"Just like Emmett," Mr. Reynolds mumbled, looking down at the floor in front of me.

I was gripping my desk, staring at the spot at my feet, frozen but shaking at the same time, and my heart was still pounding. I swear, if the fire alarm had gone off right then I wouldn't have been able to move. I would've just sat in my seat, hearing everyone run out and I wouldn't have cared. Because I'd have sat right where I was, staring at that spot, staying with Emmett Till and Thomas.

Chapter Twenty-Two
Emmett Till

After school I headed straight to Miss Georgia's. There was something I needed to see. An album. Not the flowered or plaid photo albums of her grandnieces and -nephews and even kids she didn't know who, for a long time, didn't go to school. Those were the albums she let me see. I'd always been jealous of those kids, imagining them running around playing all day and not having to go to school. Now I knew why — they weren't allowed to go, and that was a whole lot different than getting out of going.

The album I wanted to see was the black one. I'd only seen it that one time, when I was about five years old, but I didn't understand it then. Miss Georgia was babysitting me and had gone to pull some okra out of her garden. I was happy to discover a new album, but pretty soon I saw it was mostly yellowed newspaper clippings with a few pictures of people. I was confused when I got to the newspaper photo of an old stuffed rag doll with a ripped up face. It reminded me of the ugly Thumbelina baby doll Rosie got from her cousin after her cousin was done messing it up. It wasn't Thumbelina, but it did start with a *T*. It was a shorter name, and I thought maybe it was the boy doll that went with Thumbelina because it had on boy clothes.

When Miss Georgia had come through the door with her basket of okra, I held the album over my head so she could see the picture, just like the librarian did at story time. "How come you got a picture of this doll? It's even uglier than the one Rosie —" but Miss Georgia had dropped the basket of okra, grabbed the album out of my hand, and snapped it shut before I finished.

She put it up high on her mantel. "That ain't an album for you to be lookin' at," she said, real cold.

I was so surprised at how she was acting that she was picking the okra up off the floor before I asked, "Why not?"

"You're too young. Too young to see that."

"When will I be old enough?"

She never told me, but I knew the answer now. That album was about Emmett Till.

I smelled the smoke of Miss Georgia's fireplace before I got there. That's when I realized it must be cold out because I was shivering like it was the dead of winter.

Miss Georgia lost her smile when I said, "I need to see Emmett Till. It's time."

She froze for a long moment but then gave one nod, walked slowly over to the mantel, and pulled the album down.

I read all the newspaper articles about what those guys did to Emmett Till and looked at the pictures of his body. I even read about how they got away with it and said later that they murdered him, but nobody did anything about it. Both men were living normal lives, free, while Emmett Till was dead, and his family would never be normal again.

We didn't talk because what could you say about something like that? And, like I'd told Miss Miller on the first day of school, there wasn't anything you could do about it now, anyway. I spent a long time sitting on Miss Georgia's hearth rug while she sat in her chair, both of us staring into the fire.

All I could think about was what happened to Thomas. It was almost twenty years after something as horrible as Emmett Till, which you'd think would stop people from ever doing anything like that again, but it was still happening. "When's it going to change?" I said into the fire, so quiet I didn't think Miss Georgia heard.

But she did. "I don't know, Red. I don't know."

I told her something that I hadn't thought about much until now. "There are a few really little kids at my school who are black. Sometimes the white kids play with them at recess but mostly they don't. They eat by themselves in the cafeteria, too. Rosie says the junior high has more black kids, but they all sit separately, too." I looked at Miss Georgia, her face streaked with color in the firelight. "Segregation is supposed to be over."

"Change don't happen overnight."

"It's not overnight, it's been years."

She didn't say anything for a while. "It all depends on history."

I snorted. "Yeah, like I said, history's stupid."

"So, change it."

"What? You can't change history, that's the whole point. It's already happened."

"Not your history."

"My history?"

She leaned forward, took the album out of my hands, and put it in her lap, staring at the black cover. My history? Was she talking about Emmett Till and what white people did? About Thomas and what I did? I wasn't sure I wanted to know, but it was too important not to. "What do you mean?"

She whipped her head toward me, and her voice was sharp. "I mean you're makin' history every day, Red." She slammed her cane on the floor and leaned both hands on it, peering at me through the flickering light. "When I was young I wrote letters, along with the white women of Atlanta, to tell politicians that we women wanted our say. We wanted to be able to vote just like men could. And guess what? We won. Oh, yes, we did. That was 1920. My letters counted, you better believe it. Nothin' in my letters said I was black, so those politicians read them just like the white women's, and my letters made a difference. I made history for me and all women after me." She stared at me hard. "What kind of history you goin' to make?"

I sure didn't want to be a part of the history that was in Miss Georgia's scrapbook, but I didn't know what to do about it, either. Walking home from Miss Georgia's, I turned around and looked into the blackness where I'd come from. I'd never really thought that I had anything to do with history. For the first time I could see why Miss Miller could get excited about history. You couldn't be a part of science the way you could be a part of history. You'd have to be some science genius to really be a part of science, and that would end up making you a part of history. So when it came right down to it, it was all about making history.

Chapter Twenty-Three
The Dunlops

I saw the light on in the shop and a picture of Emmett Till flashed into my mind again, being dragged into someone's shed at night. I shuddered. Inside, Beau was just finishing up changing the oil in Mr. Harrison's car. I guess my face looked so dark he thought I was mad.

"Now, Red. I know you don't feel too kindly toward Mr. Harrison, but he's just giving us some business. He's trying to help in his own way."

I didn't say anything because it wasn't really Mr. Harrison I was thinking about. I looked at the hymn Daddy had put on the wall. *Buried in sorrow and in sin.* That line always made me think of Mr. Dunlop. And I thought about how he was just the type of man who would've gone after Emmett Till and lynched him.

Beau was tugging on my sleeve. "Ain't too many people in this world who are all bad, Red."

I turned away from the hymn and looked at him. "There's Mr. Dunlop."

"I think he's as much sad as bad."

"He's downright mean, Beau!"

Beau shrugged. "He is kind of a bully."

"Kind of?"

"He's mostly hot air, like most bullies. If you stand up to them, they usually back down. You know what? Sometimes, I even feel sorry for him."

"Sorry for him! Beau, you —"

The shop door creaked open, and Mama said, "Beau, I can take you home whenever you're ready."

"Yes, ma'am, Miz Porter, thank you. I'll be right there."

"Red, your supper is warming in the oven," Mama said, before crunching her way through the gravel over to our car.

Beau wiped his hands off on a rag. "Besides, there's good Dunlops, too, right? Like Rosie?" He started to smile, then stopped midway. "How come I ain't seen you with Rosie lately?"

I picked up a socket wrench from the work bench, holding it by the socket and spinning the wrench part around, listening to the rapid click-click-click-click-click. "We had a fight."

Beau's eyes got real big. "You didn't hit her, did you?"

"Naw, not that kind of fight. She said some stuff that made me mad and I . . . I guess I said some mean things to her." I stared at the wrench as I kept spinning it.

"Rosie's a sweet girl, Red. You want to lose her like that?"

I dropped the socket wrench and it banged onto the bench. *Lose her?* That's what people said when someone died.

Beau tugged at his hair. "If Rosie ain't hanging out with you, then you know who she's spending all her time with?"

I was still staring at the wrench. "Probably Darrell."

"Uh-huh. And his gang."

My head jerked up, and I watched Beau lumber over to the door, the fluorescent light shining off the bald patch on the back of his head.

He turned to me as he put his cap on and said what I already knew too well. "That gang is always getting into trouble, Red."

"Rosie wouldn't do anything wrong."

"I know, but my mama says, if you wallow with pigs expect to get dirty." He touched the bill of his cap and gave me one last stare before leaving.

I followed the line of trees from the shop, and when I got to their shed I could already hear Mr. Dunlop yelling inside their house. I couldn't tell what he was saying at first, but then his words came clearer.

"You're the fattest, laziest, ugliest thing I ever seen. You gonna eat me out of house and home."

I was thinking that was a pretty bad way to talk to Mrs. Dunlop, until he said, "I feel sorry for them boys in your class. I bet they can hardly stand to have you sitting in the same classroom," and I realized he was talking to Rosie.

I ran for their house and up the front steps real fast, as if what he was saying was poison and I was scared Rosie might die of an overdose before I got there. I banged on the door loud and hard, not like usual, and I kept pounding until the door opened.

"What you making all that racket for?" It was Mr. Dunlop. His eyes were small and dark, like they were hiding something inside of him at the same time they were trying to see inside of you.

"Can Rosie come outside? Now?"

I was hoping he wouldn't slam the door in my face on account it was after dark already, but he said, "Huh! If she can still fit through the door."

I was standing there shaking on the front porch, not because I was freezing. I felt like punching Mr. Dunlop, but I knew I couldn't get away with it. It seemed to take Rosie forever to get her coat.

"Come on!" I hollered.

Mr. Dunlop squinted at me. "What's your hurry, boy?"

I wasn't going to answer him, not even look at him.

Mrs. Dunlop said in her pansy little voice, "Oh, Ray, let the poor child come in. It's freezing out there."

"No, thank you, ma'am!" The words were polite, but I didn't say them too politely.

Finally Rosie got to the door, and I took her hand and pulled her down the steps and started running, stumbling because it was dark. Still I had to get us as far away as possible.

"Slow down, Red! I can't see! Why are we running so fast?"

"To get away from him!" I jerked my head back to her house, glaring at the shed as we hurried past.

She didn't say a word, just let go of my hand and looked at the ground.

I kicked some leaves. "You shouldn't listen to your daddy. That stuff he says is a bunch of lies."

"Daddy's just upset right now. That's all."

"Seems like he's always upset!"

She nodded sadly. "He is, Red. You know he wasn't always like this. He was real happy when he was a trucker."

I never thought he was real happy, but she was right that he didn't used to be so bad. "Why doesn't he go back to being a trucker then?"

She crossed her arms and stared at me. "He can't. Ever since Mama got sick he feels like he has to take care of her."

"But you know how to do that. You don't need him around."

She shook her head fast. "I tried telling him that, but he doesn't trust leaving us for any length of time because of Darrell."

I kicked some acorns off the path.

Rosie let out a big sigh. "Being stuck, not going anywhere, that's what makes him mean. And," she added, barely loud enough for me to hear, "he hates not making any money."

Rosie looked away, and I remembered that argument Mama and Daddy had years ago. They hardly ever argued. It was about hiring Mr. Dunlop to work at the What-U-Want. Mama said we should help him out. Daddy said he couldn't stand Ray and, at the time, I was sure glad that Daddy won. Now I could see Mama's point a little bit, at least, and I wished life weren't so complicated.

Rosie was beautiful in the moonlight, and it killed me to

see her looking so sad. Feeling bad reminded me why I'd come to see her in the first place.

"Listen, I'm sorry I said that stuff about you guys buying the shop."

She shrugged. "It's all right."

"Your daddy's still wrong to talk to you like that. Why don't you just walk away?"

She stared up at the moon. "You wouldn't understand, Red. You come from a perfect family."

"What? My daddy's dead! I have a bratty little brother, my mama's trying to move us to —"

"I mean, before." She hugged her arms around her chest. "And even now. Your mama still cares for you and J, and you'll always have good memories of your daddy."

I knew she was right about that. My daddy called me things like Boy Wonder. You wouldn't want to remember the things her daddy called her.

She sniffled. "My family isn't like other families. We're not exactly *The Brady Bunch*."

"No one is."

"Yeah, but my family is . . . a whole lot different."

"I know," I said quietly. "Everybody knows that, Rosie."

Her voice was even quieter. "But nobody does anything about it."

I shrugged. "Well, it's nobody else's business, so they can't do anything."

"Sometimes I wish they would." Her head dropped down and she spoke so softly I could barely hear her. "I'm so tired of it. Sometimes I feel like nothing will ever change."

I tried to think of something to make her feel better. "In a few years you can leave. You don't have to stay there forever."

"But I'll worry about Mama. And what about Darrell?"

"What about him?"

She gazed back toward their place. "What if he ends up just like Daddy?"

I couldn't say much to that. Everyone figured Darrell would end up just like Mr. Dunlop.

Rosie looked at me. "See? That's what I mean. Nothing's ever going to change."

Chapter Twenty-Four
The Fight

Miss Miller had already explained the whole Foxfire project, and most people had started talking with their families and interviewing people. A lot of kids didn't even mind the project, but some of them were still stuck on what to write, so Miss Miller decided we need to brainstorm.

She went to the blackboard and picked up a piece of chalk. "Who are some pillars — important people — of our community? Living or dead."

Emma Jean raised her hand. "My daddy. He's the sheriff."

As if we didn't know.

Miss Miller wrote SHERIFF SCOTT on the board in her perfect cursive handwriting.

Kids called out other names like Reverend Benson and the principal, Mrs. Pugh. Emma Jean said Lou Anne's mama.

Bobby Benson asked why.

Lou Anne rolled her eyes. "She's the head librarian at the county library."

"Why is that important?" he asked.

Miss Miller rubbed her forehead. "Please tell me that's a rhetorical question — one that doesn't need to be answered because the answer is obvious."

Bobby shrugged. "OK, fine, librarian can go on the list."

"Thank you, Bobby," Miss Miller said.

Lou Anne raised her hand and said my daddy was an important person in our community.

Bobby snorted.

"He was a deacon," she said, "and a storeowner and he was Kiwanis Man of the Year."

I smiled at Lou Anne, and she turned a little pink.

I raised my hand.

"Yes, Red?"

"Miss Georgia."

Bobby snorted again. Some kids laughed.

"Why is that funny, class?"

"Because," said Bobby, "she just an old black woman."

Miss Miller took in an angry breath and stared him down. "Old means she's wise. Black simply means her race. And woman means she's the half of the population that is capable of having babies, which, in case you hadn't noticed, is how you got here in the first place."

While the class giggled, she turned to the board and wrote MISS GEORGIA in even bigger letters than the preacher.

Someone called out, "Mr. Reynolds," and Miss Miller, her face turning pink, started writing his name on the board.

"He's not really part of our community," Emma Jean said.

Miss Miller shook her head, blushed some more, and let

out what sounded almost like a giggle except that she was a teacher. "Of course, Emma Jean, you're right. He's a contributor to our community, but he's not exactly a part of our community."

"And," said Emma Jean, "my mama said we shouldn't be listening to him, anyway."

Miss Miller swallowed hard and tried to smile, but it looked more like she had one of Mama's sick headaches. She picked up the eraser and started wiping Mr. Reynolds's name off the blackboard.

Bobby piped up, "My daddy said Mr. Reynolds is a wolf in sheep's clothing."

Miss Miller dropped the eraser and it bounced off her green dress, leaving a big chalky white mark down the side of it. It felt like we were all holding our breath, except Bobby, who had a big smirk on his face. I wanted to smack him.

"Why does your daddy say that?" Miss Miller's face was pink, but her voice was real quiet and even.

"Because he spouts off dangerous stuff."

"Dangerous?" she said.

"Yeah, he's one of those Black Power people, demanding rights for no good reason."

"Well, apparently, you weren't listening very well, Bobby," Miss Miller said, "because people have been dying in the past decade just to earn equal rights."

"Still, like my daddy said, they're happier in their own place."

I wheeled around in my desk to face Bobby. "How do you know they're happier? Did you ask them?"

"My daddy knows what's best for them."

"That's plain ignorant, Bobby! How can he know —"

"Are you calling my daddy ignorant?" Bobby stood up.

"Boys!" Miss Miller said. "Everyone is entitled to his own opinion. Mr. Reynolds is only telling people what the court decisions are and what the law says. I'm sorry if your daddy doesn't like it."

"Dumb-ass lawyer," Bobby muttered.

"What did you say?" Miss Miller asked.

"If the lawyers hadn't messed things up, everybody would be happy."

"What?" Lou Anne said, her voice all screechy. "What about all the kids who couldn't even go to school for five years? You think they were happy?"

Bobby grinned. "Sure. They were lucky!"

"Some of them probably wanted to learn something," she said, "unlike you, Bobby."

"Nah," he replied, "they're not that smart, and we shouldn't go wasting our money on them. They'll just end up as janitors, anyway, like Monkey Man."

I stood up fast. "Shut up, Bobby! And his name is Mr. Walter!"

"Aw, quit acting like you care, Porter. We all know you're part of" — he stopped to give the class a sly grin before turning back to me — "the Brotherhood."

I lunged across my desk at Bobby and everything was a blur of arms and faces, and I honestly don't remember what happened, exactly, but I know my fist hurt something fierce and I felt the pain on my chin as my head jerked to one side and then the other.

I do remember hearing a lot of voices, including Miss

Miller's, until there was banging on the door and Mr. Walter burst in, booming, "WHAT'S GOING ON?" We got quiet real quick and that's when I heard the principal's high heels clicking down the hall. And her voice. "I will not continue to have this mayhem in my school!"

Miss Miller went white and clutched her peace necklace. She opened her mouth like she was going to say something to Mr. Walter but closed it again.

Mr. Walter turned back to the hallway. "It's just what I thought, Mrs. Pugh," he called out, "It's that mouse again. That's why they're all in an uproar. I'll set some traps this evening and hope to get it this time."

The high heels stopped and there was sputtering until we heard, "Well, see that you do!" and the high heels started up again, but got farther away.

Mr. Walter turned back to the classroom and said loudly, "Sorry about the interruption, Miss Miller."

"Thank you," she whispered.

He nodded as he backed out of the room, his voice still loud, maybe for Mrs. Pugh to hear, or maybe for me, "Go on back to your learning, now."

Chapter Twenty-Five
The Map

Mama was real mad about me getting in a fight at school and spent so much time on the phone talking with Miss Miller you'd think they were best friends. Miss Miller talked Mama out of punishment at school because she said I was only defending myself and trying to show "the other boy" what was right. Mama knew it was Bobby and that helped my case a little because she wasn't overly fond of the reverend or his family.

She did give me a punishment at home, though.

"Red, you're going to clean out that shop so it's ready for selling!" She slammed the kitchen door after me, and I slammed the shop door loud enough for her to hear. No way was I packing up the shop. We were staying right here in Stony Gap.

I decided I could do one thing, though. I'd clear out the desk, because if we did move I wanted it empty and ready for the truck. We wouldn't need all the receipts and invoices, anyway. I got an old oil-filter box and threw in all the stuff from the top of the desk and the middle drawer — pencils, stapler, paper clips, scissors, rubber bands. The bottom drawer was Daddy's file system and had all those envelopes with the notes about each car we serviced, sort of like how a doctor keeps track of each patient's problems. I threw them all in the trash, except for the one that said RAMBLER, Miss Georgia's car.

I dumped out the contents of the Rambler envelope — a bunch of invoices, receipts, and Daddy's drawings about how to fix things. Seeing his drawings made me realize how much I missed them. Mama said it wasn't doodling, it was the way Daddy thought things out. I could remember watching his series of drawings as he was figuring out what kind of car to buy after the Plymouth ended up in that ditch and was too rusted out to bother repairing. He started with Corvettes, which I was real pleased about, moved on to Camaros, and finally ended up with the Chevy Biscayne. I'd wrinkled up my nose. "A station wagon?"

"It's the most practical, with two growing boys."

"How about the Corvette?"

"That's only a two-seater."

"That's all we need. Mama says those kind of cars scare her, and J's a mama's boy, so he can stay home with her. Me and you can go out riding."

He'd laughed and roughed up my hair and called me his partner. But we still got the station wagon.

I picked up one of Daddy's drawings of the Rambler's brake system and smiled, even though my throat was blocked and sore. I was about to put everything back in the envelope and throw it out when I noticed one really old brownish piece of paper that was folded into thirds. When I opened it up it crackled, and one of Daddy's drawings fell out. I stared at it because what I saw first was a stick-figure person. It was weird to see a sketch of something that wasn't mechanical. Plus, the stick man was lying sideways next to a church, his head almost touching it. I could tell it was a church because it was a big square with a cross on top. In random places around the page, Daddy had written the number 3.

"Why?" I asked Daddy, but I didn't get an answer.

I couldn't figure out what it meant, but then I realized that the old paper it had fallen out of might be a clue. When I opened the crackly old paper up all the way I discovered it was a map! It was a pretty bad map, real roughly drawn, like whoever did it was in a hurry. It had the squiggle of the creek, but it didn't really follow the flow. It had *PORTER* written on the left side of the squiggly line and *DUNLOP* on the right. That's the only reason I knew it was the creek because that's what divided our property. There was a triangle of land on the top right, the Dunlop side, that stretched from the creek to the top of the paper. It was shaded in with a few diagonal lines and underneath the triangle it said NO *CONSIDERATION*.

At the top left, the old-fashioned flowery handwriting said, *DECEDENT, G. FREEMAN*, and underneath that, something that looked like *FIERI FACIAS*. Fiery faces, maybe? Either the person that wrote it didn't know how to spell or it was some foreign language. What did it mean? "I wish you could explain it to me, Daddy."

Then I looked at the bottom left-hand corner. It was hard to read because there were brown splotches and tiny, pale scratchings, but I recognized the initials *F.S.P.* They were the same as mine! Frederick Stewart Porter. It had to be Old Man Porter!

I looked down again and saw *D.R.D* and figured it had to be a Dunlop. I squinted at the numbers that were partly covered by the brown splotches . . . *4 JULY 1867.* Independence Day. More than a hundred years ago. And then I realized something. . . . This had to be that old brown piece of paper Mr. Dunlop gave Daddy when they had that fight at Easter! The one that made Daddy so mad.

But I still didn't know what it meant. I wished Thomas were around to work on this puzzle with me. I picked up Daddy's drawing. Maybe it was the Freedom Church because that was George Freeman's church, and George Freeman's name was on the map. I tried to remember all the details of the Freedom Church. I knew Old Man Porter loaned the congregation the money to build. Miss Georgia's grand-daddy was the minister — that must've been the G. Freeman at the top of the map — and he died in the church fire. I guess that's why Daddy had him lying down dead next to the church. But why would Daddy need to draw a picture? What did he need to figure out? Except for the *3*s, the story was pretty clear. Church burns. Minister dies in fire.

Another thing that was curious was the triangle of land marked on the Dunlop side of the creek. And the words *no consideration*. Did that mean the church had been on that triangle of land? Was Old Man Porter trying to hold old Mr. Dunlop responsible for what he did — like burning down the church? Was he trying to take the land away from the Dunlops and give it back to the Freedom Church people? He made the old Mr. Dunlop agree to something because he made him initial the map, and it was dated, too. You only do that with important stuff.

I wasn't sure what *decedent* meant, but Daddy had a dictionary lying down on one of the shelves in the desk because he never could spell too well. I looked the word up and it meant a dead person. So, the paper was from after George Freeman had died and the church had burned. I wondered if the *3*s on Daddy's drawing meant three acres or some other kind of survey measurement where that triangle of land was. At any rate, it made me mad to think that the Dunlops had gotten away with something for more than a hundred years.

I thought about our sign: PORTER'S: WE FIX IT RIGHT. And I thought about something else. Daddy's words. *Maybe you should, son.* This was what he was talking about! He'd given me that long look and realized that I was almost a man and could help him, *should* help him.

"Don't worry, Daddy," I said, "you can count on me."

The shop door opened, and I quickly stuffed the map and Daddy's drawing in my back pocket. I breathed easier when I saw it was Beau, not J or Mama. Still, even with Beau, I wasn't ready to share this just yet.

"I know your mama wants you to pack everything up in here and you must be working real hard . . ." He looked around as he said it, wrinkles lining his forehead as he noticed, I guess, that I hadn't packed up anything. He tugged his hair with one hand and held out a bottle of Coke in the other, as his voice trailed off, "so I bought you a Coke."

"Thanks, Beau." I walked down the steps from the office two at a time, took the Coke, and had a few gulps. "I've been working on clearing out the desk."

"Ooh," he said, smiling, as he let go of his hair.

"Hey, Beau? Do you have any idea where the Freedom Church was that burned down a hundred years ago?"

He shook his head. "Nope. Nobody knows. Not even Miss Georgia, and she's the oldest person around."

I guess I hadn't really expected to find out that easily.

I was tipping my head back, taking another big swig, when Beau said, "But I know your daddy was looking for it."

My throat closed up and the Coke came out my nose. Coughing and sputtering, I managed to choke out, "He was?"

Beau was patting me on the back, only being as big and strong as he was, I was practically falling over. "I'm OK, Beau." I wiped the Coke off my nose with my sleeve. "When — when was Daddy looking for the church?"

"Just recently, like a couple months before he passed."

So the map was definitely what Mr. Dunlop handed to Daddy. "Do you know why he was looking for it?"

"Nope. He just said it was important to him, that he had to make things right."

I touched the envelope in my back pocket. I knew this was a special message from Daddy! "Where was he looking?"

"I don't rightly know."

"Well, how did he even know what to look for?"

Beau brightened. "The Freedom Church altar! It was a big flat rock." He spread his arms wide as he said it. "They built the church around it." His arms arched up to join above his head. "Your daddy, he figured that he should be looking for a big flat rock." He drew his arms out to the side again.

I felt my shoulders slump. "Beau. There are a ton of big flat rocks around here."

Beau tugged his hair. "Oh, yeah, I guess you're right about that. Maybe that's why your daddy never found it."

I sighed and leaned against the workbench, putting my Coke down. Plus, after a hundred years, even a big rock could be completely covered in these woods, what with ivy, Virginia creeper, moss, downed trees.

"You thinking of looking for it, Red?"

"Yeah, and I'm going to find it, too."

Beau grinned. "That'd make your daddy real happy."

I had to get as much information as possible about the Freedom Church, and Miss Georgia was the only one who'd know. I couldn't risk getting into anymore trouble with Mama, though, so I ran to the house first.

I stuck my head in the screen door. "Mama, I almost forgot. I've got to go interview Miss Georgia for our class project. It's real important."

She kept spreading peanut butter on a piece of bread. "What have you accomplished in the shop?"

"I finished cleaning out the desk."

Her knife stopped, but she still stared down at the bread. "Did you find anything interesting?"

"No," I said quickly.

She turned her head to look at me. "If you find anything unusual in there you let me know."

"Why?" I said, "What do you think is in there?"

"Nothing," she said as quickly as I had. "But we can't throw away any important papers about . . . the house or the land or insurance or anything like that."

"I wouldn't." That was the truth, at least.

She let me go, eyeing me like she didn't believe I was telling

189

her everything. But there was no way I was going to share the map and Daddy's drawing. It was like a special message from Daddy. Almost like he wanted me to find it because who else would look in the old Rambler envelope? Plus, I felt like if I solved the mystery, maybe it could help us stay right here. And even if it didn't help, there was no way I was leaving Stony Gap until I made sure Mr. Dunlop gave back the land he owed Miss Georgia. I was going to fix it right. I knew Daddy wanted that.

I ran all the way to Miss Georgia's with the map safely in the back pocket of my jeans. I didn't want to tell her about it, either. Maybe it was selfish. It was like a little piece of Daddy that I didn't want to share with anyone else. But I told myself it was because I didn't want to get Miss Georgia's hopes up. What if I never found the church? I couldn't stand to disappoint her.

Miss Georgia was on her porch, so I collapsed on the steps. "Can you tell me everything you know about the Freedom Church?"

"Good evenin', Red. How are you today? Other than for-gettin' your manners?"

"Sorry. I'm fine, ma'am, how are you?"

"I'm fine, thank you."

"So can you tell me about the church now?"

"Why are you all fired up to know?"

I had a good answer for her. I told her all about Miss Miller's Foxfire project. "And I'm going to write down the whole story of the Freedom Church. Every bit of it."

She wasn't smiling anymore. "Why you want to write about that?"

"Well, it was my great-great-granddaddy — Old Man Porter — who sold your granddaddy the land, right?"

She nodded.

"Then Old Man Porter gave the congregation a loan for the supplies to build the church."

"That's right."

"I know the church burned down and your granddaddy died in the fire, but I don't know how the fire started. Some people say lightning, but I've heard others say that Mr. Dunlop's great-granddaddy had something to do with it."

"I suspect he did."

"What else do you know? Like, do you know about where the church was?"

She stared out to the right, into the distance, the direction that the Freedom Church once stood, if that triangle on the map was right.

I could feel my heart start pounding louder because I had a feeling she knew something. She knew something more than I did. And if she told me I might be able to solve the mystery.

"I don't know exactly where the church was, but" — she cleared her throat — "I know for sure my granddaddy didn't die in no fire."

I sat bolt upright. "What?"

She shook her head. "The fire had been put out that afternoon. In the evenin' he went back after the metal collection box that was in the church, hopin' to retrieve the money he owed your great-great-granddaddy."

"Did he find it?"

"He didn't get as far as the church. He was shot within three steps of it."

"Three steps," I breathed. The *3s* on Daddy's drawing! And the stick figure — George Freeman — lying on the ground almost touching the church. It all made sense. "Who shot him?"

She shrugged. "Can't say for sure. We think a Dunlop was involved."

Of course, who else would it be? "How'd you find all this out, Miss Georgia?"

She blinked a few times and swallowed. "Because my daddy was there."

I guess she saw my eyes grow big and my mouth drop open.

"Uh-huh. He was a boy about your age at the time. My grandmother, his mama, was worried about George Freeman goin' back anywhere near that church because she knew it'd been burned down by a posse. So my daddy, he went after him, to try get him to come back home, forget about the money — which was probably either stolen or burned up. He'd almost caught up with his daddy . . . so he saw what happened with his own eyes."

I swallowed hard. It was bad enough losing your daddy. I knew that. I couldn't even imagine seeing him shot dead right in front of you.

Chapter Twenty-Six
Ima Butt

Hearing about Mr. Dunlop's great-granddaddy shooting George Freeman made me even more bound and determined to find Freedom Church. And it made me think about Thomas and how things hadn't changed much in a hundred years. You could do terrible things to certain people and nobody got too bothered about it, as long as those certain people were black.

I spent all day Saturday scouring the woods on the Dunlop property, staying low so Mr. Dunlop wouldn't see me. I tried to find a big flat rock that might've been an altar in the Freedom Church. The best one I could find was in the middle of the creek. I knew creeks could change their course a little bit over time, and it had been a hundred years, but it couldn't have changed that much. It's not like they would've built a church right on the banks of the creek.

As if my day weren't bad enough, I got home to find Mr. Harrison's Chrysler parked by our house. *Shoot!*

I ran across the gravel but stopped at the kitchen door,

which wasn't all the way closed. I listened through the screen and heard Mama and Mr. Harrison talking in the dining room, but it was hard to hear them because J had the TV on loud watching *Kung Fu*. After we watched the pilot back in February, he'd wanted to shave his head like that *Kung Fu* guy, Caine, but Daddy said J had to watch a bunch of episodes first to see if he still really wanted to.

I tried to concentrate as hard as Caine in *Kung Fu* and pick out just the voices of Mama and Mr. Harrison from the background noise. It was hard, but I heard Mr. Harrison say, "Believe me, that's what your husband would tell you."

"My hus-band," Mama said, pronouncing every syllable like she does when she's mad, "wanted to do the right thing."

"Betty, I think you've been under a lot of strain lately, so you're a little misguided. No man would want to sell his family short."

"It's not selling us short," Mama hissed. "All I'm saying is that we should —"

I pulled the screen door open so I could stick my head inside and hear what Mama was about to say and, *shoot*, that thing made such a loud creak I froze on the step.

"Red?" Mama called out. "Is that you?" She looked out from the dining room, and I quickly acted like I was just walking in.

"Yeah, hi, Mama. Is Mr. Harrison here?"

"Yes," she said, her lips tight. "He was just leaving." She looked over to where Mr. Harrison must've been. "We'll talk more about this later, Gene."

Mr. Harrison walked into the kitchen, jerked his head to the dining room, where Mama still stood, and rolled his eyes, smirking at me. I stared him down. It was one thing for me to roll my eyes at Mama, but it was a whole different thing for a snake like him to do that to her.

Mama held her hand to her forehead, squeezing her temples. "I have a terrible headache. I'm going to bed. There's fish in the fridge that Mrs. Scott brought by. Good night, Red."

There was so much I wanted to ask her about what she was saying to Mr. Harrison. What did she mean about Daddy wanting to do the right thing? And why did Mr. Harrison think that was selling us short? But it'd been so long since me and Mama had done any real talking that all I said was, "Good night."

She went in the living room, and I heard her kiss J good night. "As soon as that show is over, off to bed, OK? We have church in the morning."

"Do we have to?" he whined. "How come you don't make Red go to church? I want to stay home and play, too."

"Good night, J," Mama said.

"But how come —"

"Look, the ads are over and your show's back on," was all she said.

I wondered if she knew how I felt. I couldn't look at that pew. It reminded me too much of Daddy and how I'd disappointed him.

It was when I was eight and still stupid. Bobby Benson, being the preacher's son, couldn't afford to get in trouble himself but loved getting other kids to do his dirty work. He dared me to scratch IMA BUTT into the back of the pew we usually sat behind and see how long it took people to notice. I don't know why I did it except that he said, "Ain't you man enough?" So, during the church picnic, I snuck in with my penknife and did it.

It didn't take long at all for someone to notice. Reverend Benson starting calling families that very afternoon. Daddy kept bringing it up all week. It was like he knew I'd done it. He asked me what he thought that kid was thinking, and if I were the parent of the kid who'd done it, what would I do, until we talked about it so much that the kid became me without our even saying so.

"Why'd you do it, son?"

"Bobby wanted to see if I was man enough."

He looked down at me. "Do you feel like a man now?"

"No."

"Next time, you think for yourself and decide what makes you a man, a good man." He sighed. "Now, what are you going to do about it?"

"Cover it up," I said.

He shook his head. "Covering it up doesn't make it go away."

"No, I mean, sand it down good and put some stain on it. No one will ever know."

He raised his eyebrows. "Oh, people will know, all right, because you're going to tell them. Then you can fix it."

Daddy took me to the preacher to apologize, and when Reverend Benson said, "I'm shocked to find it was a Porter," I couldn't even look at Daddy because I was so ashamed.

"So was that hard?" Daddy asked me afterward.

I nodded. "Especially the part about him being shocked it was a Porter."

"Really," Daddy said, "I think that was the best part."

"What?"

"That means we have such a good name in our community he didn't expect that kind of behavior from us."

Somehow that didn't make me feel any better.

"Son, we're all going to do stupid things we regret. Any common person can pretend he didn't do it. It takes a real man, a Porter, to stand up to what he did, admit it, and apologize, and fix it as best he can. That's how you gain respect."

When I got home from sanding and staining the pew, he took the afternoon off of work to take me and Thomas fishing, so I guess he wasn't that mad at me. Thomas was quietly singing, "Big Red's a butt-head," and Daddy pretended he didn't hear except I could see him twisting his lips trying not to smile. And when Thomas started laughing, Daddy couldn't hold back any longer because that's what Thomas's laugh does. Even I couldn't help laughing. When we dropped Thomas off, he looked at me real serious and said, "Don't be like Bobby Benson. Don't be . . . a butt-head." Then we both cracked up.

J came in the kitchen even though *Kung Fu* was still on TV. "Why are you smiling?" he asked.

"Why aren't you watching your show?" I said.

"It's boring. There's no fighting."

"Does that mean you're not shaving your head?"

"Not unless he starts fighting some more. Are you making supper?"

"Not making it, but there's some food the sheriff's wife brought by." I opened the fridge and took out the casserole dish.

"I wish I could have a Coke," J said.

"Well, you can't." I took the lid off the casserole. "How about some —" At first, I didn't even know what it was. Once I figured it out, I knew I didn't want to eat it.

"Ew!" J said, looking in the dish, "It's fish Jell-O!"

I picked up a small trout with a serving spoon and it made a sucking sound as I lifted it up, the wobbly gelatin stuff still clinging to it. I let the fish slide back into the dish, only it didn't land in the dish. It hit the edge and bounced off it like a Super Ball onto the floor and, I swear, flopped around a couple of times as if it were alive.

J screamed, then went into a fit of giggles.

I don't know what came over me, but I scooped that fish back on the spoon and said in a wobbly Jell-O fish voice, "I'm gonna get you, J!" and chased him around the kitchen table, balancing my spoon of Jell-O fish. He was squealing and laughing and stumbling over chairs. When he ran through the dining room and into the living room, I followed him with my Jell-O fish and my wobbly voice, "Come to Fishy, J. There's gonna be some *changes* around here! I'm gonna catch people instead of the other way round!"

He was giggling so much that it was easy to catch up with him except that, when I lunged, the Jell-O fish fell off the spoon and slid across the floor, landing with a squelchy flop at the front door.

We stared at it for a couple of seconds in silence, until Mama and her headache both came out of her room looking fit to be tied.

"Boys!" she said in a screamy whisper. "What is going on?"

We couldn't help it. Our eyes moved toward the door and the fish lying in front of it.

Mama's eyes did, too. Slowly, she pointed her finger at it. "Since when do we throw perfectly good food on the floor?"

"It's not perfectly good," J said, "It's Jell-O fish!"

She closed her eyes and said slowly, "It's a fish aspic."

"Ass pick?" J said, his voice rising at the end as he tried not to laugh.

"A fish aspic is made from the congealed stock of boiled-up cartilage —"

"Ew!" J's face was in full puke mode.

"Oh, for goodness sake," Mama said, putting her hands on her hips, "it's healthy and —"

"Gross," I said.

Mama looked at me like the whole mess was my fault, which I guess it was.

For once the kid stood up for me. "He's right, Mama. It's gross!"

Mama looked at J and back at me. "What kind of an influence are you being, Red?"

I pointed at the fish. "That's just wrong."

J giggled and said, "Ass-pick" again, which made him bust out laughing.

Mama glared at both of us. "Clean up this mess." When she turned to me J made a face behind her back and stuck his hands on his hips like hers. I'd never seen him imitate her before. He was doing such a good job it was hard to keep a straight face.

"And, Red, think about what your brother is learning from you."

I nodded because if I'd opened my mouth I would've busted out laughing from watching J shake his finger at me from behind Mama's back.

J waited for her door to close before whispering, "I know what I learned." He imitated the fishy voice I'd made earlier, "There's gonna be some *changes* around here!"

Chapter Twenty-Seven

Vandalism

The next night, just as I was about asleep, I heard a car pull up, no headlights. When I heard voices and banging I jumped out of bed to look out my window.

The first thing I saw was a late '50s Plymouth Fury convertible parked kitty-corner between the shop and the What-U-Want. I could tell from the clanging and "Shhhh!" sounds that people were inside the shop. I tried to yell but all that came out was a squeak. Our hall light went on, which seemed to unfreeze my body, and I opened my window and started crawling through the pine tree.

"Red! Don't you go out there!" Mama had a hold of my undershirt and was pulling me back inside.

"Let go!" I yelled, trying to pull free.

Then we both saw it. Mr. Harrison's Chrysler coming out of the shop. The engine revved a few times and, even though it was dark, I could make out the driver.

"Who is it?" Mama asked.

It was Darrell. Two guys I didn't know ran out of the

shop and jumped in the Fury. They screeched off but I heard them say, "I didn't know he was gonna steal a car!" and "Crazy!"

J came running into my room. "I wanna see! I wanna see!"

Mama turned to J and let go of me long enough that I dove through the pine branches and tumbled outside.

"Red! Come back! Someone might still be in there!"

I got up and flew to the shop. I ran through the door and turned on the light. I couldn't believe what I saw. They'd spray-painted the shelves of tools, the workbench, and the floor. Tools were scattered where they shouldn't be. I ran up the stairs at the back of the shop to see if anything in the office had been hurt. I was real relieved when I saw that Old Man Porter's desk was fine and nothing had even been touched. I walked back down the steps and Mama and J were standing at the door.

J's eyes were wide. "Red, you're in big trouble now!"

"It wasn't your brother," Mama said. "Let's go back inside. I'm calling the sheriff."

I wasn't going anywhere. I just stood in the shop, shaking my head. Before I knew it, the patrol car pulled up and Sheriff Scott went in the house. In another minute he and Mama were in the shop.

He yawned and cleared his throat. "You know, Betty, I think I'll take you up on that cup of coffee, if you don't mind."

When Mama was gone the sheriff looked at me, awake as could be. "You got any idea who did it?"

I puffed up my cheeks and blew out, looking at my feet.

"Don't want to say who, huh?"

I started rubbing some dirt off my left foot with the heel of my right.

Sheriff Scott looked around the shop. "Shame to do such damage. Your daddy worked hard for this." He sighed. "Reminds me, I got to bring my car in here for some servicing. Oil change. And tires. Last winter just about wore them out."

He walked over to our stack of tires and looked at them, rubbing his hand over the treads. "I've used Goodyears for a long time now. I like a Goodyear tire but I might could use a change."

He made his Kiss of Death and put his hand on a Dunlop tire. "What do you think, Red? Should I be looking at a Dunlop this time?"

I chewed my lip. I knew what he was doing. And I appreciated it. I didn't look up, but I kind of moved my head a little like maybe it was a nod if that was the way you wanted to take it.

He left before Mama came back with the coffee.

"He's gone already?" she asked. "Well, come on back inside."

"I will in a minute." After she left I looked around the shop one more time and noticed that the hymn Daddy wrote had fallen off the wall. Amazingly the frame and glass didn't break, not even a crack. I hung it back up on the nail. It was like Daddy's spirit was still there. "It's OK, Daddy," I whispered.

Buried in sorrow and in sin
At hell's dark door we lay,
But we arise by grace divine
To see a heavenly day.

Chapter Twenty-Eight
Kung Fu Guy

The sheriff told Mama that Darrell was going to juvie, that he'd played one too many high jinks, especially something as stupid as stealing Mr. Harrison's Chrysler. I felt kind of bad about it because I figured Rosie might actually miss Darrell, but Mama said Darrell had made his own choices. And they weren't real good ones. Plus it might be good for him to get away from Mr. Dunlop.

After school, me and Beau cleaned up the shop, got the paint off the tools, and repainted the walls and shelves. By Thursday, Beau had put in so many hours Mama insisted he go home early. I was tired and sore, but nothing was going to stop me from looking for Freedom Church, so I headed over to the Dunlops'.

I'd made my own map of our land, the Dunlops', and Miss Georgia's, shading in red all the places on the Dunlops' land where I'd already looked. I pulled out the old map from my pocket and sighed. I'd looked all around that triangle of land on the Dunlops' land that said *NO CONSIDERATION*. I just didn't see how a church could've been there. The next place I was going to look was where the Dunlops' property bordered Miss Georgia's. Maybe the church had been real close to George Freeman's home, just over the Dunlops' property line.

I guess I was concentrating so hard as I crunched through the dead leaves, looking ahead of me, that I didn't even hear someone sneak up and grab me from behind.

I let out a scream and tried to break loose at the same time as I heard Mr. Dunlop say, "What are you doing, boy?"

I turned around. He was still holding onto my arm like a C-clamp screwed tight. His other hand held a shotgun. And he was smirking, real pleased with himself at how much he scared me. I wished I hadn't screamed.

He shook me but still didn't let go. "You're a little chicken, and a sneak, just like all the Porters. What are you doing here?"

"I was just . . . looking for rocks!" It was the truth.

He stopped grinning. "How stupid do you think I am? I'd like to tan your hide." He gave me one more shake and shoved me away from him. "Now get off my land!"

I ran all the way home and collapsed on the steps of the What-U-Want, panting. All I could think of was how those men with shotguns had grabbed Emmett Till, only I got away without anything but a scare. Still I was shaking, and I was glad no one was home to ask me why I was in such bad shape. I'd about calmed down when a Mustang sped by. Poindexter. And he was headed for the Dunlops'. I groaned. Much as I didn't want to go back there again, I had to know what was going on.

I hid under Rosie's and my climbing tree, crouching

under the branch we used to jump over the bushes from. But now I was hiding behind the bushes and looking through them to the Dunlops' front porch, where Mr. Reynolds was talking with a grinning Mr. Dunlop. His *cli-ent*. It made me sick. At least I'd get some more dirt and maybe make Miss Georgia and Miss Miller see the truth.

I couldn't hear what they were saying because they were talking low, but Mr. Dunlop pointed over to our land and Mr. Reynolds followed his gaze. Unfortunately that meant they were looking over toward me, and Mr. Dunlop narrowed his eyes and stuck his head out toward the bushes. I froze. He couldn't see me, could he? I was glad sweat didn't make any noise because it was breaking out all over me.

Rosie came out on the porch with a couple of glasses of iced tea. Mr. Reynolds bowed his head all polite and I could hear him say thank you. Mr. Dunlop was slow to take his eyes off my hiding spot, so he stuck his hand out for the glass without looking and knocked it clear out of Rosie's hand. It landed on his foot and he hollered like a snake bit him. I wanted to laugh so bad until I saw what he did next.

"You fat klutz!" He out and smacked Rosie across the face with the back of his hand, sending her reeling.

I stood up so fast to go help her that I near knocked myself out on our jumping branch that I forgot was right above my head. I tried to steady myself and was seeing those popping bubbles in front of my eyes, but that didn't stop me from seeing what Mr. Reynolds did.

He grabbed Mr. Dunlop's wrist and twisted it behind his back in one swift move, like something that *Kung Fu* guy on

TV would've done. It was real impressive. Mr. Dunlop's eyes were bulging from shock or pain, I don't know which. Mr. Reynolds's voice was loud and clear, and his face was raging red. "I don't ever want to see that again, do you hear? I am an officer of the court, and it's my duty to uphold the law! That, sir, is against the law! Do you understand me?"

The way he said "sir" made it sound a whole lot more like "scum," like he knew exactly what Mr. Dunlop was.

Mr. Dunlop gave as much of a nod as he could what with being twisted up in pain, and Mr. Reynolds let him go. I don't know which one of them was more red-faced. And what was amazing was that Mr. Reynolds still held the glass of iced tea in his other hand and hardly spilled a drop.

That seemed to surprise him as much as it did me. because he stared at the glass for a moment before handing it to Rosie, who was standing in the shadows at the other end of the porch.

"Here, miss," he said, much more kindly, "I believe I've had enough." Rosie took the glass with a shaking hand. He turned back to Mr. Dunlop, his eyes shooting daggers. He didn't look like a Poindexter anymore. He looked more like Caine, that *Kung Fu* guy on TV, the hero. He gave one more darting-daggers look at Mr. Dunlop. Mr. Dunlop blinked first. Making an about-face as tight and tough as a soldier, he marched off that porch.

Once the Mustang was out of sight, Mr. Dunlop sneered at Rosie and told her to get inside.

"Daddy, I'm —"

"Inside!" he yelled, starting after her, and she let out a

little cry and ran through the front door, Mr. Dunlop following on her heels.

The cold breeze blew again and I shivered — harder when I heard Mr. Dunlop cussing up a storm and slamming things around inside. Rosie screamed, and I forced my wobbly legs to run around the bushes, stomp up the front steps. I banged on the Dunlops' front door. I kept banging on it until it opened. Mr. Dunlop loomed over me, letting out another string of swear words when he saw it was "a two-bit Porter" at the door.

He jutted his jaw out just like one of those Rock'Em Sock'Em Robots, and my hand was itching to knock his block off. "What do you want, boy?"

"To see Rosie."

"She's busy."

He started to shut the door and I knew it was now or never. I put both hands out to stop the door. "I don't think so!"

Mr. Dunlop started breathing heavy, and he bared his teeth. "What did you say?" He said it so slowly it slowed my brain down, too, giving me a chance to think. And I thought about what Beau said about standing up to bullies. But I sure wished Mr. Reynolds were still around, so I thought of a way to make him still be around, sort of. "I just saw Mr. Reynolds and he . . . he said I should come see Rosie."

Mr. Dunlop flinched, then eyeballed me to see if I was lying.

I figured I was in deep enough I might as well be sure the lie worked. I had to make it sound lawyer-like. "And he said for me to call him immediately if for any reason she was unavailable."

He narrowed his eyes at me, but I saw him take a gulping swallow. "So, you're his little toady, huh? Figures. Can't expect more than that from a Porter." He spat on the porch, just missing my sneaker.

Much as I wanted to give him a swift kick where it'd do the most damage, I stood there silently, hoping my plan would work.

He half turned his head inside. "Rosie! It's your little puppy dog back to see you again."

When I got her far enough away from her house, I spun her around to look at me. "You don't have to put up with that, you know!"

She blinked back tears. I didn't know why I was yelling at her. I knew it wasn't her fault. But I also knew there wasn't much I could do about it, and that made me so mad I couldn't help yelling. "He shouldn't treat you like that!"

That's when she started crying. *Shoot!* I hadn't meant to do that. I swallowed hard and stepped over to her. "I'm sorry, Rosie."

She had her face in her hands but still managed to choke out, "It's all right."

I took a step closer. "And I'm sorry about Darrell. I didn't want him sent to juvie, honest."

"I know," she sobbed.

When I put my arms around her, it was like she was in a little cocoon, all wrapped up and safe. I even patted her back. It felt like the right thing to do.

As I held Rosie, feeling her warmth and her shaking sobs, I wondered what was going to happen to her. She was nothing like Darrell, but still, being treated bad had to do something to you. Something had to give. Just like with cars. You could drive a car while the radiator got hotter and hotter and keep ignoring it for a while, but all of a sudden, one steamy day, it would blow up in your face.

Chapter Twenty-Nine

J

I told Mama what had happened and even though her face went white, including her lips, all she said was she'd tell the sheriff what I'd heard but we didn't know for sure what was happening and all we could do, really, was be the best friends to Rosie that we could. It made me mad, but she reminded me about what Daddy always said, that a man's home is his castle and you can't interfere with someone else's family. Still I think even Daddy would've interfered at this point.

I went over there after school on Friday and several times Saturday morning, spying, but Rosie always seemed somewhere else. Mama went over, too, coming up with all kinds of dumb reasons, like bringing Mrs. Dunlop a magazine article about quilting or asking to borrow cake decorations when she wasn't even baking a cake.

By Saturday afternoon Mama said I'd best concentrate on my Foxfire paper because our first draft was due Monday. I wondered if Miss Miller had told Mama what she told me, that my English grade "couldn't withstand another poor mark." I was so mad at Mr. Dunlop and everything he stood for that I had a lot to say about the Freedom Church. First about what Old Man Porter did to help George Freeman and his congregation, then about everything that the Dunlops did to destroy it. J was distracting me, though, because he was outside crying. At first I ignored him because if he wasn't bawling for Mama, then he wasn't really hurt, but after a while it got plain annoying.

"What's wrong, J?" I called out my window as I kept writing.

He quit crying and his gravelly footsteps came as close as the pine tree by my window would allow, before I heard him slide down against the side of the house. His crying started up again, louder this time.

"Will you quit your boo-hooing?"

"I c-cain't."

"Yes, you can. Just shut your mouth."

"It won't stick," he moaned.

"I'll give you some glue."

"It won't work." He started wailing.

"Shoot, J! What is your problem?"

"My — my — Band-Aid won't stiiiiiick."

I let out a big sigh. "Aw, for heaven's sake!"

I got up and leaned out my window. J was sitting against the house, trying to put a ratty old Band-Aid on his knee.

"Of course it won't stick! You need a fresh Band-Aid."

"I don't want a fresh Band-Aid. I'm saving this one." He dropped his head to his knee and cried such big sobs I even started feeling bad for him. I pulled myself out of my window, scratching myself on the pine, as usual, and dropped onto the gravel next to him.

"Come on, J, it couldn't hurt that much." I looked at his knee. "You don't even have a cut!"

He started bawling so loud it hurt my ear.

I stood up to get away from the noise. "I'll get you a new Band-Aid, even though you don't need one." I tried to take the old Band-Aid away from him, but he wouldn't let go of the dirty used-up wad.

"Nooooooo! It's mine! Daddy put it on me the day he died!"

I stared at him and slid down the side of the house to the ground. He kept crying, and I put my arm around him. I didn't know what to say, but he spoke first.

"How come he did more stuff with you than with me?"

"Well — because — for one thing, I liked to hang out in the shop and you didn't."

J stopped sniveling and looked at me. "Yeah . . ." he said slowly.

"And maybe because I was older there was just more stuff I could do with him, more things to talk about, since I'm practically a grown man myself."

J wiped his eyes and stared off into the distance like he was trying to take it all in.

"He did stuff with you, too, right?" I went on. "He took you to get ice cream since you were both so fond of it."

"Rocky Road," he said.

"Right. And how about piggyback rides? He didn't give me piggyback rides."

J grinned. "You're too big, Red!"

"See, that's what I mean. He did different stuff with us because we're different." I remembered something that I'd never felt like telling J, until now. "You know something else?"

"What?"

"Daddy said you're smart and tough and fearless. He said you can tackle anything. And if you don't get to college on a sports scholarship it doesn't matter, because you're smart enough to get in without it.

"He said all that?"

"Yup. He thought the world of you . . . Bamm-Bamm."

J smirked and stared at the shop for a while. He was fingering his Band-Aid, and I guess he saw me looking at it because, real quick, he said, "I'm still keeping this."

"You should."

"Don't tell Mama about it because she'd probably throw it out."

I nodded. "Tell you what, you need a good place to keep that. I've got an idea."

I led him into the shop. "Give me your Band-Aid."

He hung onto it.

"You'll get it back in a minute, I promise."

Slowly, he handed it over.

I went up the steps to the back of the shop and opened up the first-aid kit. I remembered a tiny little tin that had aspirins in it, because once in a long while Daddy had a headache and would grab a couple of pills. I found the tin and lifted its lid. There were about half a dozen aspirin left, which I threw in the trash.

I put J's Band-Aid inside and was just snapping the lid shut when he asked, "What's this?"

I turned around and J had come up the stairs and was looking at my map on Old Man Porter's desk, the one I'd made to keep track of where I'd looked for Freedom Church. Normally I wouldn't share anything with J, mostly on account of he has a big mouth. But I figured it was up to me to teach him about real life, since Daddy wasn't around. So I told him that I was looking around the Dunlops' property for where Freedom Church used to be, and I showed him which part of the map was ours, which was the Dunlops', and which was Miss Georgia's.

I handed him the little tin with his Band-Aid in it.

He shoved it deep in the pocket of his shorts. "How come Miss Georgia's part is so small?"

"Because a long time ago Mr. Dunlop's great-granddaddy stole some of her land."

"How?"

"He shot Miss Georgia's granddaddy in the back when he was walking into church and took it from him."

J's dark eyes flared at me. "No! No way!"

I nodded. "That's why we don't get along with Mr. Dunlop."

"Oh," he said, turning back to stare at the map. "I thought it was because he's an asshole."

He said it so seriously, I busted out laughing.

"Well, he is!" J protested.

I couldn't stop laughing, which started J laughing, too, and we made our way back to the house, weaving across the gravel, hanging onto each other just to stay up.

Chapter Thirty
Mama

Even if Mr. Dunlop never gave back the land he stole from Miss Georgia's family, I still felt like I had to find that Freedom Church. For her. For Daddy. For me. If J could hang on to an old Band-Aid for months like it was something holy, I ought to be able to find the church. On Sunday I got a shovel from the shop because I figured it was time to start digging for that thing. In a hundred years, the rock they used as an altar must've gotten covered up with dirt or bushes or something. It sure wasn't in plain sight.

I wished for about the hundredth time that me and Thomas were friends. He'd probably have some good ideas about where to find the altar stone. Plus, I kind of wanted him to know that I was trying to do something good, to unbury the past and find the land that belonged to black people since long ago. I dug hard and long in the woods, everywhere there was a hump that might be covering a rock that was supposedly so huge you couldn't miss it. I didn't find a thing.

When it got so dark I couldn't tell the difference between dirt, rocks, and leaves, I dragged my shovel home. Beau was sitting on the front steps of the What-U-Want, even though it was closed, tugging his hair.

"What's wrong, Beau?" I put the tools on the porch and down next to him.

"It's the strangest thing, Red."

"What?"

"Your mama. I wanted to work on a couple of oil changes, but she's all dressed up and she said she wants to be all alone in the shop."

"The shop?" I stood up. What was she doing in there? Packing?

"See, ain't that strange?"

I flew across the gravel, even though Beau was calling out to me about how Mama wanted to be alone, and I burst into the shop like a hurricane.

It was so cold in the shop that I could see my breath and dark enough that Mama looked like a ghost standing at the top of the stairs in the office. Slowly she turned and I saw her face all puffy and red and streaked with tears. I'd never seen Mama in the middle of crying before. When she saw me she whipped her head back around to face the wall.

I saw what she was staring at. The wedding photo. I walked up the stairs and looked at it, too. Mama and Daddy looked so happy and real young. Then I noticed the frame. It was one of those that had the wedding date on it, OCTO-BER 22, 1958. October 22? Today!

I stood there staring at the picture now, too, remembering

how they always went somewhere special on their anniversary every year. They closed up shop for the day and didn't get home until real late. It was after midnight, last year, which was the first year they left me in charge, since I was eleven. I know because I woke up and couldn't believe it was so late. I even went out and asked them where they'd been and why they came back so late. They said I made them feel like a couple of teenagers being grilled by their daddy, and they stood there giggling like a couple of teenagers, too.

Thinking of Mama giggling made it hard to listen to her sniffling and gulping.

When she turned around again she whispered, "I really miss him."

My voice was quiet, too. "Then why do you want to move and leave him behind?"

She looked at the photo and spun her wedding ring around and around her finger. "Because if I can't have him anymore I don't want to have pieces of him all around me." She took a step back from the picture. "If I can't hear his voice I don't want to hear him everywhere I go." She turned away from the wall. "If I can't see him I don't want to look at everything that was his." She wiped the tears from her eyes.

That's when I realized that me and Mama had opposite ways of grieving. She loved Daddy so much that, without him, she was like the shell of a snail that'd lost its living-inside part. Like a shell you'd put on your nightstand, sitting there doing nothing until it got covered with Bazooka wrappers and a busted whistle and the baseball cards that aren't worth putting in the album, and your mama would come in your room and say, "Boys. I just don't understand them," and throw it all out, even the shell. Unless she was one of those mamas who'd turned into a shell herself and given up on cleaning and cooking and just about everything else. For Mama it hurt too much to be reminded of him. For me it hurt too much not to have everything of Daddy all around me.

"I can't leave until I find Freedom Church," I said, as much to myself as to her.

Mama did a double take and spun her ring again. "What do you mean?"

"Daddy was looking for it."

She swallowed and nodded but didn't look at me.

"I want to find it for Miss Georgia. I *have* to find it for Miss Georgia."

Mama put her hands on Old Man Porter's desk, leaned over it, and let her head drop down. I held my breath, knowing that she could see the sign I wrote, ON PAIN OF DEATH THIS DESK HAS TO BE MOVED! staring her in the face.

But she didn't seem to see anything. Her eyes were glazed over.

"It's Porter's Shop Road, Mama. Our name is here. What kind of place would it be if Mr. Dunlop was the one representing it? We owe it to this place. We owe it to Daddy."

Finally she nodded, sniffing. "Well, Mr. Harrison said it's harder to find a buyer in the fall and winter, so nothing's going to happen right away." She gave me a little smile. "Let's try to make the best of the time while we have it."

She hugged me, and I'd forgotten what that felt like. She wiped her eyes again, and it was hard to be too mad at her. I even gave her a hug back.

That night, Mama had me pick out my favorite ice cream from the store — mint chocolate chip, of course — along with Hershey's syrup and even sprinkles, so we could make sundaes for dessert. J whined so much that it wasn't Rocky Road, and how come I got to pick the flavor, that Mama told him he had to wash the ice-cream bowls. When he moaned about that, she added in the supper dishes.

"You should've kept your mouth shut," I told him.

Mama put her hand on her forehead and sighed, waiting for us to start fighting, I guess.

When I picked up a towel and said, "I'll dry," she about fell out of her chair.

Doing dishes together wasn't bad. We had sword fights with the peanut butter and jelly knives and used the Melmac plates as shields when the fighting got too tough. We played Clint Eastwood and the bad guy because J loved saying, "Do you feel lucky, punk?" over and over, and flicking water at me until Mama told us to stop dripping soapy water all over the kitchen floor. Then we had a towel race to mop up the mess, scuffing along the linoleum, until Mama came in and said we'd done enough and it was J's bedtime.

J immediately whined about it, but I got a smile out of him when I said, "Come on, punk, don't you feel lucky?" By the time I'd chased him around the house a few times and gave him a piggyback ride to his bedroom, he was having an all-out laugh attack.

Mama smiled. "Thank you, Red. Would you like to watch this new TV show with me?"

Mama had never asked me to watch a TV show with her before, and I thought it was going to be some sissy show but it turned out to be the complete opposite.

It was called *M*A*S*H*, which stands for Mobile Army Surgical Hospital, about a bunch of U.S. Army doctors and nurses who live in tents near the fighting during the Korean War and patch up all the wounded guys. It was a serious idea, but mostly the show was real funny.

In the opening credits there was this scene where all the nurses are running over to the helicopter to get the wounded guy out. Mama said to the TV, "That's what I like to see, women doing something constructive with their lives." It sounded funny, her talking to the TV like that, but it was also good to see some life come back into her eyes.

The next day, I went up to Miss Georgia's with Daddy's shoe box full of photos me and Mama had looked at after we watched *M*A*S*H*. They were all black-and-white instant pictures from Daddy's Polaroid Swinger. He took so many photos because they spit right out of the camera as soon as you took them and you didn't have to wait. Mama said we should own stock in the company, seeing as how Daddy spent so much money on their film.

I knelt down next to Miss Georgia's glider on the front porch as we went through the pictures. She chuckled at the photo of me when I was five, sitting in the front seat of her Rambler, pretending like I was driving. "You always did like cars."

We both laughed at the photo of J naked in his crib. That kid had always had too much energy. When he was a baby he used to wriggle clear out of his diaper.

"There's you and Thomas," Miss Georgia said quietly, picking up a photo I hadn't seen when I was going through the box with Mama the night before.

Thomas and I were standing bare-chested in front of the fort we'd made out of car parts. Our arms were stuck up in the air like *Vs* for victory, Thomas's right hand holding up my left. And we were smiling fit to bust. I sure didn't feel like smiling now.

I heard a sniffle and thought for a second it might've come out of me before I saw the tears in Miss Georgia's eyes. She'd picked up a photo of Daddy standing there smiling into the camera, one arm around Mama and the other around Miss Georgia.

"You can have that one if you want, to remember him by," I said. I didn't think Mama would mind too much. She had a lot of other pictures of Daddy.

She sniffed a few times. "Oh, Lordy, I'll always remember him." She handed the photo back to me. "You keep it so you have somethin' to remember *me* by."

"Oh, Lordy, I'll always remember you," I said, and that got her laughing again.

After we went through all the photos, I asked to take a photo of her.

"Why you want a picture of a wrinkled-up old lady?"

"I don't," I said, "I want a picture of you."

"Oh, you is your daddy's son, all right! You goin' to

be a charmer, you are. Still, you got a picture of me right there."

I told her it was for my Foxfire project, and she said she didn't want to get in the way of my education, so she smiled for the camera. I also took photos of her house, which she was OK with, but when I opened the freezer, she stopped me.

"What in the world are you doin'?"

"Taking a picture of mint chocolate chip ice cream."

"Why you want to take a photo of a carton of ice cream?"

"It's history, too," I said. "It's to remember my favorite ice cream when I'm old."

She laughed. "Red, I don't think you'll ever outgrow that."

I figured she was probably right, but she still gave me a bowl of ice cream.

When I got home, Beau came out on the front steps of the What-U-Want, one hand tugging his hair and the other one beckoning to me.

I walked up the steps and followed him inside. "What is it, Beau?"

"Rosie was in here a little while ago. She . . . she bought a lighter."

I walked over to the display of Zippo lighters on the counter by the cash register and put the camera and box of photos down next to them.

"She said it was a present for Darrell."

I shrugged. "OK."

Beau shook his head. "Darrell's in juvie. I asked the sheriff and he said those boys aren't allowed so much as a matchstick, never mind lighters, so why would she·buy one, Red?"

I started to get kind of a creepy feeling. Who was it for? Why would she lie to Beau? That wasn't like Rosie. I picked up a lighter and started flicking it.

The way Beau looked at me all upset wasn't helping. "I don't know, Beau. I'm sure there's some good reason."

He tugged at his hair. "Well, I think she's spending too much time with Darrell's old friends. I'm walking home by way of Kenny's from now on. I want to be sure she's OK."

I stopped flicking the lighter but kept staring at where the flame had been, thinking about Rosie, until J ran in the shop.

"What'd you do wrong at school this time, Red?"

I snorted. "Nothing."

He gave me a big grin. "Then how come your teacher keeps calling?"

I froze. "What?"

"Uh-huh, seems like she calls every day and Mama talks with her a real long time, too."

I tried to think of what Miss Miller could be complaining about. I was doing my work. I was paying attention. I ran to the house and Mama was just hanging the phone up on the kitchen wall, and frowning. "Red? That was Miss Miller."

"I didn't do anything wrong!"

Mama looked confused. "I-I'm sure you didn't."

"Well, why's she calling?"

"Oh, we just chat. About a lot of things . . . life."

"Life? But she's a teacher."

Mama broke into a smile. "Yes, Red. She's a teacher. She's also a person. A very interesting person." Mama leaned against the kitchen wall and her face got serious again. She opened her mouth to speak a few times before any words actually came out. "She thinks women can do anything. She seems to think I can do more than I thought. I guess I still think of myself as a wife and mother. But maybe I should be branching out." Mama looked at me. "What do you think of her? As a teacher, I mean?"

"She's good."

Mama twisted her lips. "I hope you're being respectful to her."

"I am. She . . . she treats us sort of like we're, I don't know, grown-ups, I guess. Sort of like what we think actually matters. Not like we're just dumb kids."

"Well, I'm glad. I like her ideas."

"You do?" I figured Mama to be more like the preacher's wife because Mama was always trying to do the right thing. You had to dress up for church because that was respectful. You had to help the poor and sick and elderly because that was kind. I figured she'd think kids should just shut up and do what they're supposed to, not think for themselves.

"Why does that surprise you, Red?"

"Well, because, you're always trying to get us to do the right thing."

"That's exactly what I'm always trying to do." She smiled like I'd just made her point for her, but I wasn't sure I really got it.

Chapter Thirty-One
Emergency!

I was still looking for the altar of Freedom Church on the part of the Dunlop property near Miss Georgia's, only now I was being a lot more careful and constantly looking over my shoulder. I spent Saturday morning prowling around, crouched low now that most of the leaves had fallen and it was easier to be spotted. I sure wished Mr. Dunlop were the churchgoing kind.

It was a real sunny day, but it was cold and I finally realized what was missing. I should've been smelling the smoke coming from Miss Georgia's chimney. That was her only heat. I decided to stop by and see how she was doing.

"Hey, Miss Georgia!" I called as I got close because I was starting to worry. I ran up the steps to her porch. "Miss Georgia?" I didn't hear anything, so I pushed her door open. She never locked it. "Miss Georgia?" When my eyes adjusted to the darkness from the bright sunshine outside, I looked over at the fireplace, still wondering why it wasn't going, and saw the lump on the floor.

Miss Georgia! I froze for a moment before scrambling over and kneeling down next to her. Her eyes popped open.

"Miss Georgia! I thought you were —" I stopped myself because I didn't want to say *dead*. "Dying." I don't know why I thought that sounded any better.

She smiled a slow, painful smile. "Just dyin' to see a friendly face."

"What happened?"

"My leg just done cracked and fell down under me. Couldn't drag these old bones over to that fool phone to call me an ambulance."

"I'll do it!" I ran to the phone and called 911.

When I hung up, her eyes were closed, but she was breathing. And she still clutched on to her cane with one hand.

"The ambulance is on its way," I told her.

She didn't answer, but I saw a slight smile on her face. I pulled the quilt off her bed and placed it on top of her, because it was so cold, and then I put the afghan from her sofa on top of that. Then I figured she still might be cold and I pulled another blanket off her bed and added that to the pile.

"You tryin' to bury me alive?" she said, her eyes closed and her voice thin, but there was still that hint of a smile.

I paced next to her, wondering if that ambulance was coming by way of California until it finally got there.

The two ambulance guys went to work on Miss Georgia right away, putting needles in her and an oxygen mask over her mouth. She'd gone limp and she looked worse than when I'd found her.

"Is she all right?"

"Out of the way, please, son," one of them said as they hurried her stretcher into the ambulance.

"We're taking her to the county hospital," the other guy said as he shut the door and drove off, siren going and light flashing.

I felt goose bumps crawling up my legs all the way to my scalp. I stood by myself on the front porch. I'd never been standing on her porch like that, alone, with her house empty. It was a bad feeling. For the first time I looked around and saw how run-down the place was. Everywhere you looked — porch, screens, shutters — things needed fixing. And I decided to do something about it.

I ran all the way back home and told Beau and Mama about Miss Georgia. Beau stood there tugging his hair with both hands while Mama called Miss Georgia's son. She gave him the information about the hospital, asking him if she should go be there with Miss Georgia. He told her he was on his way and not to worry.

When I told them my idea of fixing up Miss Georgia's place while she was in the hospital, Beau clapped and Mama squeezed my shoulder, smiling. The three of us sat down at the kitchen table and made a list of jobs that needed to be done and who could do them.

That night Mama called the hospital and found out that Miss Georgia had multiple fractures, so when she got out she'd have to be in a wheelchair, maybe forever. Beau slowly added something to the job list, his tongue working as hard as his fingers. After he left I looked at the list. *bild ramp fer frunt of howse – beau.* Maybe he couldn't spell, but he sure could think of everything. I picked up the pencil and after *Beau* I wrote *and red.*

· · · · · ·

We spent all day Sunday at Miss Georgia's. Mama cleaned inside and out, making J the runner to keep him busy until she took him to his buddy's Halloween party. I was way too old for that kind of kid stuff anymore but I couldn't help grinning when I saw that Mama left a couple of Cokes and a pile of Reese's Peanut Butter Cups on Miss Georgia's front porch for us. She knew that was my favorite candy.

After me and Beau had us a Coke and chocolate break, we built the wheelchair ramp. And I painted the porch, but I didn't sand out the IMF that Thomas and I had carved in the porch railing. I think Miss Georgia kind of liked it now. I made the entire porch light blue, so she could have sky all around her and feel like she was a cloud.

We even worked after school on Monday and on Tuesday, Miss Miller and Rosie came to help. I found out that some of the time Rosie wasn't home she was helping grade papers and stuff with Miss Miller. Beau was sure relieved to hear that Rosie hadn't been hanging out with Darrell's friends much.

I was just happy to see her again. "Hey, Rosie, how are you do—" but she gave me a big hug — in front of everyone! — and I forgot what I was even saying. I felt my face get hot, especially when J started laughing and making smoochy sounds.

Rosie stopped him, though, by giving him a hug.

"Ew! Get off!" J said as he squirmed away from her and took off running.

Except for the hug, Rosie gave all her time and attention to Miss Miller and Mama. They were chatting and giggling and pretty soon I didn't mind being by myself, although I did keep looking over at Rosie because she looked different, and I was trying to figure out what it was. Her hair was longer. And straighter. And she was taller. Or maybe more . . . developed.

When I realized that, I felt my face flush again, and I concentrated on pulling all the vines off the fence around Miss Georgia's vegetable garden. I was painting the fence when Beau came over. "Can I have me some paint, too?"

"Sure," I said, and poured some white paint in an old Jiffy Pop foil pan.

"I need a little black, too."

"That's still in the back of the car, I think."

"Okie dokie," he said, lumbering off to the Chevy.

I figured he was going to do some touch-up on the house, but after a while, when I looked up from my work, he was sitting hunched in the middle of the grass behind Miss Georgia's house.

"Beau," I called out, "what are you doing?"

"I'm painting the grave markers."

"Grave markers?"

"Yup. Miss Georgia's daddy and granddaddy and —"

I dropped my paintbrush and ran over to where he sat.

"George Freeman's grave? Let me see."

I'd forgotten about those graves, but now I was curious

to see them. They were wooden markers, of course, because most black people couldn't afford gravestones back then, but the wood was rounded and shaped like a regular headstone would be.

Beau sat back on the grass and smiled at his work. "This here is her granddaddy's."

I sat down next to him. It was sure different from Daddy's big granite headstone with all our names on it.

G. FREEMAN
Aug. 1829—Jul. 7, 1867

I looked at it for a moment and then tilted my head because something about it wasn't quite right.

Beau looked at me and nodded. "I know. It didn't have no day, just *Aug* for August and the year, 1829. I guess they knew when he died, though, because that one had the whole date."

"July seventh?"

"Uh-huh." He picked up a little pad of paper in one hand and pencil in the other. "See here? I wrote it down so I could whitewash the whole thing and then paint the right date."

Maybe because it was the pad of paper Daddy always used for sketches I remembered Daddy's drawing and the map and realized what was wrong.

"Beau, it couldn't have been July seventh." I knew. Because the map said July fourth. I remembered thinking that it was signed on Independence Day.

"Uh-huh, it was."

I shook my head. "It couldn't have been." I'd looked up what *decedent* meant, and it meant *dead*. So on July fourth, G. Freeman was already dead.

Beau looked down at the pad of paper. "I wrote exactly what it said on the marker. I know it said Jul 7." He said it so it sounded like *Jool seven*.

"It wasn't."

"I swear it said Jool seven, 1867, because I remember thinking that they both ended in seven: Jool seven and 1867."

"Maybe it was just hard to make out, Beau. Maybe it was a one that looked like a seven."

"Nope, it was Jool seven."

"Would you quit saying *Jool seven*? It's July seventh!"

He pointed at the marker. "I know it, that's why I painted it right there."

"But it wasn't July seventh!"

"What's all the fuss?"

I whipped around and hadn't noticed that Rosie had come up behind us.

"Red thinks I put the wrong date on —"

"You did put the wrong date!" I said, cutting him off.

Beau tugged at his hair. "I don't think so. I'm sure it was a seven."

Rosie crouched down and looked at the marker, patting Beau's shoulder.

"It wasn't a seven," I said, "I know that for sure!"

"How can you know that for sure, Red?" Beau asked.

He and Rosie both looked up at me. I blinked. I didn't want to tell them about the map. I tried to think of something to say, but my mind seized up.

"How come you the only one who knows that?" Beau asked.

Rosie squinched her eyes at me, and I was sure I was busted.

All of a sudden, she smiled. "You know how close Red and Miss Georgia are. That's probably how he knows."

"But I should've —"

"No you shouldn't, Beau," she said, patting his shoulder again. "Nobody knew. Except Red."

She smiled again, and I smiled back, but I didn't feel good about it.

Mama and Miss Miller had come over by then, and Rosie explained what was going on.

"I can fix it," Beau said, whiting out the seven. "Soon as it dries, I'll paint a one."

Mama allowed as how the way they made ones and sevens back then could've been real similar. "And besides," she added, "these markers haven't been painted in forever, so what with weathering and mold and goodness knows what else, I think you did a wonderful job, Beau."

Miss Miller agreed. "They were no longer slaves whose owners might've kept all that information precisely because they were considered, well" — she rolled her eyes — "*property*, so who knows how accurate the date is."

Beau didn't look a hundred percent convinced, and neither was I. There was something that bothered me about the whole thing. Maybe the date was written wrong on the grave marker a hundred years ago, like Miss Miller said; maybe it had been hard to read, so Beau got it wrong, like Mama said; or maybe, I thought, there was another explanation. Maybe

Old Man Porter and old Mr. Dunlop got the date wrong on their map. But how could you make a mistake like that? Wouldn't they know if it was really Independence Day or not? I tried to think of other possibilities. What if George Freeman was shot on July 4, and they thought he was dead, but he didn't actually die for three more days?

Later, at home, I checked the map when I was by myself and it definitely said "4 July." I guess it was possible it was a seven, but it sure looked like a four to me. And I didn't want to show it to anyone else, not yet. The bottom line was, the only person who was likely to know for sure was Miss Georgia.

"No, Red," Mama said, "I am not calling long-distance to the hospital and bothering Miss Georgia about a silly date."

"It's not a silly date!"

"Why are you so het up about this? Beau changed it already."

"I just want to be sure."

She sighed. "Did you notice that his birth date had only the month and the year? I don't mean to be disrespectful to the deceased, but I don't see how it matters that much whether the man died on the first or the seventh or the seventeenth."

I had a feeling it mattered a lot, but I'd have to wait until I could talk to Miss Georgia in person.

Chapter Thirty-Two
Beau

A couple of mornings later Beau didn't show up. Mama called his house, but she didn't get any answer. Pretty soon we found out what happened. Beau's mama was dead.

Mama said it was expected because Beau's mama had been sick for a real long time but that even though Beau knew that and was prepared, it's always a shock. And she said that while she hadn't made me go to church since Daddy died, I had to go to the funeral. She didn't need to tell me. Of course I was going. Beau was our family.

We sat with Beau in the family pew. Miss Miller and Rosie both gave him hugs and sat in the pew right behind us. When Mr. Reynolds walked in and sat next to Miss Miller, I saw Reverend Benson's face go all blotchy, and I thought his eyes were going to pop out of his head. There was no mistaking the icy glare he was giving Mr. Reynolds. I turned around, but Mr. Reynolds didn't seem aware of the reverend at all. I think Miss Miller was. She had on that sick headache kind of smile and was looking everywhere but the pulpit.

Mama sat between J and Beau, holding Beau's hand like he was a little boy. I was sitting on the other side of Beau, who sat there stunned. I remembered feeling exactly the same way when I'd sat in this same pew four months earlier for Daddy's funeral.

I didn't like being back here. I didn't like the memories of that day. I didn't want to think about Thomas and how he hadn't been able to come to the service and, even though he went to the burial, I ignored him. And I didn't like having to listen to Reverend Benson. I was tuning him out like I used to until I noticed Mama's breathing turning into sharp exhales like when I was in trouble.

"Our dear friend, and Beau's mama, Ida Yates was solid as a rock, even in these turbulent times. She knew her place and she knew everyone else's," Reverend Benson said. "She knew how to be kind to black folk. She knew they're happier with their own kind." He narrowed his eyes at us and, I figured, the pew behind us with Mr. Reynolds in it. "They prefer to go to their own neighborhoods, their own schools, their own churches."

Yeah, their own churches that happened to be thirty-five miles away, so old people, like Miss Georgia, could hardly go anymore. Mama's hand was gripping Beau's so tight now that he winced, and I had to reach over and, one by one, peel her fingers off Beau's hand until she finally noticed and gripped her purse instead.

"Putting notions in people's heads," the reverend went on, "is just plain dangerous. They start demanding things. They don't know where they belong anymore. No one knows where they belong anymore. Everything's in an uproar." His voice was turning into a roar. "People get hurt!" He pounded the pulpit. "People get killed!"

I heard a murmur running through the congregation of amens and a couple of people saying, "That's right," along with Mr. Reynolds clearing his throat over and over like he had something caught in it.

"Ida Yates knew her place and her responsibility, too. Why, when she got sick, she hired a black housekeeper, giving that poor woman a job to keep her off welfare."

Mama's foot was shaking up and down.

"This community has lost two very good souls recently." He nodded over at us. "Deacon Porter wouldn't hold no stock in breaking society apart. Uh-uh, no, sir!"

If "breaking society apart" meant being a bigot like Glen Connor or Mr. Dunlop, then Daddy sure would break it apart. Reverend Benson was twisting Daddy into something he wanted Daddy to be, not the man Daddy was, and I didn't like it one bit! I knew Mama felt the same as me because her foot was jiggling wildly now, and she was sitting up so straight you'd think her spine was a drive shaft.

The more Reverend Benson went on and the more Mama's foot bounced up and down, the more I wished he'd shut up. Apart from spouting lies, he was making Mama mad, and that would only make her more determined to run away and live in Ohio.

After the service we stood in the receiving line and Mama had a fake smile plastered on her face. People came up to Beau and hugged him and said nice things about his mama and said they'd come by and to call them if he needed any-thing, but I knew from experience that he wouldn't remember one word.

The sheriff's wife fawned all over Beau, telling him what a model citizen and wonderful American his mama had been. When she shook Mama's hand she held it extra long and said, "That was some sermon, wasn't it, Betty?"

Mama's voice was as phony as her smile. "That was some sermon," she repeated, less enthusiastically than Mrs. Scott. "And here I was, expecting a funeral service."

Mrs. Scott's smile faded fast but the next group of people came up to pay their respects, so she walked slowly off.

When the preacher reached us and held Mama's hand, talking about his wonderful sermon and how everyone was on the same page, Mama's toe was tapping the floor a mile a minute and her skin was drawn so tight across her face I thought it might rip.

Reverend Benson shook my hand and said, "Well, it's good to see you, stranger. The way you're avoiding us, people might get the impression that you aren't a real Christian, and where would that leave you? So what do you say, Red, you ready to rejoin the flock?"

I had a lot I wanted to say to him, none of it good, but he looked at Mama for the answer. And, after a long moment, she gave him one. "Red prefers to think for himself."

I felt my mouth drop open, and I figured Reverend Benson was shocked, too, because his smile turned fake and ended up all teeth. "Oh, you got to watch out for that. That's likely to get a boy in trouble." He gave a phony chuckle.

"Matter of fact, he *has* gotten himself in a bunch of trouble, hasn't he?" He bent down and peered at me. "Skipping school? Vandalizing property? If you're not careful, you'll get yourself sent to juvie like Darrell Dunlop." He straightened and turned to Mama. "Good dose of religion would cure that. We're always here to help. At Open Doors Baptist Church, *our doors are open*." He chuckled again, this time for real. "That's what I always say, right?"

"Yes," said Mama, losing even her fake smile, "that's what you always say. I need to take care of Beau now."

"Of course, of course. Beau, I'll be by later to check on you, and we'll say a prayer for you mama."

We headed for the car. Except Beau. He just stood there. Mama looked over at me, and I took Beau by the hand and led him to the car. I opened the door and guided him into the front passenger seat and buckled his seat belt for him.

Mama sniffled and patted his arm. "Beau, you'll be taking all your meals with us for a while because I won't have you sitting and eating alone. That's no good for anyone, believe me."

By the time we got back home, it smelled real good. Mama had cooked food ahead and left it in the oven so it was warm. I was still leading Beau by the hand.

Mama put on her apron. "Red, please set the table."

I dropped Beau's hand. "Table?" I said, like it was some foreign word.

"Yes," Mama said, "the table." She glanced at the piles of papers on the dining room table. "The kitchen table. Plates, forks, and knives, please."

While I was setting the table, J came in from outside, got the Ritz crackers down from the cabinet and put some in his Flintstones bowl. He headed into the living room, walking right past Mama at the oven.

"Where are you going with that bowl?" she asked him.

"To watch TV."

"Oh, no, you're not. We're sitting down to eat together."

He turned and stared at her. "Why?"

Mama twisted her wedding ring around her finger. "Because we're civilized. And that's what civilized people do."

J looked through the dining room to the TV in the living room and back at Mama. "We ain't been civilized in a real long time."

"We *haven't* been civilized —" Mama stopped correcting his English and looked at her hands. She twisted her wedding ring a few more times. "You're right, J," she said quietly. "But that's going to change now. We're all going to eat together."

J shrugged and went to his usual place at the table.

Mama gave me the eyeball, so I sat down, too.

After she set the casserole dishes in front of me, Mama steered Beau over to the table to join us and sat down at her place, which left one seat for Beau. Daddy's.

Beau tugged his hair.

"Sit down, Beau," Mama said, and picked up a spoon to start serving the mashed potatoes.

But at the scratch-squeak of Beau pulling the chair away from the table, Mama, J, and I stared at the gold vinyl. When Beau let go of it, the chair let out a puff of air like a sigh.

"That's Daddy's chair!" J said.

Beau froze. It felt like a lifetime that Mama's serving spoon hung in the air above the potatoes, I held my breath, and Beau stood like a statue.

"But . . . I guess it's OK for you to sit there," J said, and it was as if the whole room finally let its shoulders down and the house was allowed to breathe again.

Chapter Thirty-Three
M*A*S*H

The weather had turned cold now that it was November, and the leaves had all just about fallen from the trees. I thought that'd make it easier to find a big altar stone, what with all the greenery dying, but it didn't. As I looked for the stone, I kept trying to make sense of the dates on my map and on George Freeman's grave that didn't match up. It made me real uneasy, but I couldn't figure out just why.

It was late afternoon on Sunday once I got home from searching, and I could hear J's loud voice coming from the kitchen and Beau trying to calm him down. Mama said Beau would be hanging out with us now because she had to teach him how to take care of himself, and even teach him how to drive. It was weird how Beau knew a car inside and out but never learned to drive one.

I walked in the kitchen to see Beau tugging his hair, Mama standing with her hands on her hips, and J whining.

"I'm only seven!"

"You're almost eight," Mama said, "and you can throw dirty clothes into a machine just as well as I can."

"But, Mama, I don't know what to do with them after that!"

"When the washing machine stops, you take the clothes out and put them in the dryer."

"I can show you how," Beau said. "Your mama explained it to me. I can even show you how to fold all your clothes up real good."

J glared at him. "Thanks a lot, Beau!"

I had to grin, even when Mama said that doing our own laundry applied to me, too. It couldn't be that bad. Heck, tossing clothes into a couple of machines was easy, and I could skip the folding part and stuff my clothes in the drawers.

Mama carried on about how women had better things to do than spend their whole lives picking up after men. She went on so much she sounded just like she did at the beginning of both *M*A*S*H* episodes we'd watched, and I had to grin.

Mama stared at me. "What's so funny, Red?"

"I was just thinking, 'That's what I like to see, women doing something constructive with their lives.'"

"Where did that come from?"

"You!"

"What?"

"You say it when you watch *M*A*S*H*."

"I do not!"

I about busted out laughing. "Yes, you do!"

She stopped and thought a minute. I don't know if she believed me, but she sniffed and said, "Well, it's true, anyway. Women are just as strong as men. Not in the same ways, maybe, but we can do anything you all can do. And, what's more, you can do the same things I can. As a matter of fact, it's about time you both learned how to cook for yourselves."

"What?" J cried. "It's all your fault, Red! You and your big, fat mouth!"

She glared at us with a look that said we'd better shut up right then. "If you're expecting some woman to do all your cooking and cleaning for you, you've got another thing coming. By the time you're grown, women aren't going to be putting up with all of this, oh, no, they're not!"

She was sounding like Miss Georgia now. And she wasn't finished. "I'm not raising any lazy men around this house. You'd best pitch in and learn how to take care of yourselves. The times, they are a'changin', boys."

We rolled our eyes. It was a bad choice.

"Excuse me?" Mama's hands were on her hips, and her eyes were shooting daggers.

"Yes, ma'am," I mumbled.

I guess J wasn't watching Mama because he rolled his eyes again and said, "Yes, ma'am, *sir*!"

On top of learning how to cook fried chicken, mashed potatoes, and biscuits from scratch, J got to wash dishes afterward. I didn't offer to dry because the job I got took even longer — raking all the leaves out from under the crawlspace of the house. In fact, J was out on his bike before I'd made it three-fourths of the way around the house.

While I was working on the far side of the house, outside the dining-room window, my rake hit something hard under a pile of leaves. When I heard a clink, I realized it was glass. It was hard to see since it was almost dark, but I brushed the leaves away and found more than a dozen empty Coke bottles. "What the —" It only took me a moment to figure it out.

"J!" I hollered.

"What!" When he saw an empty bottle in my hand, he took off, spraying gravel, and peddled like mad behind the What-U-Want.

I went the other way, caught him, and dragged him into the back of the store. "Beau! Can you come here?"

Beau came loping to the back.

"Have you been missing some bottles of Coke out of the store?"

"Yes," Beau said slowly. "But I been putting money in the cash register drawer to pay for them."

"But you weren't drinking them!"

"No, but I figured whoever took them must need them."

"It was J!" I said, shaking J by the arm. "And he didn't need them. He stole them!"

"Well, I didn't know," J whined.

"Didn't know what?" I said. "You knew you weren't supposed to take them. You even told me Mama said we couldn't take any Cokes. That's why you were hiding the empties." I was so mad I gave his arm another shake. "Shoot! It's bad enough you stole them. You make a crime even worse when you try cover it up, J. That's just shameful!"

J's sniveling turned into bawling, which made Beau go all soft and mushy. "I'm sure he didn't mean no harm, Red. He's just a little boy."

I stared at J as I answered Beau. "If he's big enough to steal and lie about it, he's big enough to pay for what he did.

J, you're going to have to earn some money so you can pay Beau back."

J quit crying long enough to whine. "How am I gonna do that?"

I thought for a minute, adding up the cost of the Cokes he stole, and came up with an answer. "You have to do all of Beau's chores for a week, and that includes his laundry!"

Beau and J both started protesting, but I insisted, telling J, "What would Daddy have said, huh?" That shut him up good.

"And," I added, "you have to clean up your mess. Go get all those empty bottles, wash them out, and stack them in the back to be collected. You hear me?"

"Yes, sir." He didn't even say it sarcastically. He said it like I was, well, like I was Daddy. And he went right off and started collecting the bottles.

J got sent to bed early, which was just as well because we had to watch the news and then it was time for *M*A*S*H*. I even got Beau to watch *M*A*S*H* with us. At first, he didn't want to.

"I seen it before, Red, and they talk so fast I don't even know what they're saying," but I finally convinced him.

Mama watched *M*A*S*H* like it was the news, so she ignored you until the commercials came on. I figured I'd better give Beau a quick explanation of the show before it started. I about busted a gut when Mama said her line about women doing something constructive with their lives, but Beau, hearing her say it for the first time, got all serious and nodded his head, saying, "You're right, Miz Porter. It's real good to see that."

He kept talking when the show started, too.

"Is this Vietnam?"

"No," I said, even though I'd already told him, "it's Korea."

"It looks like Vietnam."

"Except it's Korea," I said again.

"Well, it could be Vietnam."

"Beau! It's Korea, OK? Now, just watch."

When the commercials started, Mama turned to me like she'd been holding her thoughts in during the show, and said, "He's right, Red, it is about Vietnam."

"No, it's not! It's Korea!"

"Yes, it's set in Korea. But it's really talking about Vietnam. And how a lot of people would like for us to get out of there. Stop losing money, stop losing lives."

"Then why don't they just come out and say that?"

"You can't just come out and say that," Mama said, running her finger around the rim of her iced tea glass.

"Why not?"

"Because speaking out against the war is not . . . a popular opinion."

"Your mama's right," said Beau, "people would think you weren't being patriotic. Nobody wants to be unpatriotic."

"So nobody says anything?"

"Well," Mama said, "some people do, like the hippies and peaceniks, but they're considered the crazies. Nobody wants to speak up and be one of the crazies."

"So everyone just sits there and says nothing? How's anything ever going to get better?"

Mama looked down at the braided rug like it was suddenly real interesting to see how those colors coiled around into a tiny little circle of black in the center.

"It's all confusing to me," Beau said.

"It's not just you, Beau," Mama said, and I could tell she wasn't just saying it to make Beau feel better because her eyes had that faraway look as she held her iced tea glass with one hand and ran her finger around the rim with the other. "It's a confusing time. Even in the 1940s when we were at war, we knew where we stood. And in the 1950s it seemed like we had it all." She sighed. "Then the cracks started showing because we'd only been covering up the problems. It seems like the past few years it's been nothing but war and uproar, assassinations, fighting battles like civil rights, women's lib—"

"But those ain't all bad things, Miz Porter."

"Oh, I don't mean it's all bad. Some of it's good — change we needed, like civil rights. In fact, we need more change when it comes to civil rights. We still aren't treating people equally or fairly." She sighed.

I wondered if she was thinking about Thomas. I was.

"But," Mama went on, "change can still be hard for people. It's confusing and sometimes even painful." She smiled at me. "Like growing pains."

I didn't know if it made me feel better or worse that the rest of the country was in an uproar like my life seemed to be ever since Daddy died. On the one hand it meant I was like everyone else in the country. On the other hand, if grown-ups couldn't even make sense of everything that was happening, how the heck was *I* supposed to?

Chapter Thirty-Four
Beau's Plan

Before school Monday morning I was puzzling over the old map when I smelled something unusual in the kitchen. Hot food. I bumped into J as we ran for the kitchen.

Beau was making pancakes. Mama didn't even have to teach him because he said his mama had taught him how. She made some Nescafé, though, with milk and sugar, and set the NASCAR mug in front of me.

"Your coffee, sir," she said with a smile, and I couldn't help grinning back at her.

I must've eaten eight pancakes before I stopped for a breath because they were real good and I was still making up for going a long time without hot breakfasts. Even J was cramming them in.

"Boys!" said Mama, "You have plenty of time before the bus comes. Slow down or you'll get a stomachache."

"Miz Porter?" Beau said, sitting down in Daddy's chair, "I got me an idea how you can stay right here in Virginia."

That stopped me from eating. "How?" I said with my mouth full.

"You can sell your place and still stay in town. Y'all can just move into my house. I got three bedrooms. Miz Porter, you could have Mama's, and the boys can share. For free, because it's done paid for."

I looked at Mama.

"I — I don't know what to say, Beau."

"Miz Porter, your family has always been more than kind to me." He reached up to tug at his hair. "Now that Mr. Porter's gone, it seems only right that I should help take care of ya'll for a change."

"But, Beau, that would be too big of a change. There are three of us . . . all living at your house?" She looked across the table at J bouncing in his seat and shook her head. "You'd never get any peace and quiet."

"But . . . I don't like peace and quiet, Miz Porter. I get lonely all by myself."

Mama chewed her lip and looked around the room, her eyes settling on everything like maybe, hopefully, she was figuring out how to move it to Beau's house. When she gazed into the dining room and beyond, Beau lit up.

"I got me a nice big color TV, Miz Porter. We can sit and watch all those TV women who are like you."

Mama tilted her head. "What women?"

"You know, those women who are doing something constructive with their lives."

I held my breath because if I'd said that, Mama would know I was poking fun at her. But she didn't look mad at all. In fact, she held her head up and was half smiling. "That's a lovely offer, Beau, but I —"

"You just think about it, OK? It's a real big question. I need a lot of time for questions like that to run around my brain before they settle. So you take your time, all right?"

She smiled. "All right, Beau. I'll think about it."

When Mama turned away I gave Beau two thumbs up.

At school, Miss Miller let us work on our Foxfire projects "independently or in small, *quiet* groups," she said, her eyes flicking to the door. She patrolled up and down the rows of desks just to make sure we kept it down to a low hum.

She stopped at the front of my row, my desk, and crouched down. "I know you were concerned about the date on that grave marker," she said, "so I tried to find out at the county courthouse."

I stared at her, because I didn't know you could look that kind of stuff up, and also I was surprised she'd go out of her way like that for me.

"Unfortunately during the Civil War and for some time afterward, the county didn't keep birth and death records, not very thoroughly, anyway, and the state didn't take over doing it until the early 1900s, so I'm afraid he's lost in that gap."

I tapped my pencil on my desk a few times. "Does that mean there'd be no information about Freedom Church, either?"

She nodded. "Bill — Mr. Reynolds has combed those records and he hasn't found —"

"Why is he looking that up?"

Her face went a little pink, like maybe I'd caught her at something. "I-I think he just wants to find out the truth."

I let that sink in for a moment. Since he was a lawyer and he had to follow the law, maybe it was a good thing for him to be working on this case. Maybe he could find where on the Dunlop land the church had been. I knew he could stand up to Mr. Dunlop. And I knew he didn't like Mr. Dunlop, either.

Miss Miller was talking, and the edge in her voice is what got me to tune in. ". . . and while I know you don't care much for him, he is —"

"I changed my mind about him, Miss Miller. I think he's OK. Mostly."

"Oh." She smiled, and her voice went back to normal. "Well, I'm glad to hear that. Mostly."

She stood up again to continue her patrol, and I got an idea. I scribbled the words on a piece of notebook paper and tore it out of my binder. "Miss Miller?"

She was halfway down the row, but she turned around and walked back to me.

I dropped my voice to a whisper. "Could you give this to Mr. Reynolds and see if he can translate it?" I folded up the piece of paper so no one could see the words *Fieri Facias* and handed it to her.

"OK," she said slowly. "Is there anything he needs to know about it?"

I shook my head. "I don't even know if it means any-thing, but it's the only thing on the —" I stopped myself just before saying *map*. "It's the only thing I can't figure out."

"Ah, like a piece of a puzzle." She smiled. "I'll let you know what he says." And she went and put it right in her suede purse so I knew she realized how important it was.

• • • • • •

When I got home from school Reverend Benson was in the living room. Mama was crouching on the sofa, looking pale and small. He insisted I join them because, he said, "If you're grown up enough to decide whether you go to church or not, you're grown up enough to understand this discussion."

"Is it Rosie?" I asked.

Mama shook her head. "Rosie's fine."

"You see, Red, your mama has this notion of y'all moving in with Beau."

"I know," I said.

Reverend Benson cleared his throat. "Well, your mama being a widow and Beau being a single man, that would be living in sin, the two of them living together without being married."

"It's not like that! Plus, it's not just them; it's me and J, too."

"Ex-act-ly," he said triumphantly, turning to Mama. "Think of the message you're sending your boys. They'll believe they can pick up with any floozy — oh, not that I'm implying you're a floozy, no ma'am —"

Mama's foot started shaking up and down.

"— but just think of how it looks. Think about your reputation. And your responsibility to your boys, to your whole community, and to Beau." He stood up and grinned at both of us. "I know you'll do the right thing."

Mama had barely shut the door behind him when I was after her. "You don't have to listen to Reverend Benson. You don't even like him!"

Mama started tapping her foot. "Whether I care for

253

Reverend Benson is not the point. In this case, I'm afraid he's right."

"But that's just dumb, Mama. Everyone knows Beau is like my brother. Daddy and you always thought of him like a son. So, who's going to think bad about you?"

"It's not just me. I have to think about Beau's reputation, too. They might think I'm using him by taking over his house without paying him rent or anything."

"Then we'll pay him!"

"With what, Red? We're in debt. Even after selling our property, there are so many bills to pay, we'll only have a tiny bit of money, and that won't last long. Back home, we can live with your aunt Patty, at least until I get on my feet." She shook her head. "How could we possibly pay Beau rent?"

"By getting a job!"

Mama froze, and her face went thoughtful, almost surprised. "Things *have* settled down, now," she said slowly, "and you boys are in school. . . . You're right, I suppose I could look for a job."

"I meant me, Mama, not you."

"Why not me?" Mama asked.

"What can you do?"

"What can I do? There are a lot of things I can do, young man! You, on the other hand, need to go to school and do your studies so that one day you'll be able to take care of yourself." She marched into the kitchen and I heard pots and pans banging, so I guessed that was the end of that. I just hoped she'd think of some job she could do because without Beau's house as an option, Ohio was getting closer and closer.

Chapter Thirty-Five
Mama and Rosie

Mama plopped the macaroni-and-cheese dish on the table and sat down to supper with the rest of us. She didn't serve herself, though, only the rest of us. She was busy folding and unfolding her napkin as she told Beau that we couldn't move in with him and explained what Reverend Benson said.

Beau swallowed his forkful of macaroni. "Oh. OK. Reverend Benson knows what's right, so whatever he says I guess we have to follow."

I snorted.

"Well," Mama said, her foot starting to shake, "I'm not sure he's right about everything, but I think he may be right about this issue."

"And peach pie," J said.

"What does peach pie have to do with anything?" I asked him.

J looked at Mama. "Reverend Benson said his wife is always in the kitchen, where women should be, spending their time making his favorite things to eat, like peach pie."

I looked across the table at Beau and I bet my eyes were as big as his. I swear we both scooted our chairs back from the table at the same time, ready for Mama to blow a gasket.

Her foot was shaking faster than a timing light, and she was rocking her fork between two fingers as fast as a gauge gone berserk. Her eyes and lips were tight. "I don't have time — or the inclination — to bake pies all day."

"But I like your pies, Mama," J says.

"Then you should learn how to bake them."

"I'm not a girl! I shouldn't have to cook stuff!"

Mama's fork flew out of her hand and clanked on the floor at the same time her hand hit the table so hard the lid fell off the sugar bowl.

J's mouth dropped open. First, he stared at the fork on the floor, then at the sugar bowl, and finally at Mama.

Even Mama looked surprised, but that didn't stop her from talking. "I thought I'd made it crystal clear that cooking and housework are not just for women to do, but apparently there's still some confusion." She stood up from the table and marched out of the kitchen.

"Man, J," I said, "how stupid are you? Don't you know saying stuff like that is only going to make her mad?"

Mama reappeared in the kitchen with her coat and purse, glaring at me now. "It's not just the talk that upsets me, it's the thought behind it. I have a perfect right to be angry about that. It's my *life*!" She dropped her purse on the counter as she put on her coat. "You all can clean up after supper. This kitchen floor needs scrubbing, J," she said pointedly, "and the whole house needs dusting and vacuuming." She glared at me and Beau.

"Yes, ma'am, Miz Porter," Beau said.

"I'm going out. And I want you *gentlemen* to think about —" She let out a sound between outrage and disgust, storming out of the kitchen and out the door. We listened to the car door slam and the gravel spin as she took off.

J tired himself out scrubbing the kitchen floor and went to bed without a fight. Beau had vacuumed, I'd dusted, and we were finishing cleaning the kitchen by the time we heard the Biscayne wagon crunch its way back onto the gravel. I was surprised to hear two car doors open.

I heard Mama say, "I could've dropped you right at your front door."

"No, Mrs. Porter." It was Rosie's voice. "I want to walk the path because Daddy'll be asleep by now, so I can sneak in — I mean, I can go in without waking him up, like the car and headlights might. Thank you for taking me out to supper."

I looked at Beau. The two of them had gone out to supper?

"Thank you, Rosie," Mama said. "I really needed your company."

"Oh, anytime. That was fun." Rosie giggled. "I wonder if anyone heard us singing, what with the windows all the way down. You have a real nice voice, Mrs. Porter. You should sing more often."

Rosie was always wanting people to sing. She tried to get me to join her in that song from the Coke ad, "I'd Like to

Teach the World to Sing." After enough times of me singing "in perfect harmony" off-key on purpose because I thought it was so funny, she got fed up.

"You remember how that song goes, right?" Rosie asked.

They started singing that "I Am Woman" song. We watched them through the screen door, Mama's arm around Rosie's waist, Rosie's arm around Mama's shoulder, walking toward the shop, and I was surprised to see that Rosie was taller than Mama.

I heard Beau next to me humming along with them, and then start singing softly.

I stopped him when he sang, "I am woman."

"Beau! It's not a song that's meant for you."

He looked at me, then back out at Mama and Rosie. "I think it's a song that's meant for everyone, Red." And he went on singing about wisdom borne of pain.

He was still singing as Mama stood alone in the moonlight by the shop, watching Rosie walk down the line of trees to her house.

Chapter Thirty-Six
What Happened to Rosie

Miss Miller was on recess duty and called me over. "Here's your answer from Mr. Reynolds," she said, handing me back my piece of paper. "If you have any questions, I may be able to explain it better."

I opened up the paper and read Mr. Reynolds's handwriting. I couldn't make out any of it, not because his handwriting was bad but because most of the words he used I didn't know. *Writ of execution, debtor, judgment rendered, recorded lien, foreclose.* I looked up at Miss Miller.

"I know," she said, "That's why I had him explain it to me in plain English. Basically what it means is that if someone can't pay their debt, the person they owe the money to can take away their property — land, for example — in order to get paid back." She looked at me. "Does that help?"

"Not really. I mean, I understand what you said, I just . . ."

"It just doesn't help you solve the puzzle."

"Right."

"Well, maybe it will. Sometimes we need to let things mull around for a while before we figure them out."

I was letting things mull around that afternoon while I was looking for the church, but it wasn't making any sense yet. Who was it that couldn't pay a debt? And who was going to get something for it? Was Old Man Porter making the Dunlops pay for something? Maybe the Dunlops were supposed to pay George Freeman. Maybe they never paid. Is that why the old Mr. Dunlop shot George Freeman in the back? I was getting frustrated that I couldn't figure it out.

I was also getting pretty discouraged about ever finding that altar, so I was almost relieved when I saw Rosie sitting on that big rock in the middle of the creek, knowing I could just sit for a while and talk with her. She was hunched up and moving funny, so I figured she had her transistor radio and was singing and moving to the music. When I got closer, though, I realized what was happening. She was crying.

I plunged right into the water, not even trying to pick my way across the stepping stones. "Rosie!"

She flinched. "Red! You scared me!"

My jaw dropped when I saw her face. There was a big bruise on one side, so half of her face looked blue-ish.

She tried to cover it up by putting her hand on her cheek, but she winced in pain.

"What happened, Rosie?"

She looked away and wouldn't answer.

"Did your daddy do that to you?" My voice came out like a growl.

She kind of shook her head. "Red, don't go doing anything, you'll just get hurt."

My voice dropped even lower. "He's not getting away with this."

But I didn't know how to stop him. It wasn't like me and Thomas could glue her daddy's hands down with contact cement, although I sure would like to try. I had to do something.

I convinced her to come back home with me. "Mama!" I yelled. I coaxed Rosie into the kitchen as she tried to cover her face with her hands.

Mama came in from the dining room. "I'm right here, Re—" She stopped when she saw Rosie. "What happened?"

"Her daddy!" I said.

Rosie burst out crying again, and Mama ran over to us, pulling Rosie into her arms.

I walked straight to the phone and picked up the receiver.

"What are you doing?" Rosie squeaked.

"Calling the sheriff."

Rosie gasped.

"He's right, honey," Mama said, putting her head against the good side of Rosie's face, "We have to."

"The sheriff?" Rosie breathed, as I dialed the number. "What are you going to tell him?"

I looked at Rosie, one side of her face all swelled up. "The truth."

• • • • • •

Mama, Rosie, and I were sitting at the kitchen table with cheese and Ritz crackers that none of us were eating when Beau came to the kitchen door, wiping his hands on a grease rag. "I done fixed two cars today all by my—" He saw Rosie, who'd forgotten about her face and tried covering it, but it was too late. Beau's jaw set and his face went hard. "I think I'll go stop by the Dunlops'."

"Now, Beau," Mama said, holding Rosie's hand, "you don't need to go over there. The sheriff went and we're waiting for his call now."

"Don't you worry, Miz Porter, I'm going to be respectful and all, just pay them a visit and let Mr. Dunlop know I know what's going on without saying as much." He turned to go. "And let him know that Beau don't like it. No, sir!"

I tried to go with him, but both Mama and Beau insisted I stay put.

"He thinks I'm harmless," Beau said, "but he don't know Beau."

I finally agreed because Beau convinced me that Mr. Dunlop would only get madder if I were there. But I sure couldn't help picturing Mr. Dunlop as a Rock'Em Sock'Em Robot, whose head I knocked off over and over and over.

Mama decided to "have some girl fun," so she and Rosie went to look in her closet for more clothes she could fix up for Rosie. As soon as they left the kitchen, I hightailed it over to the bushes by the Dunlops so I could watch what Beau did.

He was standing at their front door talking to Mr. Dunlop, whose face was peeking out from the crack.

"I bet you want to wring the neck of the person that done that. I know I sure do! Yes, sir, if I ever catch that guy, he's gonna wish he were dead by the time I finish with him. In fact, I'm gonna sit right here on the porch all night long and watch out for him and make sure he don't come back."

The door opened wider and Mr. Dunlop half stepped out. "You gonna do no such thing, you big —"

But just as he said *big*, Beau marched up the steps and loomed over him like an angry black bear and Mr. Dunlop stepped back with a snort. "Fine, you fool enough to sit here all night in the cold, go ahead!" He also flung some choice words at Beau, but Beau just smiled and said, "Thank you very much," touched the bill of his cap, and sat on the top step of the Dunlops' porch.

I felt a lot better knowing Beau was there, so I went on home. The sheriff called to say he'd read Mr. Dunlop the riot act and, what with Beau there, it was safe for Rosie to go back home. Rosie didn't want to leave her mama alone, anyway, so Mama walked her over, along with J, and brought them supper. Mama made it real clear that I was to stay at home.

When Mama and J got back to the kitchen, J asked her, "Why were you so nice to Mr. Dunlop? I thought you were going to yell at him like you did when I said Reverend Benson likes his wife to bake —"

I gave him the evil eye, and J must've been getting smarter because he actually shut up.

"It's best not to annoy wounded animals," Mama said. "They might lash out even more."

• • • • • •

The next morning, after Rosie got on the bus, Beau came back home. After school, I told him what a good job he'd done, especially standing his ground on the porch and scaring Mr. Dunlop.

"I don't like acting that way, Red. But the ugliness is always going to be there unless you face it."

"You were the one who felt sorry for old Mr. Dunlop," I reminded him.

Beau nodded slowly. "I still do, a little bit."

"Why on earth would you feel sorry for him?"

"It must be hard not having anybody love you."

Only Beau would be kind enough to think that. I was just glad nobody was leaving Rosie alone with Mr. Dunlop. Mama called the Dunlops' house "Grand Central Station," what with all the visitors that day, from Reverend Benson, his wife, and other church ladies to the sheriff.

"I'm taking Rosie out to dinner tonight," Mama told me as she wiped down the kitchen counter. She stopped to give me the eyeball. "You, young man, are forbidden to go over there because Mr. Dunlop does not like you."

"Mr. Dunlop doesn't like anyone! That's no reason for me not to go."

"He doesn't like you, in particular, because he knows that you'll stand up to him. That's rare in this town. You stay away from that man, that's the rule."

I didn't like the rule, but I kind of liked the reason for it. I walked over to the shop, trying to hide a smile, when I heard Mr. Dunlop yelling, "I don't need your help!" and J came running down the path from the Dunlops', practically crashing into me.

"What were you doing over there, J?"

"I'm keeping my eye on Mr. Dunlop like everybody else."

"How?"

"I asked him if he had any jobs I could do for him 'cause I ain't got my Cub Scout badge yet."

"But you're not even a Cub Scout."

He grinned. "I know. That's how come I ain't got a badge yet."

I couldn't help laughing. "That was a good one, J!" I had to admire how brave J was, going right up to Mr. Dunlop like that, but I also knew how annoying J could be and it wouldn't take much pestering for Mr. Dunlop to get real mad at him. "You shouldn't go over there anymore, though."

His face fell. "Why not?"

"Well, for one thing, do you really want to do any chores for him?"

"No!"

"Then you don't want to go back again."

His forehead was still scrunched up.

"You done good, Bamm-Bamm. Daddy would be real proud of you."

His grin was so wide he looked as goofy as that cartoon kid, Alfred E. Newman, on *MAD* magazine.

Later, when I saw Mr. Reynolds's Mustang race by — with Miss Miller in it — I figured they were going to the Dunlops' and I headed over to my hiding place so I could watch.

I heard Mr. Reynolds before I got there, his voice loud and angry.

"All I'm saying, sir, is that times are changing, and you

will no longer get away with abusing your own children — or women or blacks or any class of people, for that matter."

"Times ain't changing that much!" Mr. Dunlop barked back. "Not here!"

"Oh, really? You might be interested to know that as of 1967, in *Loving versus Virginia*, the Supreme Court held that mixed-race marriage is perfectly legal in the United States."

By that time I was in my hiding place and Mr. Dunlop was having a conniption. Mr. Reynolds was walking backward off the porch, being tugged along by Miss Miller, but all the while he kept talking.

"Yes, sir, blacks and whites can indeed get married right here in Virginia. I'm simply telling you what the law says. And, in spite of how you feel about the schools, the Supreme Court outlawed segregation in public schools in *Brown versus Board of Education* of Topeka, Kansas, and right here in Virginia" — by this time Miss Miller had dragged him to the car and started pushing him into it — "in the case of *James versus Almond*, the school board was ordered to open up the schools they closed" — Miss Miller shut his car door and Mr. Reynolds quit talking all of a sudden, surprised that he found himself behind the wheel of the Mustang, and looked over at Miss Miller getting in the passenger seat.

She patted his shoulder and smiled at him as he pulled out the keys and started the engine. As they drove away I couldn't help but think that they acted like a little old married couple already.

"I'm gonna lay you out!" Mr. Dunlop shouted after them.

I tried to keep from busting out laughing, thinking, *No, he laid you out . . . again!*

Mr. Dunlop went inside, and I was just finishing laughing and getting up to cross back over the creek when he came out on the porch. With his shotgun. I crouched down again real quick and watched him pace the front porch, muttering about teaching people a lesson. I got up my nerve to run when he turned to pace away from me. I didn't look behind me, but ran flat-out for our house, expecting any minute that he'd shoot me in the back just like his great-granddaddy shot George Freeman. I never ran so fast in my life.

I flew into the kitchen, grabbed the phone, and called the sheriff. I told him about Mr. Dunlop, and that Mama was out with Rosie. "She took her out to dinner. She could be bringing her back home any minute!" I stopped to let him speak and also because I was out of breath.

I knew it was bad because for the first time in my life I heard the sheriff swear. "What kind of gun?" he asked.

"Shotgun."

"Could be worse," he muttered. "Red?"

"Yes, sir?"

"You get your little brother and Beau and lock yourselves in that store right now, you hear? Ray ain't too fond of y'all."

"Yes, sir. I know."

The three of us were sitting on the floor in the back of the What-U-Want playing gin rummy when I heard Mama knocking on the front door.

"Boys! Are you in there?"

I ran to the front and unlocked the door for her. "What happened?"

"Yeah," said J, catching up with me, "was there a shootout?"

"No," Mama said, staring J down, "there was no shoot-out. Sheriff Scott took Mr. Dunlop in for questioning and plans to stay with him tonight. Meanwhile, Rosie is packing —"

"Packing?" I said, "Why?"

"In the morning the sheriff is driving her to Waynesboro, to her aunt and uncle's, for a while."

Beau tugged his hair. "Poor Rosie."

"She's lucky!" J said, wheeling on Beau. "She gets to miss school!" J turned back to Mama. "How long?"

"Just a week or two," Mama said, "until things settle down."

I caught Mama's eye and crossed my arms at her. Did she really think things would settle down and everything would be OK? She looked away quick like she didn't see me, but I know she did because her foot started tapping real fast.

Chapter Thirty-Seven
Kinship

Miss Georgia's son called to tell us he was bringing his mama home from the hospital. He also said she caught pneumonia at the hospital and not to be surprised that she looked kind of weak. Finally I could get the answer on when George Freeman died.

Mama organized a homecoming for Miss Georgia at her fixed-up house. We made a lot of food. All four of us. I made biscuits, from scratch. Beau made baked beans. J even made sandwiches. Mama surprised me when she told us that since Miss Miller had worked on fixing up Miss Georgia's place, she'd invited her *and* Mr. Reynolds. When I opened my mouth to remind her that Mr. Reynolds hadn't helped at all she cut me off.

"— and because he's her friend, he's welcome, too."

When we loaded everything into the car, Mama had another surprise. "Beau has his permit now, so he's going to drive." She was real calm about it, until we hit the road.

"Don't grab the wheel like that, Beau! Try to relax." Mama's voice was so tense she was making me all twisted inside. Poor Beau's hands were shaking enough for me to see them vibrating even though I was in the backseat.

Beau braked for about the hundredth time and we all lurched forward. Again.

"When are we going to be there?" J asked.

"Shut up," I hissed at him.

J shot me a devil look and gave a little kick to Beau's seat. I kicked him right back.

"Ow! Mama! Red's kicking me!"

Mama swung round in her seat like she was about to dive at us. "Boys! Stop it! We don't need any distractions up here! Beau is trying to drive, in case you hadn't noticed!"

"We noticed," J mouthed off.

Mama took a deep breath and puffed up about twice her normal size. It was ugly. That's when I realized our car was drifting way over to the left. Where the road dropped right off. Into the ravine.

"Beau! Look out!"

Mama spun around and yanked the steering wheel to the right, all in one move, faster than I'd ever seen her do anything.

We were all quiet after that. So quiet, I think we were all holding our breath. It took forever to make it the last quarter mile to Miss Georgia's.

I saw Miss Miller and Mr. Reynolds sitting on her front porch, waving, then not waving, then waving again as we crept closer.

When Beau slammed on the brakes, parking next to the Mustang and the Rambler, Mama said, "That was a fine job, Beau," like nothing unusual had happened.

Beau grinned. "Thank you, Miz Porter."

Me and J just looked at each other like the front seat was crazy, but even J knew better than to say anything.

We said hey to Miss Miller and Mr. Reynolds. At least we got there before Miss Georgia, although I don't know how, since it felt like it took an hour to go half a mile. Me and Beau quickly got the firewood out of the trunk and piled it up by her fireplace. Beau went ahead and got a fire set for her, even though the sun was still out. It was cold at night now, especially if you were old and skinny like Miss Georgia.

"She's here!" J yelled.

I ran to the door, wanting to see Miss Georgia come wheeling up the ramp we'd built.

Miss Georgia never stopped staring at the house the whole time her son was getting her wheelchair out of his Plymouth Fury station wagon, lifting her out of the car and into the wheelchair, and pushing her up the ramp. Her eyes were kind of watery, and she kept pressing her lips together. Inside that big old wheelchair she looked like a fragile baby bird in a nest. When Mr. Jones got her situated in front of the fireplace, we all kind of stood there, just watching her as she looked around the room.

"George," she said finally, "I believe you done brought me to the wrong house, you fool!"

We laughed and everyone started talking at once.

I tried to ask Miss Georgia about the grave markers, but J shoved past me with our plate of sandwiches and biscuits. "Lookit, Miss Georgia, we made this stuff for you!"

She raised one eyebrow. "You mean, your mama made them."

"Nuh-uh, I made the sandwiches, and Red made the biscuits. Mama's making me and Red and Beau do all kinds of work around the house so we don't turn into lazy old men."

Miss Georgia's son dropped his head and groaned. "Oh, don't start that, please, or Mama will be telling my wife — again —" And he started imitating Miss Georgia's voice, "I hope you're not spoiling that lazy old man who calls himself my son! You'd best be coming up with more chores for him before he turns into a fat old slug!"

"You got that right!" Miss Georgia snapped, but she was smiling.

So was her son. It was funny to think of Mr. Jones as her son, since he looked old enough to be someone's granddaddy, at least, maybe even great-granddaddy.

Miss Georgia thanked J and even took a sandwich from his plate. "I'll save this if you don't mind. I don't have much appetite right now, but I'll surely enjoy it later." She looked around her again and whispered, "James, look what these good people have done."

"Miss Georgia?" I said, "Can I ask you about —" but she didn't seem to hear me.

She was reaching past me, her arm kind of wobbly, grabbing Beau's hand. "I heard about your mama, Beau, and I'm real sorry. Sure am. She was a fine lady. A real fine lady."

"Thank you, Miz Georgia. I sure do miss her."

Miss Georgia nodded and patted Beau's hand.

"She was my only kin. Now I ain't got no one."

Miss Georgia stopped her head in midnod and sat up like she was about to blast right out of that wheelchair. Her voice was raspy but firm. "Don't you talk like that, Beau! You got plenty of folk around here. It ain't a question of kin. Sometimes your own kin ain't worth dog spit."

Mr. Jones rolled his eyes and groaned again.

"It's kinship what counts," Miss Georgia went on. "Don't matter where it come from. You understand that, Beau?"

Beau was at attention now, too. "Yes, ma'am, Miz Georgia! Kinship. I got it."

"That's right, you got it. Lots of it." And she sat back in the wheelchair and had a coughing attack. I ran to get her a glass of water.

When she finally stopped, Mama asked, "How are you feeling, Miss Georgia?"

She smiled. "Old. That's how I feel. Old. And tired."

Mama rushed to fix her a plate of food like that'd help her feel young again.

I couldn't wait any longer to ask the question that had been burning a hole in my brain for weeks. "Miss Georgia, we fixed your grave markers out back —"

"But I got the date wrong at first," Beau interrupted, tugging his hair. "I'm real sorry, Miss Georgia, ma'am, but I fixed it up, soon as Red told me what I done wrong."

"Yeah," I said, "because it was July first, right?"

"Not Jool seven," Beau added.

"He means July seventh," I said.

The whole time, Miss Georgia's head was turning back and forth between the two of us. "What are y'all talkin' about?"

"Your granddaddy," Beau said.

"He died July first, right?"

"Red said it wasn't Jool seven — I mean July seven, right?"

"Oh," Miss Georgia's forehead scrunched up, "I believe it was."

Beau tugged his hair again. "You believe it was July seven or you believe it was July first?"

"I . . . I —" She sighed. "Boys, right now I can't hardly remember my own name."

Mama came up behind me and said real quiet, "Red, we need to go now."

I wheeled around. "What? We just got here!"

"Miss Georgia's very tired. Miss Miller and I are going to get her ready for bed. You boys all wait outside."

"Can't I just ask one question about —" but Mama had her hands on my shoulders and was steering me out the front door, and Beau followed.

J was already outside. "We didn't even get to eat," he whined.

I listened to the crickets and the low voices of Mr. Jones and Mr. Reynolds talking as I paced in front of the house.

Beau turned our Chevy's headlights on, sat on the ground in front of the bumper, and made shadow animals against the house. When J still complained about being hungry, Beau cracked him up by making food shadows of anything J called out.

I didn't care about eating. Or shadow play. I had a mystery to solve. I couldn't stand having to wait another day.

When I looked over at Mr. Reynolds, his arms crossed,

talking to Mr. Jones a mile a minute, I realized it was time. Time to show him the map and ask him why it said *Fieri Facias*. And if George Freeman didn't die until July seventh, did the map mean what I thought it meant?

I walked over to him. "Mr. Reynolds, can I talk with you in private, please?"

Mr. Jones nodded like it was OK with him and, except for Mr. Reynolds looking a little surprised, I guess it was OK with him, too, because he followed me to George Freeman's grave.

The crickets seemed even louder now, like they were screeching a warning with everything I said.

I told Mr. Reynolds about the date on the grave marker and arguing with Beau and asking Miss Georgia about it. Finally I pulled the map out my pocket and started to hand it over to him, but pulled it back when his head jerked and he said, "Is that the paper Mr. Dunlop gave your daddy?"

"How do you know about that?"

"Your mama told me that your daddy was upset about a paper Mr. Dunlop gave him, but she never actually saw it." He tilted his head at me. "Where'd you find it?"

"In his desk."

"She said she looked in his desk and couldn't find it."

"Well, she wouldn't have looked in an envelope called Rambler."

"Rambler?"

"That's Miss Georgia's car. Daddy kept notes about the cars he worked on." I looked down at the paper in my hand. "But he had a different kind of note for this."

"May I see it?" Mr. Reynolds asked.

I handed it over, and he looked at the top of the map carefully. When his eyes got to the bottom of the page, a gasp escaped from his mouth. He looked up at the top again.

"What does it mean?" I asked. "How could George Freeman have been killed three days after that map says he's already dead? There's got to be some mistake, right?"

Mr. Reynolds didn't answer, but he rubbed his thumb back and forth by the initials at the bottom of the page.

"It's dirt," I told him. "It won't come off. It's been there for a hundred years." Why did he care about that, anyway? I needed to know what the words meant.

He shook his head and started scratching at a spot with his fingernail. "I don't think it's dirt." He looked straight at me. "I think it's blood."

I took a step back. "Blood?"

Mr. Reynolds nodded solemnly. "A blood oath."

I felt my stomach lurch. Because this is what had been niggling at my brain until I figured it out. And after I figured it out, I almost wished I hadn't: *How could Old Man Porter have known three days ahead of time that George Freeman was going to die . . . unless he was somehow involved in the murder?*

Mr. Reynolds answered the question even though I didn't want to hear it. "I suspect your great-great-granddaddy wanted to get rid of George Freeman before the loan was paid off. That way, he could take their land back." He stared at the map. "That explains the *Fieri Facias*. As far as the *No*

Consideration, well, that means no money. . . ." Mr. Reynolds face turned pink, and he looked somewhere between hollering and puking. "I think that means he was willing to give Daniel Dunlop that little piece of land for free . . . if he would . . . you know . . ."

"If he would what?"

"Murder George Freeman."

I heard my name a few times before Mr. Reynolds shook my shoulder. "Red? I may need to use this as evidence. I've got to get to the truth."

He took a small pad of paper and a pen out of his jacket pocket. "I'll make a quick copy for my purposes, but I may need the original later, OK?"

He handed me back the map, but I wasn't sure I even wanted to touch it.

"Take care of it, now," he said, pushing it into my hand. "It may prove to be important."

Mama called over that it was time to go. She got in on the driver's side, saying, "Miss Georgia says she'll talk with you tomorrow, Red, OK?"

Mr. Reynolds cleared his throat. "Are you going to ask her about the date of death?"

I nodded. I couldn't talk yet.

"We need to know that before we can be sure of what happened. Will you let me know what she says?"

I nodded again, or maybe it was a shiver.

In the car, my back pocket felt weird, like the map didn't belong there. It was uncomfortable. Just like I felt.

"How's Miss Georgia?" Beau asked.

Mama looked across the seat at him, then glanced at us in the backseat, swallowed hard, and said nothing. I saw her watery eyes, though, and how much she was blinking.

I finally found my voice. "Is she OK?"

Mama's voice was shaking, like it was between angry and crying. "She's ninety-three, you know. She's very, very old." She grabbed a Kleenex from the box on the dashboard and blew her nose.

Beau tugged his hair. "Miss Georgia sure did like how you painted her front porch, Red. She said she could see all the way to freedom." He turned around in his seat to look at me. "What did she mean by that?"

"Freedom Church," I said. Beau's eyes grew wide, but I shook my head.

Mr. Harrison's 300 was parked in front of our house with him inside. He had the dome light on, looking at some papers. When he saw us, he started grinning like a fool.

Mama took J into his room to put him to bed. I stood in the kitchen, with Beau tugging his hair and me fuming, while Mr. Harrison sat on the living-room sofa, still grinning.

He started talking before Mama even made it all the way in from the hallway. "I got you a big-time buyer, Betty."

"Oh?" She sat down on the sofa.

"New. York. City." He pronounced every word and paused after he said all three, like he was waiting for her to clap or something.

"Oh," Mama finally said.

I could see Mr. Harrison from the kitchen doorway, and

he didn't look too pleased that Mama sat there stony faced. I smirked at him even though he wasn't looking at me.

"This fella wants to build himself a fine home and bring his rich city friends here to visit in the winter. Think of the money they'll be spending in our community. You'd make your husband proud. It's just what he would've wanted you to do."

I froze long enough to hear Beau moan and say, "Careful, Red —" before I flew into the living room.

"We aren't moving!"

Mr. Harrison kind of chuckled and gave Mama a wink. "Well, it sure looks like a For Sale sign out front, son."

I crossed my arms and set my jaw. "I'm not your son, and we're not moving."

Mr. Harrison ignored me. "It's a good deal of money, too," he told Mama.

"We don't care about money!" I yelled. "We care about doing what's right!"

Mr. Harrison let his head roll back and his ugly mouth open wide and nasty laughter come shooting out. I ran past Beau in the kitchen and out of the house, fearing I might shove something down that ugly mouth of Mr. Harrison's if I didn't get out of there right away. I heard Beau calling after me but I was too full of hatred to stop.

Chapter Thirty-Eight
What the Bible Said

The next day I went to see Miss Georgia, like I'd promised. Outside it was as dark and gloomy as I felt. And misty — if I hadn't known how to get there so well, I could've gotten lost in the mist. The dampness made the dead leaves stink, and I felt like I was breathing rotten air.

When I got there, her son's Plymouth Fury wasn't in front. He must've already left. It was weird not seeing Miss Georgia on the porch, but smoke was coming out of the chimney, so I figured she must be inside.

The door was open a crack and I knocked.

"Come in, Red," she called.

"How'd you know it was me?"

She turned in her wheelchair and smiled. "I may be old, but I ain't all the way gone. Not yet."

I slumped down in front of the fire.

"You lookin' pretty glum."

I told her about Mr. Harrison and the buyer. "I don't want to leave," I said. "This is my home."

"I hear you, Red. I hear you."

It was exactly what Daddy used to say to me, and it sent a shiver through me. "Miss Georgia, I have to ask you about that grave marker."

She coughed as I was trying to answer, and she kept on coughing.

I got a glass out of her strainer and filled it halfway. Good thing, because her hand was so shaky that a full glass would've spilled all over her. She drank some, and it seemed to stop her coughing. She handed the glass back to me and nodded at the fire like I was supposed to sit back down, so I did.

"You and Beau wanted to know exactly when my granddaddy died."

"It had to be July first, not the seventh," I said.

"Why do you say that?"

I didn't say, *Because if it was July first, then my great-great-granddaddy planned your granddaddy's death.* All I said was, "That's what I heard."

"Well, I think you heard wrong."

I swallowed hard. "Why?"

"I thought about it, and I remember my daddy said the congregation had a party and a few days later they went to church, collected the rest of the money, and that Sunday night the church burned down." Her voice was weak and shaky but she took a few raspy breaths and went on. "I'm pretty sure the party was on July fourth because my daddy talked about a special Independence Day celebration. They had a big celebration because they'd gained their financial independence, too. They'd be payin' off their debt on the church. Then on Sunday, which was July seventh, they gave thanks, and on Monday they were goin' to pay the debt and go to the courthouse to record the deed."

My heart was pounding and my voice was so shaky, all I could do was repeat her last three words, "Record the deed?"

"That's right. They were ready to pay Old Man Porter everythin' they owed him. Then they'd own the church and the land, free and clear." Miss Georgia smiled and her face looked at peace. "Free and clear."

My face must've looked the exact opposite of peaceful. So Old Man Porter knew three days ahead of time . . . three awful days when he knew George Freeman was going to be murdered. And did nothing to stop it. In fact, he planned the whole thing. Three days when Old Man Porter might've passed him in town and George Freeman might've lifted his hat and thanked him for loaning his congregation the money so they could build the church. The money they were about to pay back. What did Old Man Porter do? Say "you're welcome"? Nod back at him? *Smile?* It made me sick to think of it. What kind of person does that to another person? A Porter.

"No," I said out loud. "No, it couldn't be."

Miss Georgia said something, but I wasn't even listening, until she put an old *Farmers' Almanac* on my lap. It was from 1867. She opened it up to July and pointed at the days. The day of the month was the fourth and the day of the week was Thursday. And the seventh was a Sunday.

I was hoping against hope that something was wrong.

There had to be an explanation. There just had to be. "What if people couldn't remember exactly what the date was or wrote it down wrong by mistake?" I blurted out. "Miss Miller said that birth and death dates didn't get recorded real well back then, so if folks didn't have a place to keep those records, the dates could be wrong."

"Well, she's right about that."

I breathed a sigh of relief.

"My folk had a place to record that information, though."

"But the church burned down."

"It wasn't in the church."

"Where was it?"

She pointed up at the shelf above the fireplace. "Bring down that Bible and we'll solve this once and for all."

I pulled the Bible out from underneath that black album with Emmett Till's picture.

"Open up the back cover," Miss Georgia said.

I stood in front of the fire. I should've been warm but I was shaking. Cradling the Bible in my left arm, I opened the back cover with my right, gripping onto it with hope. I looked at the names written carefully on the page in black ink. The first one read:

GEORGE FREEMAN, B. AUGUST 1829, D. JULY 7, 1867.

There it was. Written in the Bible. In black-and-white.

There was no getting around it.

It was us.

I felt the Bible slip out of my hands and hit the floor with a *bang*.

Chapter Thirty-Nine
The Desk

I don't even remember running, but the next thing I knew, I skidded to a stop in the gravel in front of the What-U-Want, gasping for air. Everything looked different. Nothing looked right, almost like it didn't belong.

I knew one thing that didn't belong. I ran to the shop and yanked open the door. For the first time, the shop smelled dirty and stale. I sprinted up to the office in the back, to Old Man Porter's desk. I stared down at the sign I wrote, not that long ago. ON PAIN OF DEATH THIS DESK HAS TO BE MOVED! It was going to be moved, all right. I ran down the steps, grabbed an ax off the tool rack, and ran back up the stairs again.

The first chop cut the sign in half and the ax stuck in the desk I hit it so hard. I wrestled it free and hit the desk again. And again. Over and over. *Pound, pound, pound.* Until chips were flying as wildly as the swear words coming out of my mouth. Over and over. *Bang.* Heave. *Bang.* Heave. *Bang.* And I went for the legs of the desk and chopped them off one by one until the deformed wooden structure was tilted at an angle and I kept going at it because I wanted to lay the whole thing flat on the ground, like a coffin. *Pound, pound, pound.*

"Red!" Mama screamed. She was standing at the bottom of the steps, looking up at me, her eyes wide and both hands covering her mouth.

All the noise stopped, except for my panting. And I realized I was sweating. And I saw that I had wood chips all over me, bits of the chopped-up desk.

I looked at Mama and she was slowly taking her hands down from her mouth. "What are you doing?" she whispered.

"I'm getting rid of the desk!" My voice came out loud and screamy, especially compared to her whisper.

She shook her head a tiny bit, like it was too stiff to move very far. "Why?"

When I told her, her hands went back to covering her mouth and her eyes got wide again. That's when I heard Beau moaning, and realized he was just a little ways behind her, tugging on his hair.

"That's bad. That's real bad. Mr. Porter, he said something bad had happened, but I didn't know it was this bad."

Mama let out a whimper, too.

"Did you know about that, Miz Porter?"

Mama shook her head. "All I knew was that we were somehow involved. I didn't know . . . I thought maybe we didn't try hard enough to stop Mr. Dunlop . . . I never thought . . . Porters?" She looked at me like she couldn't quite believe it. Water was collecting in her eyes, and her voice was a whisper again. "He just said he wanted to fix it. But how —"

"See, Mama?" My voice was shaking. "See why we can't move?"

She put her hand against the wall below the office as if to balance herself.

Beau looked up at me. "What do you mean, Red?"

"Freedom Church was never on Dunlop land. Old Man Porter stole it from George Freeman and his congregation. We don't even *own* all this land. We can't sell until we find Freedom Church and give it back to Miss Georgia. Right, Mama?"

Her mouth was hanging open, but I saw her head do a definite nod. I felt like I'd finally gotten through to her before she turned around and walked like a robot out of the shop.

Beau watched her leave and then turned to me. "Red, are you OK?"

I shook my head, staring at the ax that was still in my hand.

"Did you apologize to Miss Georgia already?"

My head jerked over to Beau. "I — she doesn't know yet."

He tugged his hair. "Well, you're going to tell her, right?"

"Yeah. Of course."

He nodded. "I'm going to go apologize to her, too."

"Why? You aren't even a Porter."

His shoulders sagged and I realized what I'd said.

"Beau, you should be happy right now that you're not a Porter. It's not your folk that — that did it."

He looked up at me, his eyes shining in the shop lights. "It seems like everybody ought to say sorry for something as bad as that."

My eyes flew around the shop. "This is a shameful place." I raised the ax and gave the desk another blow. And another. And another one, until I was getting all worked up again.

"Why do you keep doing that?" Beau called up to me.

"Because I want to get rid of my great-great-granddaddy!"

"But that's just a desk. That won't get rid of him. He's still your people."

"I don't want him to be my people!" I threw the ax to the ground and it tumbled down the stairs. "My people aren't like that!"

Beau stood there, both hands tugging at his hair. He looked down at the ax lying at his feet, then up at me.

All the power went out of my voice. "My people aren't supposed to be like that." Not Porters. Not Frederick Stewart Porter. Not me. Except I realized something that made me shiver even though I was sweating. Old Man Porter had asked a Dunlop to do his dirty work for him, killing George Freeman, just like I'd asked Darrell Dunlop for help from his gang, and that ended up hurting Thomas. Maybe we weren't all that different.

I couldn't stand my name now — his name. Even my nickname was the same. Red. Because of my hair. I even looked like him! I couldn't even stand my hair — his hair.

"Beau!"

He jerked at my loud voice. "What is it, Red?"

"I need to borrow your electric shaver!"

"Why?"

"Because Mama got rid of Daddy's."

Beau squinted up at me. "I don't see no hair growing on your face."

"I know. I'm shaving my head."

"You — you want to be like that *Kung Fu* guy, too? I thought that was just J."

I kicked the desk. "I don't want to have the same hair as Old Man Porter, so I'm going to shave it all off."

"But, Red," Beau said, tugging his hair, "it's just gonna grow back again."

"Then I'll shave it again."

"But it'll grow back."

"I'll keep shaving it!"

Beau sighed. "All's you can do is hide it for a while before it pops back out."

"Fine! Then I'll hide it!" I tugged on my hair, just like Beau, wanting to pull it all out.

"I don't think it's how you look what makes you different. I think it's how you act."

We stood in silence for a while until Beau spoke again. "The way I see it is you got a chance now to make the name Frederick Stewart Porter stand for something different."

"How? It's a pretty bad legacy."

"I know it is. But you can do it."

"How," I said again, not as a question. I didn't really expect an answer.

"Because you ain't just that nasty old Frederick Stewart Porter's great-great-grandson. You's also your daddy's son."

Chapter Forty
Confession

I hardly slept that night and by the time the sky was turning
from dark to red, I'd about convinced myself that I shouldn't
go see Miss Georgia just yet. It'd be better for her if I could
tell her I'd found the church when I told her the other news.
But when I walked into the kitchen, Beau was already standing there, holding a plate of pancakes.

He looked at me with his puppy-dog eyes. "I made you
your favorite breakfast, Red, because I know it'll be tough
going up to Miss Georgia's this morning."

I felt a gnawing in my stomach but it wasn't hunger.

"I don't know, Beau. I was thinking I might go
look for —"

"I know it must be real hard," he went on, like he hadn't
heard me, "but it sure is brave of you to go see her."

I looked down at my sneakers.

"You want I should come with you?"

"No." I still hadn't quite decided if that was where I
was going.

"I know it'll mean the world to her to have you tell her the truth."

I swallowed hard.

"And also" — he put the plate down on the kitchen table with a clank — "it'll mean the world to your daddy."

I felt the sigh come out of me more than heard it. I was worn out like I'd just been in a fight. And lost.

I let the kitchen door slap behind me as I headed up to Miss Georgia's.

Orange sunlight was trying to peek through the morning mist as I stood in the wet grass for a while, staring at Miss Georgia's front porch. Looking up, I could see the blue painted ceiling, Miss Georgia's sky. Finally I crossed the path and walked up the steps, one at a time.

I knocked on her door. Softly. Kind of hoping she wouldn't hear. Then at least I could tell Beau I went. I tried. But she just didn't answer.

"Come on in, Red."

My eyes dropped down to my shoes, and I pushed the door open.

"I knew you'd come back, Red. You're not one to run away from things."

If I could've melted through the floor right then, I would have. I closed the door behind me with a click.

She turned in her wheelchair and looked at me. Really looked at me.

I stared at the fire. It was the only light in the room. It was quiet for a while before I got up the nerve to speak.

"Miss Georgia? I got something to tell you. And it's not good."

"You know you can always talk to me, Red."

I wasn't sure she'd feel that way after she heard what I was going to say. "My daddy told you that Porters were somehow involved in what happened to your granddaddy, right?"

"He did."

I swallowed. "Well, it was more than just involved."

"Huh." She looked at her hands in her lap, and her voice was pained. "He was part of the posse," she whispered.

I shook my head. "It's worse than that." I swallowed again. "See, he was thinking the church wouldn't have the money to pay off their debt, so he'd be able to take over the church — and all the land."

Miss Georgia turned to me. "But they could pay. They were gettin' ready to —"

"I know. That was the problem."

Miss Georgia's face looked as gray as her hair.

I took a deep breath. "He had to stop them from paying off their debt so he could take their land." I paused, because I really didn't want to go on.

"What are you sayin', Red?"

"My great-great-granddaddy made a blood oath with old Mr. Dunlop to kill your granddaddy before he had a chance to pay his debt, so he could take his land back."

For a fleeting moment I thought she was going to laugh. "Red, how in the world did you come up with that?" Her eyes narrowed. "Is this some story Ray Dunlop been tellin' you?"

"No, ma'am." I slowly pulled the folded-up map out of the back pocket of my jeans and held it out to her. "It's something Old Man Porter wrote himself."

She stared into my eyes but reached her hand out, touching the paper but not actually taking it. I wished she would because it felt almost painful to hold that thing. For a while, it was like we were frozen, our hands on either side of the map, neither of us wanting it.

Finally she took it, her hands shaking as she unfolded it. I watched her lips as she mouthed the words *Decedent, G. Freeman* and cringed when she took a sharp breath in. She eyed the rest of the document, squinting when she got to the bottom of it. She pointed at the initials. "What does that say, Red? It's too small for me to read."

I almost groaned out loud. It was the last thing I wanted to read. My own initials. "F.S.P., my great-great-granddaddy's initials, and a Dunlop's initials. And the date. Fourth of July 1867."

She turned her head to look at me. "That why you were askin' about the date my granddaddy died? That why you wouldn't believe me?"

I nodded.

She looked back at the map and pressed her lips together until water came out of her eyes. Finally, she said, "It's true, then."

I hung my head and whispered, "Yes, ma'am." I backed away to the wall opposite the fire and slumped against it. I looked down and saw, rather than felt, my hand clutching my stomach, just like Daddy had done when we heard Mr. Dunlop's gun go off.

"I'm really sorry, Miss Georgia. I'm so, so sorry." Sorry seemed like such a weak word. I wanted a word that was a whole lot more powerful than the kind of word you use when you bump into someone by accident. "I wish it'd been different. I wish it'd never happened."

Miss Georgia's face was frozen, along with her whole body. I couldn't help staring at her. I wanted her to start yelling at me, calling me and my family names, or throwing stuff, because that's what we deserved. I kept waiting, but the only thing that happened was some water coming out of her eyes.

"You must hate me, Miss Georgia."

Her voice was real quiet so I had to strain to listen. "Why would I hate you, Red?"

I thought of Beau's words as I destroyed Old Man Porter's desk: *He's still your people.*

"Because of what . . . my people did to . . . your people." It was too hard to say it again, to say, *My great-great-granddaddy paid someone to murder your granddaddy.*

She was silent for a while before saying, "Well, ownin' up to it, that counts for a lot." She stared into the fire as she fingered the map. "Old Man Porter was a piece of work. We knew he was a two-faced, lying —" She stopped herself. I don't know why. She didn't need to stop on my account. "He didn't want us around. Your great-granddaddy was only some better, but your granddaddy, he was a decent man, yes he was. And your daddy, well, we all know what a good man he was."

I looked away. I wasn't sure if she was being sarcastic, because my daddy had hidden the truth from her, a pretty important truth.

"I-I'm sorry Daddy didn't tell you the whole truth." I looked at her, almost like I was asking her a question. "I don't know why he didn't."

She nodded. "Maybe he was hopin' it wasn't true. Maybe he was still gettin' used to the idea. Maybe he was comin' around to it."

I shrugged. That answer didn't make me feel any better.

"I suspect your daddy was hopin' to find the church, and he was goin' to tell me the whole story once he could give me some good news along with the bad."

I froze, because that was exactly what I was planning on doing until I ran into Beau. Maybe that's what was going on. Maybe Daddy wasn't going to keep it a secret forever. Maybe he was going to fix it right in the end. I hoped so. But I guess I'd never know for sure.

"I think he would've tried to fix it up right," Miss Georgia went on, "because that was his way. But he didn't have the chance to finish." She looked at me.

I nodded and stood up straight. "I've been trying to find the church, too, but I guess I was looking in the wrong place. I've been all over the Dunlop property, but the piece of land the Dunlops got from Old Man Porter for killing your — as payment — probably isn't where the church was. Freedom Church must be on our land."

She coughed several more times, her whole body shaking. I started to get her some water but she grabbed my arm. After she quieted down and took a deep wheezy breath, she leaned forward, and pushed against the wheelchair.

"Be careful, Miss Georgia."

Her arms were shaking as she pushed hard to get herself up.

"I don't think you're supposed to be doing that," I said, getting ready to catch her if she fell.

She waved me away with one hand, but that made her fall back down into her wheelchair, kind of flopped over to one side.

"You OK, Miss Georgia?"

She took several breaths before she spoke. "You'll have to get It, Red. She pointed to the floor, in her bedroom. "Under there. A box."

I got up and walked over to the doorway. I looked inside and saw her bed. It was one of those high ones that you could fit a lot of stuff under. I went in and knelt down by the bed. At first I couldn't see anything, but I reached under and felt around until I bumped something. A box. I reached my other hand in and pulled it out.

It was half the size of a shoe box and a whole lot more beautiful. Made out of orangey wood, it had different patterns running through it from the knots and rings that were in the tree. It looked like somebody oiled it every day to be so shiny that it glowed like a pool of golden light.

I brought it over to Miss Georgia and handed it to her, but she said, "Open it."

When I lifted the lid, a whiff of cedar rose out of the box. It smelled sweet, like it had been saving itself up to make the whole room smell nice. The inside wood of the box was beautiful, too. There was only one thing inside. It was about the size of a baseball, a ball of some kind of white cloth.

I looked up at Miss Georgia and she nodded.

Slowly, I picked up the ball and a piece of the cloth fell away and I saw it was a long strip, so I started unwrapping it. Somehow I knew that what was inside was sacred.

When I got to the end of the cloth, there was a rock, gray with splotches of black and white. The firelight made the white sparkle and the black stand out sharp and strong.

"It's a piece of the Freedom Church altar," Miss Georgia whispered.

I stared at it. "I figured it was just granite. That's what I was looking for."

"This here's the rock you lookin' for, Red. It's granite, all right. Speckled granite."

"I never knew it was so beautiful." I picked it up out of the box. "How did you get this?"

"My daddy chipped that piece off himself." The flames in the fireplace surged and I swear it felt like the rock was burning my hand. I dropped the stone on the floor but Miss Georgia didn't seem to notice. She kept on talking. "I showed it to your daddy. Now I'm givin' it to you."

I picked up the rock again. "I'm going to find Freedom Church, Miss Georgia, I swear."

"It would sure mean a lot to me if you did, Red."

After we sat in silence for a while, she said she wanted to look at her porch again, so I pushed her wheelchair out there. She looked up at the ceiling. "I like what you done out here. So far."

"So far?"

"I don't see that peace symbol you were talking about

painting for me." She tried raising an eyebrow but it only went up halfway. Still, I smiled back at her.

Sitting on the steps, I tried not to peel the paint like I used to. It was warm for November. The sun had burned through the mist and the sky was blue and cloudless.

"Feels like I can see all the way to Freedom," she said, and looked out toward our property, struggling to sit up in her wheelchair. She was squinting and leaning her head out so far it looked like she was trying to find someone in particular. Finally she sat back with a sigh.

"I'll find it, Miss Georgia. Don't worry. I'll keep looking."

"You're a good friend, Red."

I didn't know about that. I didn't feel like I'd been a good friend to Thomas. And I sure didn't feel like us Porters had been good friends to Miss Georgia's family.

She sighed again, looking over toward our place. "I sure do like to think that the good souls are the ones who'll win in the end."

I looked out at our land, too — even though some of it wasn't our land. And even though I wasn't convinced of it, I said, "They will, Miss Georgia."

She made a sound like the sheriff's Kiss of Death. "Who is *they*, Red?"

I turned to look at her. She was bent forward, her eyes peering into mine. "Who you callin' *they*, huh? *They*," she said, "is you."

Chapter Forty-One
The Stone

As soon as I left Miss Georgia's I started combing our property line looking for where Freedom Church might've been. I searched for hours until I heard Mama calling. Something in her voice made me run to her as fast as I could.

Mama stood by the shop, her eyes so full of water she looked like she was drowning. She kept lacing her fingers together, then pulling them apart.

Beau had reached her, too, lumbering over from the What-U-Want. "What is it, Miz Porter?"

"It's . . . Miss Georgia."

I felt my heart pounding. "What happened? Is she all right?"

Mama shook her head. "She's . . . dead."

There was a silence and then a gasping sigh that might've been me or Mama or Beau, but it sounded like it came out of the shop itself.

• • • • • •

Miss Georgia's son asked me to be a pallbearer at the funeral, along with family members, including his grandson — who

I'd met before but I'd never really gotten to know because he was four years older than me — and Thomas. Even though I saw him at the service, me and Thomas didn't talk to each other. Mostly what I remember of the funeral was my black shoes, either plodding along as I was holding the casket, or stiff on the floor between the pews. I remember hearing singing and crying, and feeling bodies around me, but not seeing anything at all except my black shoes.

After the service and burial, we went back to Miss Georgia's house and my eyes started seeing everything again. I looked for Thomas but could only see his grandparents. I saw Mrs. Reed, Miss Georgia's granddaughter, and Anthony, her great-grandson. I saw exactly where Miss Georgia had been sitting just a few days before, and what she looked like, and what she said and did. And I knew what I had to do.

I found Mr. Jones out on the porch. I sat on the railing, waiting for him to finish talking to Mr. Reynolds, and rubbed my hand against the smooth paint feel of the porch posts. I could still catch a little whiff of that new-paint smell. I thought about all the times I'd sat there talking to Miss Georgia, or even just sitting there saying nothing, sometimes in the light, sometimes in the dark, sometimes when it was cold and sometimes when it was so hot you could barely breathe.

"Hey, Red."

I looked up and it was Mr. Jones, his face looking more wrinkly and his hair grayer than I'd remembered.

"Hey," I said, sliding off the railing. I pulled the piece of the altar stone out of my pocket and fingered it for a moment. "Your mama gave this to me. It belonged to her daddy." I sighed before handing it over. "I think it should stay in your family."

"Oh, I remember that." He reached out and touched the stone, then raised it and looked at it against the setting sun. He sat down on the porch step. "It's part of that church."

I sat down next to him. "Freedom Church. I'm going to find that church, you'll see." I stared at the stone in his hand. "I'm sorry about what my great-great-granddaddy did. And I think we should give you some of our land because —"

"It's not so much a question of the land, but it was important to my mama to find out what happened and set things right." He yanked at his tie, loosening it some with one hand while the other hand still held the rock. "That's why I hired young Mr. Reynolds for her."

"What? You mean . . . *you're* his client?"

"Me and my mama, that's right."

"So that's why she liked him all along!"

"Yeah, she told me I had to find a good lawyer from Richmond, and the Reynolds family is good people."

"What did he find out?"

"He's still working on it. But I think that any claims my family had have been pretty well buried."

"But Freedom Church is most likely on my property."

He shrugged like it wasn't news to him. "Even if you found it, I don't know that my family can make a claim. Bill — Mr. Reynolds — is having a hard time finding any paperwork."

I swallowed. "Did he tell you about the map?"

"He did, but he said it's circumstantial evidence and there's no one around to attest to it."

"What does that mean?"

Mr. Jones smiled. "There's no one who can prove what that document actually meant."

"I think it's pretty clear."

"Maybe, but in a court of law? That's different."

"Shoot, what's the point of being a lawyer if you can't prove anything?"

Mr. Jones chuckled. He tossed the stone up a few times, snatching it out of the air on its way down.

"We'd give your land back to you, anyway."

"Well, that's real kind of you, Red, but your mama's got to take care of herself and her boys, too. She doesn't have your daddy around anymore."

"But it wouldn't be right if we kept what wasn't ours to begin with."

He shook his head. "It's not like I'm moving back here, anyway."

"But what about your daughter? And your grandson? Your mama thought she might like it here."

"Oh, yes. Carolyn wants to go back to her roots. I swear, she would trace her roots all the way back to Africa, if she could."

I felt kind of sick thinking about my own roots, and I put my face in my hands.

"Well, you got to remember, she's the great-granddaughter of a slave, a freed slave, but still. I know that sounds like a long, long time ago to you, being so young and all."

"No, sir," I said, my voice muffled in my lap. It didn't sound long ago at all. In fact, seeing as how I was the great-great-grandson of a racist murderer, it wasn't nearly long enough.

"Son?"

I looked up and Mr. Jones had one eyebrow raised, just like Miss Georgia. "I'm glad you were here for her. You were like one of her own. I think my mama wanted you to keep this." He gave the stone back, closing my hand around it. He stood up and pointed his thumb into the darkness beyond Miss Georgia's porch. "Looks like someone wants to talk to you."

It was Thomas. I could barely make him out in the light coming from the front window. He stood a little away from the cars, his suit jacket thrown over his shoulder and his MIA bracelet reflecting the light. He was making marks in the dirt with his shoe. He eyed me but then looked away, like he couldn't quite decide if he wanted to talk to me or not.

I took a deep breath, stood up, and walked over to him.

He didn't look at me but tilted his head toward Miss Georgia's house. "It looks good."

I nodded. "She liked it. I left our IMF carving."

He gave a hint of smile as we went back to toeing the dirt. "I saw."

Neither of us said anything for a while, but I figured one of us had to bring it up and maybe it was supposed to be me. "Did you get my letter?"

"Yeah, I got it."

"I meant it. I'm real sorry."

"I know," he said quickly, giving the dirt a little kick.

"Are we . . . can we . . . still be friends?"

He put his foot down, staring at it. "I don't know. Father Corbett said it's okay for me to be angry."

I went cold then, even though my armpits were prickly with sweat like it was hot as August. I guess I couldn't blame Thomas for feeling that way, but I sure didn't like hearing it. I looked at the ground. "Who's Father Corbett?"

"My math teacher." Thomas let his breath out with the same force as the air coming out of a tire. "But I'm also supposed to forgive."

I looked up, figuring that was a good sign. I still hoped we could be friends again. Someday. "I wish it had never happened," I said.

"Yeah," he said, "me, too." He finally raised his head and stared into the distance like he was seeing far, far away. "But maybe it had to."

I didn't think I'd heard him right. "What?"

He shrugged. "Maybe we both had to grow up."

"I don't want to grow up like that!"

Thomas looked at me for the first time, the line between his eyebrows all creased. "How much choice have we got?"

His eyes were questioning, not like a teacher who already knows the answer and just wants to see if you're listening, but like Thomas. The kid who asked me if Mr. Dunlop always yelled at Rosie that way, the kid who wondered why Miss Georgia got mad when we made that Black Power salute, the kid who asked Daddy how come he respected Miss Georgia so much when other white people didn't.

"Thomas!" It was his granddaddy's voice. "It's time to move along now."

Mr. and Mrs. Jefferson were getting in their Chevelle. Thomas turned, walked slowly over to the car, and got in behind his granddaddy. I wasn't sure, but it looked like he waved at me in the rear window, so I waved back, just in case. I was still watching them drive off when I realized I'd never given Thomas an answer to his question.

Chapter Forty-Two
What Are You Up To?

When I went back to school, Miss Miller was talking about our Foxfire project. "Finish these up tonight, class, and bring them in tomorrow."

Bobby Benson groaned. "Tomorrow?"

"Yes, Bobby," she said, giving him a tight smile, "because the next day is Thanksgiving, and unless you're planning on coming to school on Thanksgiving, you'll need to bring your paper in tomorrow."

Her smile turned soft when she bent over my desk. "I know it's hard, Red, but Miss Georgia was a wonderful woman, and you're doing something very important. By writing about her family's history, Miss Georgia's legacy will live on."

I didn't particularly want to write about that legacy. It was too awful and embarrassing. By the time I got on the bus, I realized I had to tell Miss Miller that I couldn't write anything for that Foxfire project. When the bus reached the first stop, I went by J's seat and told him I had to go back to school and to ask Beau to pick me up.

"Ohhhh." J grinned. "Did you do something bad?"

"No more than you did," I snapped back.

I walked back to school, thinking of what I'd say to Miss Miller. I could tell her I really didn't get enough information and, now that Miss Georgia was gone, there was no way to get it. That was only partly lying. Miss Georgia was gone. And who was to say how much information was "enough." But what if she told me to write up as much as I had? I'd have to tell her my heart wasn't in it. That wasn't a lie at all.

When I got to school, Sheriff Scott's patrol car was out front. I hurried up the steps and heard shouting in the front office.

A man's voice I didn't recognize said, *"Animal Farm?* For sixth graders? They can no more understand that than — than a bunch of farm animals."

"That's right," a woman said, and it sure sounded like Mrs. Scott. "And it puts all kinds of ideas in their heads that they're too little to be thinking about. They're just babies!"

"I wouldn't say babies —" the sheriff started, but he was interrupted by a bunch of other voices yelling and about the only one I could make out was Mrs. Pugh saying, "I've counseled her so many times!" and then the sheriff telling everyone to calm down.

I walked quickly past the office and around the corner. Mr. Walter was coming toward me carrying two boxes, one stacked on top of the other. I saw the Marvin Gaye album sticking up out of the top box and froze.

"Mr. Walter?" I said, my voice rising.

He looked at me and his eyes were so sad. He shook his head. "I'm sorry, son."

I saw the light from our classroom at the end of the hall. I finally moved, my sneakers squeaking down the long hallway, sounding like they were echoing Mr. Walter's words. *I'm sor-ry son, I'm sor-ry son.* I walked faster, the echo getting louder and more insistent, like a train getting up speed, *I'm sor-ry son, I'm sor-ry son.* I ran, trying to get away from the sound, but it only screamed louder in my ears, *I'M SOR-RY SON, I'M SOR-RY SON, I'M SOR-RY SON!*

I was running so fast I overshot the classroom and had to grab the doorjamb and swing myself inside. What I saw stopped me cold.

Miss Miller was surrounded by boxes. Her desk was practically empty. She was taking a poster off the wall when she wheeled around to face me.

"Red?"

I looked around the room, then at the poster in her hand, *The time is always right to do what's right. — Martin Luther King Jr.* I looked at Miss Miller. Her eyes and nose were pink, but she tried to smile.

"What's going on?"

"I'm " — she swallowed — "I'm leaving, Red."

"Leaving?"

She wasn't even trying to smile anymore. She was just trying to stop from crying.

"Why?"

She blinked hard, pressed her quivering lips together, and turned away.

"We —" I said, even though I was thinking *I,* "want you to stay. We" — and again, I meant *I* — "need you to stay."

She shook her head, rolling up the poster, putting a rubber band around it, and dropping it in a box on the floor. "I've been fired."

"What! Why?"

She picked up the copy of *Animal Farm* from her desk and stared at the cover. "It seems I'm too much of a troublemaker for this community." She tossed the book into one of the boxes.

"They're firing you because of *Animal Farm*? Because of a *book*?"

"It's not the book so much as . . . well, they don't like my telling you what to think."

"You don't tell us what to think! You tell us *to* think!"

In spite of everything, Miss Miller smiled. "Thank you for understanding the difference, Red."

"Who's doing this?" I demanded.

She looked away.

I narrowed my eyes and hissed through clenched teeth. "Emma Jean Scott! Emma Jean, her mama, Sheriff —"

Miss Miller turned to face me. "It was not Emma Jean, and definitely not the sheriff."

"Mrs. Scott, then."

She shook her head. "It wasn't them." And the way she said it made me believe her.

If Emma Jean hadn't told her parents, then who'd go shooting their big fat mouth —

"Bobby!" I said.

Miss Miller flinched.

"Bobby Benson's the one who got you fired, isn't he?"

Her hesitation gave her away. "It wasn't Bobby." But the way she said Bobby's name told me all I needed to know.

It wasn't Bobby. It was Bobby's daddy. The preacher. Of course. He had power. And Miss Miller said things he didn't like. She wanted people to think and question. Like Daddy, who wanted Open Doors Baptist Church to live up to its name and be open to everyone, including blacks. Like Mama, who told him, *Red prefers to think for himself.* Like Miss Miller.

Miss Miller turned back to the wall. "I've got to finish packing now, Red."

"But — what about our Foxfire book?"

"I'll have to leave that up to you."

I heard a posse of footsteps coming down the hall. Miss Miller held onto her peace necklace. "You'd better go."

I didn't say anything, just backed out of the room, practically into Reverend Benson himself. And Sheriff Scott. And Mrs. Pugh. And a bunch of other adults, who stared at me, then at Miss Miller. I wanted to yell at them, all of them, but I figured the way they were looking at Miss Miller it'd only make things worse for her.

"Red? What are you up to?" Reverend Benson asked. He smirked and looked down on me, waiting to see me squirm.

Usually I'd say what most kids would say — "Nothing" — and slink away. But something told me that was exactly what Reverend Benson wanted to hear. So I drew myself up and looked him in the eye. *What was I up to?* "A lot," I said. "A whole lot." And I gave a big smirk right back to him.

I turned and saw Mr. Walter coming back down the hall, and I remembered how he'd held his head up high and walked out of our classroom even with people's unfriendly eyes on him, and I did the same thing. I made sure to walk tall and hold my head up high the whole way down the hall. And when I walked past him, he gave me a nod, and I gave one back to him and I felt like there was someone who understood.

Chapter Forty-Three
My Paper

"That is an outrage!" Mama said, when I told her about Miss Miller.

She was pacing the kitchen so much, me and Beau had to lean back against the counter to keep out of her way. All of a sudden she grabbed her purse from the table, marched to the kitchen door, and slammed it behind her. We listened to the Chevy peel off.

"What's she going to do?" Beau asked.

"I don't know."

"What are you going to do?" he asked.

I took a deep breath. "I got a paper to write." I wanted to give it to Miss Miller before she left town. I felt like I owed it to her.

I really did start writing it the truthful way because Miss Miller tried to do the right thing even though it got her fired. But it was hard to do the right thing. Real hard. The Rock'Em Sock'Em Robots stared at me from my dresser. There was so much bad stuff going on around me — Miss

Georgia dying, Rosie getting beaten up, Miss Miller getting fired, Mama still planning on moving us to Ohio, what happened with Thomas — that I just couldn't face writing down something as horrible and depressing as what had really happened.

I mean, who would know if I changed it a little bit? Miss Miller wouldn't know. Miss Georgia was gone. Her son didn't want anything to do with this place. Mama wouldn't even know about it. Beau wouldn't read it because he couldn't read very well. Mr. Dunlop wouldn't read it. Rosie wouldn't find out. Nobody in the world would ever know.

Except me.

And Daddy, because as soon as I started to write, his voice came into my head, saying, *I hear ya, son*, only I wished he wouldn't. I pushed his voice out and thought about the meanness of Mr. Dunlop and how just saying he killed George Freeman was the truth, even if it wasn't the whole truth. But Daddy's voice kept coming back, over and over, interrupting what I was trying to write.

"Red?"

I nearly jumped out of my chair because the voice wasn't from inside my head. It came through my window.

I looked out and saw the green cap and then Beau's face through the pine branches.

"Shoot, Beau! What are you doing out there?"

"Waiting for your mama to come home. Plus, I got you something to help you write." He pushed it through the window.

It was a bottle of Coke, already opened for me.

I was about to take a sip, when Beau said, "Don't worry, I didn't steal it like J. I already paid for it."

Now I had a new voice talking in my head. And it was mine. Scolding J for stealing those Cokes. *What would Daddy have said, huh?*

I stopped the bottle before it hit my mouth. Beau kept talking, but I didn't even hear him because of all the voices already talking in my head.

Mine. *You make a crime even worse when you try to cover it up, J.*

Miss Georgia's. *You're not one to run away from things.*

Thomas's. *How much choice have we got?*

Even Miss Miller's words from the blackboard. *The truth will set you free.*

And Daddy's. *I hear ya, son.*

"OK, OK," I yelled, "I get it!"

All the voices stopped. It was silent. Beau was outside my window, covering his mouth with one hand and tugging his hair with the other.

"Sorry, Beau," I said. "I was yelling at myself."

Slowly, he took his hand away from his mouth. "You know what to write now?"

I nodded. "Yeah. I know."

It was almost midnight when I was finishing up my paper.

I'm not proud of all our history, but I'm not covering it up, either. I'm owning up to what we did. And I'm paying for it, like I should. That's how we'll get our good name back. Now I can be proud of my land again, even if it is a little different than I thought it was. And whatever I do from now on, I'm making my own history. I hope I don't mess it up. But if I do, I'm not going to lie about it. You just have to make up for what you did. That's the only way people can trust us. And it's the only way people can respect me.

That's when I finally thought of the title for my paper. It made me think of Daddy. It made me think of Miss Georgia. It made me think of where I came from, and who I was. And it made me smile.

I turned back to the first page and wrote in big capital letters across the top:

R-E-S-P-E-C-T

This time I was happy to hear Daddy's voice in my head, saying, *I hear ya, son.*

Chapter Forty-Four
Daddy's Grave

The next morning Mama said she couldn't do anything to help Miss Miller even though she tried, and all she could do was spend the day helping her pack. I gave Mama my paper to give to her. She wasn't my teacher anymore, but I still wanted her to have it.

"We're having Miss Miller — and Mr. Reynolds — over for supper tonight so we can say good-bye to her," Mama said. "I'm glad you're up early, Red, because I'd like you to make the biscuits now."

"Why? You said biscuits are best eaten right away."

"The way things are going, who knows what today will bring? This way at least they'll be ready."

I was surprised I even got the biscuits to rise because I was in such a hateful mood. I hated that Miss Miller was fired. I hated that there were so many stupid people around and that they had such power. I hated it all the more because it made Mama so annoyed that she wanted to leave this place even faster. Now there was nothing for her here. Daddy was gone. Miss Georgia was gone. Miss Miller was going to leave.

I didn't know if Beau would be enough to keep her here. Or Rosie, since who knew how long she'd be with her relatives in Waynesboro?

We had a substitute teacher at school. She droned on and on and not one of us said a word. The classroom was quiet as a graveyard. I bet Mrs. Pugh loved it.

When I got off the bus that afternoon, our front porch was piled high with boxes.

"No," I heard myself say, like it was someone else talking, someone real sad.

I went inside slowly, and Mama was in the dining room wrapping china plates in newspaper.

"What's going on?"

She stopped. "Mr. Harrison said the buyer is in town already. He . . . he wants us out as soon as possible."

"How soon?"

Mama blinked a few times and swallowed hard. Her voice came out as a whisper. "Tomorrow."

"But — you shouldn't even be selling, Mama! Some of this land isn't even ours! We stole it!"

"I tried, Red, but Mr. Harrison said —"

"Mr. Harrison is a lowdown piece of —"

"Red," Mama warned.

"Well, he is!"

"I don't see any way around it," she said.

I stormed outside and next thing I knew, Mama and J were standing by the car, J holding a brown paper lunch bag, his head hung down, and his lips wobbly. Mama's lips were wobbly, too, but she steadied them enough to say, "We're going up to tell Daddy good-bye. Do you want to come?"

I turned away and looked at the shop. "I'll go on my own."

"All right," she said, "but be back by six o'clock. We're still having Miss Miller over for supper for her" — Mama hesitated — "last night."

Our last night, too.

I heard the car door open. "J?" Mama said, "What's in your bag?"

J's voice was quiet. "Sump'in for Daddy."

"Oh. OK," she said, and I heard her slide onto the seat and shut the door.

After they left, I got the cedar box with the altar stone from under my bed and went over to the shop. I looked at the hymn and the map on the wall. I took out the altar stone and stared at it for a good long while before putting it in my pocket.

By the time I got to Daddy's grave, Mama and J had already left. There were fresh white roses in a real vase, but I swallowed hard when I saw what J had brought in that lunch bag. His Flintstones bowl.

It was thundering in the distance and a few drops of rain fell, hitting the edges of J's bowl and slowly dripping down inside. A petal fell off one of the roses and into the bowl. I took the piece of altar out of my pocket and knelt down in front of Daddy's grave. A couple of sprinkles of rain hit the stone, turning those spots darker. Slowly, gently, I put it in the bowl next to the white rose petal.

"This is all I got for you, Daddy," I whispered. "I tried. I really did. I'm sorry."

I knelt there a long while, watching the few raindrops hit the petal and the stone.

Chapter Forty-Five
Fire!

When I got back home, our place was bone-dry. It was like the rain knew that Daddy's grave was a sad place and it had to shed some tears on it. I went in the shop and started putting the pieces of the chopped-up desk in a trash bag when I heard the door rattling.

"Can I come in, Red?" It was Rosie.

"Rosie! You're back!" I was so happy to see her I hugged her. I would've stopped myself but she seemed to want to keep hugging. I took in a whiff of her. She still smelled like lemons, like lemonade, like summer before . . . before Daddy died and everything bad started happening. "Are you OK?" I asked her.

She finally let go, nodding. "I came to tell you how sorry I am about Miss Georgia."

"Yeah. Me, too."

"Are you doing all right?"

"Rosie . . ." I didn't know how to tell her. I couldn't even say it to myself.

Mr. Harrison's loud voice did it for me. "Hallelujah and Happy Thanksgiving!"

We stepped out of the shop and saw him plastering a SOLD sticker across the For Sale sign.

Seeing it in big red letters like that made me feel even worse.

"No!" Rosie cried. "You can't leave! I'll die! I'll just die!"

Mama came out of the house, slowly, kind of jerky, wiping her hands on a towel. "Isn't there any way around this, Gene?"

Rosie took off running.

Mr. Harrison acted like nothing had happened. "Well, now, Betty, you signed those papers a while ago. We're good to go!"

Mama wiped her face with the towel as if she thought that would wipe things away. "Red? You'd better go after Rosie."

I stared at her. "You go after her. You're the one who did this!"

I took off, but not after Rosie. I ran into the shop and slammed the door. I needed to think. I took in a deep breath of the oil and dirt but it didn't work. No shop. No Daddy. No home. No Beau. No Rosie. And what would happen to them when we left them behind? I shook my head, trying to get my brain to work. I had to do something. And I had to think fast. Or it was all over.

I don't know how long I was in there but at some point I realized that my breaths were taking in more than air. I smelled smoke. Not the smoke of a wood fire. It smelled different, not like someone's woodstove, more like chemicals or . . . contact cement.

I opened the shop door. Smoke was coming from the direction of Rosie's house, and I ran down the line of trees to reach it. I stopped at the creek.

It was the shed. Sparks flew from it and swirled in the air. Flames roared up the wood sides. The fire was hot and fast and angry, like all the nastiness of that shed was finally exploding. Mr. Dunlop was there, swearing up a storm and spraying the flames with his hose, but it wasn't doing any good. I didn't get too close because the only thing worse than Mr. Dunlop was Mr. Dunlop really mad. When I heard him cussing about "those Porters" I took off.

I ran back to the What-U-Want to tell Beau what happened, even though he'd already smelled the smoke. "Figures he'd think it was us. Probably something in his own stupid shed started the fire."

"You think so, Red?"

I shrugged. "It happens. Why? What do you think started it?"

"Oh, I don't know. Just ain't a usual everyday thing, so maybe it's something unusual what started it."

"What are you saying, Beau? Are you thinking someone set the fire?"

He shrugged. "I sure don't know. Nope. I don't." And he started tugging on his hair.

"You know something, Beau."

He stepped back from the counter, farther away from me, and shook his head. "No, sir, I don't know nothin'."

When his eyes landed on the display of Zippo lighters, I realized what he was getting at. And I didn't like it. "Are you saying Rosie did it? Is that what you're saying?"

Beau tugged his hair with both hands.

"That's a terrible thing to say, Beau!"

"I didn't say —"

"A terrible thing!" I stormed out of the What-U-Want, slamming the door behind me.

Chapter Forty-Six
Rosie's Place

My feet knew Beau was right before my head could accept it because they were already running me over to the Dunlops'. The smell of smoke hung heavy in the air and burned my eyes, nose, and throat. I hardly noticed it, though, because all I was thinking about was Rosie, and how I'd ignored all the warnings.

I knew those warning signs — the way Mr. Dunlop acted and how Mrs. Dunlop didn't act at all. I'd seen the warning, like her daddy hitting her. Heck, I'd even caused some of the problems, like getting Darrell sent away, not taking Beau seriously about the lighter, and not hanging out with her more. I wish I'd been a better friend. The thing is, if you ignore warnings, they jump from being warnings to something that's already happened, and then it's too late.

When I got to the Dunlops', the sheriff's car was parked outside. I ran up the steps and pounded on the door.

Mr. Dunlop flung it open and when he saw me his eyes went all squinty and that nasty smile came on his face. "Well,

well, well. Here he is, Sheriff. Just the kid I was talking about."

Sheriff Scott stood behind him, eyeballing me. "Come on in, Red."

I slid my back against the inside of the door to stay as far away from Mr. Dunlop as I could. But I could still smell his sweat.

I saw Rosie, hovering in the corner by the wood stove, her arms wrapped around herself.

Mr. Dunlop slammed the door and pointed at me. "It's him. He's always sneaking around my property and —"

"I'll take care of things, Ray," the sheriff said. "What do you know about this, Red?"

"Nothing. I just smelled the fire."

"He's lying!" Mr. Dunlop yelled.

Me and Rosie looked at each other while the sheriff and Mr. Dunlop argued about what they didn't know. But we knew. I wondered if she was going to let me get arrested. And I wondered if I'd go ahead and let myself be arrested.

Mr. Dunlop's voice was louder now. "He's a juvenile delinquent! He vandalizes buildings and signs, cuts school, and gets my kids in trouble." He gave me a hard stare. "And all the while he's acting all sweet and dumb like his buddy Beau."

I stared back at Mr. Dunlop real mean because I didn't like the way he spat out Beau's name.

The sheriff said, "We'll look at everyone, Ray —"

"You don't need to! Look at him! You can see it in his eyes. I'm telling you, them Porters have always had it in for us!" He jabbed his finger at me, but I stepped back. "And this one's gone even crazier since his daddy went and died on him."

I just about hauled off and punched him in that big, fat, stinking mouth of his.

"He got my Darrell sent to juvie. Maybe it's time for a Porter to join him!"

Mr. Dunlop grabbed me by the shirt, the sheriff stepped forward, and Rosie yelled, "Red didn't do it!"

We all turned and looked at Rosie.

Mr. Dunlop snorted. "What do you know, anyway? You don't know nothing."

"Yes, I do."

"Oh, yeah? Like what?"

Rosie's voice shook. "Like I did it."

That made Mr. Dunlop shut up and let go of me. There was a little cry from the bedroom, so I knew Mrs. Dunlop heard. Sheriff Scott gave his Kiss of Death.

The phone on the wall rang. And rang. With each ring, Mr. Dunlop's face turned a darker shade of purple and his breathing got so heavy you could hear it. He leaped over the coffee table to the phone and ripped it clear off of the wall, so that the ring died in the phone's throat in a final raspy jangle.

Mr. Dunlop took a step toward Rosie. "I'm gonna —"

"You gonna do nothing." The sheriff pulled up his belt, the one with the gun hanging off it. "This is a case for the law."

"Law don't have to worry. By the time y'all get your butts in gear, I'll have taken care of this — this —"

Mr. Dunlop had his hand on Rosie's throat before me or the sheriff could get to him. Her eyes bulged out as if the more he squeezed her throat the less room there was inside for her eyes and something had to give.

It took both Sheriff Scott's arms to yank Mr. Dunlop's hand away and it seemed to take him forever. Finally, Rosie's little rag-doll legs collapsed under her and she slid down the wall to the floor, her eyes still bulging out.

A raging scream came out of me and I shot myself at Mr. Dunlop and was on him like a tick on a dog. I started pummeling him all over. Then I was up in the air, looking down on him like I was an angel roaring down on the devil himself.

"Get a hold of yourself, Red." It was Sheriff Scott, dangling me up in the air like that. He gave me a little shake before letting my feet touch the floor, but he didn't let go of me. And I didn't quit struggling or screaming.

"What's wrong with you, Mr. Dunlop?" My voice didn't even sound like me.

Mr. Dunlop was leaning on the sofa, breathing heavy.

Rosie was choking and coughing on the floor.

"Look at her!" I yelled.

He didn't move.

"I said look at her!"

His head jerked around to look at me, and I was glad I still felt the sheriff gripping my arms. It made me feel even stronger. "Not me, you idiot! Look at her!"

For some reason, he did. And Rosie looked back at him, before she looked away.

"No Porter did that, Mr. Dunlop. It's you! You're the one who's destroying your own family! You want to know why she did it?"

A car horn was honking real fast, over and over, somewhere down the road.

"Because you're a nasty old cuss who beats his own daughter! And his son! And you treat your wife like dirt. No wonder everyone hates you."

I finally stopped because Mr. Dunlop was shriveling up like a two-day-old balloon that's all wrinkled and useless. And I heard crying. I didn't know if it was Mr. Dunlop or Rosie.

The car horn kept honking, real loud and close, and I realized it was our own Chevy Biscayne wagon.

"What now?" Sheriff Scott muttered, letting go of me.

I ran to the door and opened it. Beau was getting out of the car.

"Fire!" he said. "Fire . . . left over from the shed . . . wind got it . . . down that row of trees . . . to the . . . shop!"

The word *shop* came out like a cry, and I heard a cry come out of me, too.

I heard the sheriff behind me, talking to Mr. Dunlop like he was a little kid. "Come on with me, Ray."

"Red?" Beau called.

"I-I'm coming, Beau!" But first I ran to Rosie and pulled her up. "Come on!"

She clutched on to me and we flew out of the house right after Sheriff Scott and Mr. Dunlop.

Beau had the door open for us, and I saw his cap ducking

back into the driver's seat. Me and Rosie piled into the seat beside him and he screeched off, on the tail of the patrol car, making me slide over and squish against him, and Rosie against me.

"Is it — is it burned down, Beau?" I said into his arm.

He moaned. "I don't know. Your mama called the fire truck and was calling over to the Dunlops', too, because I told her you might could be there, but no one answered, and the fire truck's not there yet, and your mama's trying to hose it down but she has to get up in the tree and she don't know how to get him down —"

"Get who down?"

"J. He's scared of the fire, so he crawled up that tree by your window and he's hiding up there, crying. I tried to help but I can't climb no tree, and that's when your mama said to come get you so you could get your brother — Rosie? Are you all right?"

I hadn't even noticed Rosie was crying. Now I saw the patrol car's flashing lights shining across her face, making her look scared and red one moment, and blue and dead the next.

I struggled to get my arm unpinned from between us and put it around her. "It's all right, Rosie. Everything's going to be all right."

But even as I was saying it, I didn't see how anything could ever be all right again.

Chapter Forty-Seven
The Tree

A fire engine pulled up at the same time we did. The sheriff's siren was screaming along with the fire truck's. The whole place was flashing lights and shouting people and crackling walkie-talkies yelling words and numbers into the air. Against the darkening sky, bright orange flames came out of the corner of the shop by the trees.

I jumped out Beau's side of the car because Rosie wasn't moving, and I had to get to the shop.

Beau was turning around in circles, tugging his hair. "Miz Porter? Where are you? It's Beau. What you want I should I do now?"

I grabbed him and stopped him spinning and looked into his eyes. "Beau. You got to take care of Rosie. OK?"

He let go of his hair. "S-sure, Red. I can do that."

Another fire truck with screaming sirens pulled up. I went running toward the shop, but a fireman stepped in front of me. I tried to skirt around him, but he grabbed my arm.

"I have to help!" I yelled.

"You can help by standing back."

I looked up at him. "I have to save the shop."

"We're doing all we can."

I didn't like the sound of that, and when I looked between the trucks and got a better view, I saw what he meant. The whole place was up in flames.

"Do something!" I shouted.

Right then, a huge hose started spraying the flames, but there was a big *boom* and a ball of flames shot up, right through the water.

I heard shouting all around me and everything looked like it was wavering because of the shimmering walls of heat. And smoke. I could smell it, feel it in my eyes, and even taste it. And it made things look a little blurry, so I felt like I was in a nightmare. People scurried around like nobody knew what to do, except someone had to be holding that hose because it was still spraying, even though the flames were still going.

Mama was pulling on my arm. "Red! You've got to get J down!"

She turned my head toward the house and pointed to the old pine outside my bedroom window. I couldn't see J at first. Then I saw him, much higher up than I thought he could go. And he was screaming. My name.

Mama pulled me toward the house as I looked back through the smoke and flames to the shop. My eyes were stinging so much they were watering.

"Red!" J wailed.

"I'm coming, I'm coming." I wiped my eyes and climbed my tree as far as the roof before J screamed. I couldn't help looking over at the shop, since I had a better view now. It was mostly gone. I had to look away and blink hard. I turned back and took another step up.

"Quit it, Red! You're shaking the tree! It's gonna fall!"

"It's not going to fall, J."

"Yes, it is, too! Quit shaking it!"

I stopped climbing and stood real still so he wouldn't feel anything. "OK, I stopped. But you're going to have to get down by yourself, then."

"I can't! Thomas ain't showed me how to climb it yet!"

"You got up there, J, so you can get down again."

"No, I can't!"

"You waiting for Thomas to come save you?"

There was silence for a moment, then a real quiet J said, "Can he?"

"What do you think?" I said, wishing Thomas would magically appear, too. "You know what he'd say, right?"

"You can do it?"

"Yup."

"But I can't!"

"Of course, you can."

"No, I —"

"Just listen, will you? First, look at the branch you're holding on to and grip it tight with both hands."

"What do you think I'm doing?"

How could that kid be sassy even when he was scared? "Second, you take one foot off the branch it's on —"

330

"But —"

"— and while you're still gripping on with both hands, you feel around for the next lower branch with your foot, OK?"

"But, what if I fall?"

"J, you ride your bike around with no hands! You got two hands on that branch. You mean to tell me you can't fish around with one foot for just a second?"

He didn't say anything for a moment. "I'm real good at bike riding."

"Yes, you are."

It was quiet and I listened to the wind rustling, water squirting, and firemen's voices.

"Do you really think I can do this, Red?"

"I know you can." I thought of what Daddy used to call him. "You can do it, Bamm-Bamm. You're a Porter, aren't you?"

"Yes, sir," he said, talking like I was Daddy, and in spite of everything I smiled.

"Once you find the branch, you test it and make sure it'll hold your weight, while you're still holding on with both hands, OK?"

"OK."

I finally saw some movement. "How's it going?"

"I found it."

"So now you put your other foot down there and once you're settled, you take one hand off the branch and grip another branch that's a little lower."

He started whining, but I cut him off and kept talking

to him until, one step at a time, he made it down almost to my level. I stepped onto the roof so he could get down the rest of the way.

"Just a couple more steps to go, J."

"It's Bamm-Bamm," he said. He stepped onto the roof next to me and he broke into a grin. "I'm telling Thomas I climbed this tree!"

"Well, thank goodness!" Mama said. "Now come on down, both of you!"

Beau lifted J down from the roof and handed him to Mama, who scooped J up while she laughed and cried at the same time.

There was a huge *crack* from the shop, and I saw the steps fall away from the office. The metal roof had melted onto the office area and the office was up in flames. There was still a lump where the office used to be, the foundation, I figured.

"Red," Mama called up to me. "Please come down now, OK?"

"In a minute," I said, unable to take my eyes off what was left of the shop.

I sat down on the porch roof feeling like I'd been beaten. I guess the firefighters felt the same way because they were sitting on the trucks or on the ground staring at the smoldering shop. It was like we were perched all over the place at some strange funeral.

I heard Beau's voice below me and I saw him standing next to Mama and J, still holding on to Rosie's hand. "That's what I think we should sing, Miz Porter, that hymn what was on the shop wall. I remember the words." Beau took off his cap and started to sing.

> *Buried in sorrow and in sin*
> *At hell's dark door we lay,*
> *But we arise by grace divine*
> *To see a heavenly day.*

I leaned over to see better through the branches of the pine. The headlights from the fire trucks lit up what was left of the shop. I stared at where that desk used to be and caught a glint of something. Something I'd never seen before. Something that shouldn't have been there at all. I swear my heart stopped.

Chapter Forty-Eight
Freedom Church

"There it is!" I screamed. "It's right there! I can see it!"

The black-and-white specks glinted in the strong lights of the fire trucks. Speckled granite. The altar of Freedom Church. Right there. In our shop. Under the office in the back. Where Old Man Porter's desk used to be.

"Red!" Mama called, "stop jumping on the roof, you're going to fall off!"

"What is it, Red?" Beau asked.

"The altar!" I yelled. "I found it!"

I let Beau lift me down off the porch roof, but as soon as my feet hit the ground, I ran for the shop, gravel flying behind me.

"Red! Come back!" Mama screamed.

"Stop him!" a man yelled. "It's still hot!"

Arms were grabbing for me, but no one could catch me. I flew straight to the stone. When I got right up to it, I could feel its heat. I stared at it. George Freeman's altar. Buried right here. And now raised from the dead.

I stood there for I don't know how long, but I realized there was no one around me, no one telling me to get back or pulling me away. I turned around and squinted into the headlights of the fire trucks and patrol car, not able to see anything for a moment. And then I saw why no one was moving.

Mr. Harrison was standing there. With another man, looking richer and fancier than him. The rich guy was holding some papers under his arm.

The whole place had gone silent. It was like everyone knew it was bad news.

Beau was holding Rosie's hand, while his other hand was pulling on his hair. Rosie's big eyes stared at me and her heart lips quivered. Mama was holding J and looking like she was about to cry. And Miss Miller was next to Mama, which surprised me until I remembered that she was supposed to be having supper with us tonight. It seemed like a whole lifetime had gone by since this morning.

I looked down at the smoldering pieces of wood, melted metal, and charred tools that were strewn all around me. I took a deep breath and walked slowly, listening to my crunching footsteps breaking the silence, not exactly knowing what I was going to do, but knowing that everyone was watching and waiting for me to do whatever it was.

I walked all the way up to Mr. Harrison and faced him. Pointing back to the rock, I said real loud, "That's the altar of Freedom Church."

"There you are, Mr. Cataldo," said Mr. Harrison, elbowing the fancy guy next to him, "that's what you can put on the plaque over your fireplace." He chuckled.

Mr. Cataldo wasn't laughing. "I didn't know there was a church here."

"Aw, that wasn't a church," said Mr. Harrison quickly, "it was just an old car repair shop. See? It's burned down now — that's one less building you have to get rid —"

"It was a church!" I yelled. "It was a historic church from more than a hundred years ago!"

Mr. Cataldo looked at Mr. Harrison and then at me.

"It's true!" I said. "That's the church that belonged to Miss Georgia's granddaddy. That's her family's church. Freedom Church. And that's her family's land."

"No proof of that in the county records!" Mr. Harrison said with a nervous laugh.

Miss Miller stepped forward. "Excuse me," she said to Mr. Cataldo, "but there's a lawyer on his way here right now." She looked at her watch and peered down the road. "He should already be here. I believe he has some evidence to support this boy's claim." She smiled at me.

Mr. Harrison shook his head. "It's a nice story, but that's all it is. A story."

"It is not, and you know it!" I said.

Mr. Harrison started talking back to me, but Mr. Cataldo put his hand up. "If it's all the same to you, I'd like to hear what the lawyer —"

We all heard the Mustang speed up the road, crunch over the gravel, and we watched a dazed Mr. Reynolds step out. "What — what happened?"

"Fire," someone said, as if it needed an explanation.

"Mr. Reynolds?" I asked, running over to him. He just stared at the shop, or what was left of it.

I shook one of his lanky arms. "Mr. Reynolds!"

He startled and looked down at me. "I found the altar of Freedom Church! It was under our shop the whole time. Doesn't it belong to Miss Georgia and her relatives? That means we can't sell this land, right?"

He still looked dazed.

"Bill." Miss Miller was at his side. "Don't you have some papers about the property?"

"Papers?" he said.

She raised her eyebrows at him.

"Oh," he said, lifting his glasses and settling them back on his nose again, "Yes — yes, I do." He leaned into his car, took out a briefcase, and pulled a fat folder out of it.

Mr. Harrison walked toward him. "Now, son, you're not even from these parts."

"But I am a lawyer, admitted to the Virginia bar, and I know how to research land titles, even fraudulent ones." He raised the fat brown file in one hand and shook it. "I've got enough evidence here to raise doubt about the title of this land."

"What are you saying?" Mr. Cataldo asked, joining us.

"I'm saying," Mr. Reynolds said, "that there's a cloud on the title."

Mr. Cataldo put a hand on his forehead. "What, exactly, does that mean?"

"It means there's doubt as to who really owns this land. It means you take a risk if you buy this land. It means years and years of court battles."

Mr. Cataldo glared at Mr. Harrison. "I'll need a ride back to the airport," and he headed for the Chrysler.

"A deal's a deal!" Mr. Harrison said.

Mr. Cataldo took a deep breath and turned on Mr. Harrison. "Forget it — I'm not touching this powder keg!" He took the papers from under his arm, held them up, and tore them in half with a rip that split the air.

• • • • • •

The house was in an uproar all night. Mr. Reynolds was on and off the phone talking to Mr. Jones and even to Miss Georgia's granddaughter. I convinced Mama that it wouldn't be right to sell our place, that at least some of our land had to go back to Miss Georgia's family because her granddaddy had bought it fair and square. The sheriff took Rosie home and Mr. Dunlop to jail for the night to "cool off." Miss Miller finally got J to go to bed and then took Beau home, but not before Beau grabbed my arm and grinned. "It's just like the sign said. You sure did fix it right, Red!"

I guess things were fixed "right" but that meant we were moving to Ohio, which was about as wrong as anything could feel.

I don't know if I slept at all. I guess Mama didn't because early the next morning she was sitting at the kitchen table wearing the same clothes as the night before, just like I was. Normally she'd say, "Happy Thanksgiving!" but I don't think either of us was feeling real happy.

She explained that Mr. Jones and his daughter, Mrs. Reed, said that even though part of our land belonged to their family, it didn't have a house or a store built on it at the time their ancestors owned it, so they were going to pay for the worth of the house and What-U-Want, and some of the land. And we'd be able to keep a small piece of land ourselves.

"I think that's fair all around, don't you?" Mama asked me.

"I guess, but —" I was about to ask her if getting some money meant we could stay here, either buy a house or build a house of our own on what land we had left, but she spoke first.

"It won't leave us with much money because we need to pay off our debts, so we'll still have to move."

I let all my hope out in one long breath.

"There's good news, too," Mama said, all fake cheery, "Beau will have a job because Mrs. Reed wants him to keep working here. And the sheriff is convincing Mr. Dunlop to go back to trucking."

I shook my head. "He won't because he can't trust Darrell and —"

"Well, Darrell's not around right now," Mama pointed out, "and even when he is, Sheriff Scott is making a very convincing case to Mr. Dunlop that if he doesn't change, he might not have Rosie around at all, and I believe Ray got the message." She looked over toward the Dunlops'. "Rosie's going to be okay."

I would've felt better if I knew I could stay and actually get to see Rosie. Or Beau. Or have a chance to be friends with Thomas when he visited in the summers. Now there was no hope because I'd be in stupid Ohio.

"And," said Mama, "I've decided that I'm going back to school to become a teacher, so I can support my family. Until I get my degree, I'll do some substitute teaching."

I just stared at her. I didn't know what to say. It felt like there was nothing but change happening.

"Now if you don't mind, Red, I'd like to have the house to myself for a little while to say good-bye." Her lips trembled along with her voice, even though she was trying to smile.

I swallowed hard because of the lump that was growing in my throat and stood up. By the time I pushed the door open she was talking again.

"I'm going to miss this place."

I felt my head drop down.

"At least we're all packed," she said.

My head dropped down lower.

"I suppose," Mama spoke as if she were choosing every word carefully, "we'll load up the car and take as much as we can in each trip, and then keep coming back for more."

I turned around and looked at her. "All the way to Ohio?"

"No," Mama said, and a slow but steady smile crept across her face until she was full-out grinning. "To Beau's."

Chapter Forty-Nine
Thanksgiving

"Rosie! Rosie!" I was banging on her front door even though it was barely dawn. "We're staying!"

I heard a squeal from inside, and Rosie flung the door open, her bathrobe only half on over her bright pink nightgown.

I explained everything to her and she kept blinking like she might still be dreaming, but her little heart lips were making a big smile. "You're really going to live with Beau?"

"Yep."

"Wow." She shook her head, grinning. "Your mama is one strong woman."

"Yeah." I grinned. "She is. Oh, and not only are we staying, your daddy's leaving — he's going to start trucking again! Sheriff Scott is making him."

This time she squealed and jumped up and down on the front porch, clapping her hands. And then she grabbed me and hugged me, for a long time. I didn't mind. I hugged her right back, for a long time.

When I walked back toward the altar stone I saw the NASCAR mug sitting there on top of some papers. I picked my way over the remains of the shop to get my coffee, and saw it was sitting on my paper, "R-E-S-P-E-C-T." I picked up my mug, sat down on the stone, and flipped to the last page to read what Miss Miller wrote. There wasn't a grade. And I don't think that was because she wasn't my teacher anymore. All I did was write down what really happened and how I felt about it. You don't give a grade on real life. But if she had given me a grade, I bet it would've been an A. With all the words she used like *honor* and *truth* and *respect*, how could it not be an A?

I stared at our house, the house I'd grown up in, the only house I knew. It was going to feel strange having other people living there. I guess knowing that they belonged there all along made it easier to take. Sitting on the altar stone, I was glad that I'd finally found Freedom Church, even if it did mean that our shop burned down. And even though it meant I'd found out who killed Miss Georgia's grand-daddy. Us. But I also knew I wasn't Old Man Porter. I might have his name, his blood, and his hair, but I wasn't him. I was the man of the family now, and I got to decide what Porter stood for.

I took a sip of my coffee and thought of Daddy. On Thanksgiving Daddy always made us say what we were thankful for. I was thankful that we'd be staying in Stony Gap. And that Rosie was going to be OK and Beau had a job. It still hurt that Daddy and Miss Georgia were gone. And that I'd lost Thomas, too. Maybe someday I could be friends with Thomas again. At least now that I'd fixed things right, I figured Daddy would be proud of me. I took another sip of coffee, and I swear I heard Daddy's voice far away. *I hear ya, son.*

I heard a loud voice from inside the house. It was J whining. Mama was trying to calm him down. I guess some things would never change.

I remembered that Mama wanted to be alone, so I yelled, "Hey, J!"

He pushed the kitchen door open and stood there in his green briefs and red T-shirt. "What?"

"Come on out here."

"I don't want to. It's cold."

"Then put on some clothes."

"I can't find any! Mama packed everything."

"I got something to show you," I said, "but you have to come out here and see it."

He gave me his whiny look and sighed. "Oh, all right."

"And get some shoes on!" I called after him, like Daddy used to.

J trudged out in snow boots and a yellow bath towel slung around him like a cape. With his green briefs and red T-shirt he looked like he was trying to be Robin from *Batman*. I thought about what Daddy used to call me and I couldn't help smiling.

"So who are you trying to be, J? The Boy Wonder?"

His pouty mouth slowly turned into a grin. "Yeah." A shiver ran through him. "But I'm still cold."

"Well, come on up here, Boy Wonder. You can lean against me."

J hopped up next to me.

"I got a story to read you."

He looked at my paper. "Aw, that ain't no story. That's your homework. I saw Miss Miller give it to Mama last night."

"It's real good, though. And it's true, too."

J narrowed his eyes at me. "Does it have any shooting in it?"

"As a matter of fact, it does."

His eyes popped wide open.

"And guess what else? You're in it."

His eyes got even bigger. "Are you?"

I nodded.

"And Thomas?"

I thought for a moment. "That's part two," I said.

"And it's all true, even the shooting?"

"Yup. So you want to hear it?"

He nodded so hard it felt like the whole rock was shaking. Then he shivered and leaned against me. I even put my arm around him like Daddy used to.

The sun was rising with red and orange streaks in the sky, and I breathed in the smoke from Rosie's wood stove as I started reading our true story out loud.

Acknowledgments

There are people I've never met and many I've never heard of who have inspired this book. Certainly, there are heroes such as Martin Luther King Jr., Fred Shuttlesworth, Shirley Chisholm, Barbara Jordan, Aretha Franklin, Fannie Lou Hamer, even Nelson Mandela, Bishop Desmond Tutu, and Helen Suzman, but so many more who were and are extraordinary people who deal with adversity — unspoken, unseen by some, but still present — every day of their lives. Their courage, patience, strength, and spirit move me.

On a personal note, there are many people I'd like to thank for their help with this book, but I will name just a few: my mother, for teaching me tolerance and kindness and that you make the world the way you want it to be; Jan, for always being my big sister, protector, champion, friend, teacher, and first reader (who caught my typos); Keith Bruce, for help with Thomas, and for his laughter and life insight — we will always miss you, Keith; Shirley Parrish, for help with Miss Georgia, in particular, and for friendship in general; Mary Frances Bruce, Amy Stearns, and Laurie Stearns, for reading early drafts and being my friends and supporters for many wonderful years; my agent, Linda Pratt, who should become a diplomat if she ever changes careers, because she can deliver pointers and suggest changes with such grace and good humor that you want to rush back to the table and rework things to make them right; my editor, Andrea Davis Pinkney, whose vision, determination, and encouragement drove me to take this novel to a higher level and delight in its improvement; and, of course, my family, for believing in me, supporting my work, and becoming fans of "fend for yourself" dinners. Bill, thank you for your constant love and laughter on this beautiful journey.

Without all of these people, and dozens of writer compatriots, I wouldn't have succeeded in publishing a work of which I'm proud. This book has taken a long road from its first draft over a decade ago. It has grown, faced hard facts, dealt with realities, and finally matured into an authentic story. There may be flaws or places where it stumbles, but it picks itself up and keeps going, heading for the truth. I hope it succeeds. I'm happy with its journey. I wish a similar path for all of us.

Author's Note

There are defining moments in our lives when something hits us with such force that we will never forget it — exactly where we were, who was with us, and what emotion we experienced. One such moment for me was as a child in South Africa. At that time, the country was governed by a system of apartheid, which meant keeping blacks, whites, and Asians apart from one another and giving them different levels of privilege. It was not something I fully understood until my first day of school. At the end of the day, I was in the kitchen with my mother, reporting to her, with some concern, that all the native children must've been ill because not one of them had been at school.

I remember looking out the window at the surreally brilliant sunshine, beyond my mother's pained face, as she explained apartheid to me, a system that was unfair and unjust but that we were forced to follow, and how that meant I would not see any black children at my school. I felt such profound powerlessness, magnified by the fact that my mother, an adult, the one I looked to for protection, for making things right and for making sense of my world, was also powerless. It was a shocking and frightening feeling to learn that adults could be so ridiculous and that these same adults governed my life. Under the fear, I felt anger.

A couple of years later, in the late 1960s, we lived in Virginia, and I was feeling proud to be American. I remember another conversation with my mother, also in the kitchen, where I smugly announced a critical difference between South Africa and America: We did not have apartheid in America. I'll never forget her turning from the sink and locking her eyes on mine. "Oh, yes, we do," she said in a voice shaking with emotion. "We just don't call it that." After she explained the injustices in our own country's race relations, I experienced those same emotions of shock, fear, and anger, which I took out on our mailbox. Our mailbox was not quite right after that, but I felt it matched the state of our country. Things were not quite right.

What I realize now is that my mother likely saw me through the kitchen window, and while every aspect of my behavior — being violent, destroying property, making a scene, acting unladylike — was something she normally would have stopped, she let me continue. She understood. And as a mother now, I can feel the pain of having to explain the world's ugliness to a child, without being able to make things right.

Several years later, in the early 1970s, the same time as the setting of this book, we were living in Alabama. There I witnessed racial slurs as well as the genteel cover-up of racism, both of which stunned and angered me. By then I knew it was a part of my world, but it still upset me, especially the feeling of powerlessness. What could a kid do? Except maybe share and explain one's beliefs and stand up for people who were being wronged. I didn't know it at the time, but those are actually very important and powerful things that a kid, or anyone, can do.

I wrote this book so that readers might see that, no matter what your age, you can make a difference. If you think something is wrong, change it. If you think people are being wronged, change that. You have the power to change things about your world. That doesn't mean you'll always win — often, you won't — but even making an attempt to "fix it right" does have an effect. Above all, you have the power to be whatever kind of person you want to be. No one can take that incredible power away from you.

I also wrote this story so readers would know that it wasn't very long ago that people routinely judged one another by the color of their skin or by their ethnicity. While we have come a long way, there is still a long road ahead of us. To the travelers on this road: Be brave; be strong; be leaders. As Red's father would say, *I hear ya*. We all hear you.

Seeing Red's Characters

George Freeman represents the African Americans who were run off their land, some of them killed, in the nineteenth and twentieth centuries. Early in the twenty-first century, the Associated Press researched and reported on murders and subsequent land theft, revealing huge losses of African American land between Reconstruction and the civil rights era.

Howard Carwile was a real-life white lawyer in Richmond who tirelessly represented many African Americans from the 1940s through the 1960s. White lawyers like Carwile and Judge Frank Johnson of Alabama fought for justice and equality, chipping away at a segregated South. African American lawyers such as Oliver Hill, Samuel Tucker, Henry L. Marsh III, and Constance Baker Motley, to name just a few, were particularly brave and stalwart in their efforts to achieve social justice. Any one of them is worthy of many books themselves.

Bill Reynolds is modeled after J. Sargeant Reynolds, lieutenant governor of Virginia, who died far too young in 1971. Among other forward-thinking actions, he attacked Massive Resistance; supported the election of Doug Wilder, an African American, to take his senate seat; and appointed the first girl page to the Virginia General Assembly.

Miss Miller is modeled after my sister, Jan Molnar, who is the best kind of teacher — the type who believes in and respects her students enough to hold them accountable for their actions and encourage them to question and think for themselves. Her surname, Molnar, is Hungarian for Miller.

Philip Walter is modeled after Leon Walter Tillage, author of *Leon's Story*, about growing up in a sharecropping family under Jim Crow laws. After participating in civil rights marches, he became a janitor at a school in Baltimore, Maryland. He always maintained a spirit of optimism and dignity.

Miss Georgia is an amalgamation of strong women I've known over the years, from many races and cultures, whom I respect deeply, including my mother. I named her Fannie Mae in honor of Fannie Lou Hamer, a brave woman in Mississippi who never gave up being a civil rights activist despite death threats and beatings.

The story of Emmett Till, horrible as it is, is real. In this book, set in 1972, Red wonders how something so hideous could have happened as recently as seventeen years before. In fact, there have been many lynchings since the death of Emmett Till. We now call them hate crimes. One recent hate crime resulted in the beating and death of an African American man, James Anderson, in Mississippi in 2011 — thirty-nine years after Red wonders how such things could still happen.

Finally, Red's last name is Porter for two reasons. Pullman Porters were early leaders in the civil rights movement, successfully creating a union and organizing events leading up to and including the March on Washington in 1963. I wanted to pay tribute to them. Also, a porter is a person who carries burdens and, symbolically, all of us are like Red, carrying the burden of our history and the responsibility for our current society. Red Porter is the hope for our future. He is modeled after you.

Kathryn Erskine